CATCH A FALLING STAR

LAURA CARTER

B

Boldwood

First published in Great Britain in 2025 by Boldwood Books Ltd.

Cover Design by Rachel Lawston

Cover Illustration: Rachel Lawston

A CIP catalogue record for this book is available from the British Library.

Paperback ISBN 978-1-78513-590-3

Large Print ISBN 978-1-78513-589-7

Hardback ISBN 978-1-78513-588-0

Ebook ISBN 978-1-78513-591-0

Kindle ISBN 978-1-78513-592-7

Audio CD ISBN 978-1-78513-583-5

MP3 CD ISBN 978-1-78513-584-2

Digital audio download ISBN 978-1-78513-586-6

This book is printed on certified sustainable paper. Boldwood Books is dedicated to putting sustainability at the heart of our business. For more information please visit https://www.boldwoodbooks.com/about-us/sustainability/

Boldwood Books Ltd, 23 Bowerdean Street, London, SW6 3TN

www.boldwoodbooks.com

To all the B characters in my north east first act.

PROLOGUE

LYRA

That Night

Seven Years Ago

'You're here!' my best friend, Cami, bellows across the sound of hundreds of drunk undergrads.

It's standing room only in the music venue in Newcastle-upon-Tyne, where we go to uni. She reaches out a hand and drags me through the crowd to the spot she's got us at the very front and centre of the stage.

We're waiting for the main act – rock band, my *favourite* band, The Hand Me Downs. We've had tickets for nearly a year and in that time, the band has sky-rocketed. Their next tour won't be two-thousand capacity venues; it will be arenas and stadiums.

'So?' Cami says, looking to the ceiling. 'Did you do it?'

I bite my lip from a combination of nervousness and excitement. Once I say it out loud, it will be real. 'You are no longer looking at a third-year med student but a budding documentary photographer. I quit.'

'Oh my God, Lyra, this is huge! You finally made a decision about your own life!'

I don't get to tell her that the decision will be severely life shortening, since my parents are going to kill me when they find out, because the lights dim to near darkness.

There's movement on the stage.

Jay, the drummer, comes out first and my own scream is drowned out by the many others in the space. Once he's settled on his stool and making himself look busy checking his kit, Trev, one of the guitarists, comes out, waving like he's too cool for school (he kind of is) and sets up next to a bass guitar and an electric guitar.

I deafen my own ears when brothers Guy and Scott come onto the stage together.

Scott walks up to the standing microphone and as the stage lights turn on, he speaks to the crowd. 'Alreet, Newcastle! It's good to be home.'

But I don't watch him because I'm too focused on Guy, the songwriter, with the most distinct voice I've heard. He comes to stand behind a microphone right in front of me and slips the strap of an acoustic six-string around his neck. He sets about checking the tuning of his guitar as my entire limbic system tunes into him.

And right after Scott has introduced the first song, it's Guy who leans into his microphone and counts, 'One, two, three, four.' I swear my heart beats to his rhythm.

The atmosphere is electric. The air heavy with sweat. The floor vibrating in time to the low frequency of the bass guitar, booming out of the amplifier.

As Scott's youthful yet rocky voice sings out, 'I'm addicted to you…' I let my head fall back, my arms swish around uncoordinatedly, my hips twist and turn. *Free.*

If I let myself, I could be terrified. Terrified of telling my parents that all the money they've spent on private education and extra tuition has been for nothing. I won't be following in their footsteps.

But for one night, I'm going to enjoy the not knowing, the excitement of having no clue what comes next, the relief of the unrelenting pressure to be someone I'm not disappearing.

I dance through the first set and two beers, occasionally getting shoved by fellow groovers but not caring about any of it, until I'm pulled from my reverie by the Geordie accent of Guy Walker.

'We're gonna bring down the tempo with this next one. It's called "You and Me".'

I brace myself for my favourite of the band's songs. One of the few Guy performs.

His pitch is low, his voice gravelly in the sexiest of ways. I watch his fingers move over the strings of his guitar, the rest of the band silent. His eyes are closed when that first note comes. It hits my ears then travels the rest of my body like a surge of energy. My heart beats faster, my skin ignites, the way I knew it would hearing him in person, this close.

What I'm not prepared for is when he opens his eyes, he isn't looking into the distance, across the crowd of people here to listen to him. He's looking right at me, stilling me, stealing the air from my chest. It's like the only person he can see beyond the blinding stage lights is me. As if the words he sings and the chords he strums are meant for my ears.

'There's just you and me,
Forget all these people.
Because it makes no sense,
But I can't tear my eyes,

Away from you.'

As the beat picks up, his strumming becomes fiercer, the drums kick in, then the entire band is playing the chorus of the song he wrote. It's as if the faint curve at one side of his mouth is an inside message between us, like it's the start of a smile, of something. A promise.

The song moves into another, and another, the band members stopping between tracks to drink from bottles of beer on the stage and accept towels from surreptitious stage staff. I take my camera out of my bag and snap a few shots of the night. Then as I get back to dancing, the most bizarre thing happens. A man emerges from backstage and approaches me.

'Guy wants to know if you'll join him backstage once the lads're finished.' He's a big man, *huge*. Neck and arms tattooed and bulging beneath his black t-shirt kind of big. He has the trademark accent of someone who was born and raised in the deepest, darkest *Toon*. As for the tone of his voice, it's completely disinterested, as if he's asked this question of many girls, many times before.

But this is *Guy* from The Hand Me Downs so, rightly, I'm flattered. On a Lyra-favourable interpretation, *technically*, he did just sing to me, too.

Regardless, I am of course going to say, 'N—'

'She'll be there,' Cami tells the big dude, leaning across me to be heard.

'I— Cami, *no*.'

'Relax, it's not like you're committing to having his babies,' Cami yells, making me eye the stage as if Guy can actually hear her over the sound of his band rocking out.

'What're ya saying, yes or no?' the Hulk presses.

As he does, Guy's lips curve into that knicker-melting

lopsided grin again and I nod. Not to the big guy, or Cami, or myself, but to Guy.

And half an hour later, after the band has played their last song and thanked the crowd, my cardiovascular system might explode.

This is it. I'm going to meet the man of my dreams.

'Ha way then, Flower.' The Hulk is back, and he's created a path in the crowd to get me to the backstage door.

I feel sick. Please God, don't let me throw up on Guy Walker.

'Enjoyyyyyyy,' Cami sings as I give her the wide-eyed look of a deer caught in headlights, because that is *exactly* how I feel.

I follow along a corridor that's buzzing with activity – bodies shifting around with earpieces in, some people who look like press holding cameras and microphones. I feel as if everyone in the corridor can see in my pink cheeks that I'm a fangirl and I'm about to meet my crush.

The big man leads me to a dressing room that actually has *The Hand Me Downs* written on a plaque on the door, with a giant gold star above it.

'Give 'em a minute, they're still changing,' he tells me. I wonder how he knows, until he taps the small black bud in his ear.

Feeling too awkward to make conversation with this man, who clearly isn't interested in what I have to say, and not daring to look up to the other eyes in the corridor that might be mocking me, I take my phone from my bag.

'Nee pictures unless the lads say it's alreet,' the big man tells me.

'Oh, no, I wasn't—' I'm saved from myself by my sister's name lighting up the screen of my phone.

Olivia? At this time?

'Hey, is everything okay?' I ask instinctively, speaking into my handset whilst holding my free hand to my opposite ear.

'No, Lyra. I— I don't know how to say this...'

I know, as my stomach falls into the floor, that it's bad. Bad news is the only kind that can't wait at this time of night. Bad news is what happens when my parents are on call and their pagers go off.

As my sister tells me, 'It's Dad,' I'm already backing away from The Hand Me Downs' dressing room, and right before I turn to leave, I see the man of my dreams open the door.

Suddenly, nothing seems real.

'Wait, I don't even know your name,' a voice I could pick out of a packed concert hall says. His words fall on my back as I run. To where, into what, I've no idea.

But my sister is begging me down the line, 'Please come.'

1

LYRA

April 2025

Trapped in a Lift with a Naked Butler

As I take the last of my bags from the boot of my car and push it shut, I'm still humming to the tune of The Hand Me Downs' song that I was playing on my drive into the city. It always reminds me of nights out at uni with Cami. *I miss her.*

Sighing, I gather my camera, a handbag, a half-eaten box of tacos and a hen-party gift. Who even hires a professional photographer for their hen party? Isn't there some kind of rule; what happens on the hen stays on the hen?

There were no parking spaces on the street outside Charlotte's apartment building, so I'm going to have to lug everything down to the Quayside from Deansgate Car Park, ten minutes away.

Charlotte is my older sister's best friend. She used to be mine, when we went to school together, but now that my sister and Charlotte are both doctors at the same hospital and I'm *just* a wedding photographer, things have changed.

When I step out of the multi-storey car park, I'm hit by wind whipping up from the River Tyne, dragging my hair loose from my long braid. It's Newcastle-upon-Tyne, the north-bloody-east of England, and it's freezing outside, yet I'm a flushed and windswept mess by the time I reach the old stone conversion. Great – dishevelled is precisely the impression I'm going for.

To add insult to injury, I'm not even being paid for tonight. My sister is Charlotte's bridesmaid for her wedding in May and has organised tonight, roping me in for free. I guess she's hoping that Charlotte will similarly do something nice for her when she gets married in September.

Honestly, I would much rather be at home, in my loungewear, writing articles about people I've made up, that will never be published, drowning in thick, creamy hot chocolate.

Instead, I struggle through the main entrance of Phoenix House, fighting the weather and the heavy door as I nudge, kick and bump my way inside. Irritated that I even agreed to be here at all. I'll do just about anything to avoid conflict and oft times, that means doing things I have zero desire to do.

As the door closes, I'm assaulted by a potent smell of fresh paint in the foyer and can see multiple WET PAINT signs. One of which is covering the door to the staircase, not that I had any intention of carrying this stuff up to Charlotte's duplex penthouse.

'Could you hold that, please?' I call as the doors to the lift are just about closing across a man I can barely make out, except to note he has a significant dark beard and he's dressed entirely in black.

The doors close and I'm about to mutter how I feel about that when they reopen and he comes my way.

'Let me help you,' he says. Voice deep, raspy and smooth all at once. Such a distinct combination, it makes me look from my baggage to him, briefly finding dark-blue eyes on me.

Then he relieves me of my tacos takeaway box and my heavy over-shoulder camera case.

'Thank you so much. You don't have to help,' I tell him, a little discombobulated by that voice. Or maybe just the wind. The walk. The very fact of being at the hen party of an *ex*-friend of mine, in the capacity of no one important.

'I'm going up in the lift anyway, it's no hardship.'

I consider my alternative and, though I hate to put people out, I tell him, 'Okay, thank you.'

Inside the elevator, I notice two one-litre bottles of liquor – gold flecked tequila, I think – resting on the floor. Simultaneously, I realise that, despite the really quite nice woody, peppery aftershave the bearded man is wearing, there's a resounding stench of fish and chipotle coming from my food box.

We both reach for the elevator buttons at the same time – him probably keen to get away from the smell as quickly as possible.

If it wasn't for the fact he looks a little untidy and like a potential alcoholic, I wouldn't mind hanging around his voice and scent. It would be a nice way to procrastinate.

'Sorry, you go,' I tell him.

He nods, pressing the button for the fourth floor. 'Where're you headed?'

'Fourth, too, actually. Thank you.'

He hesitates, scrutinising me from head to toe; at least, it feels as if he is. As he does so, I stare back, finding that beneath the bushy beard, he could be quite handsome, actually. But I'm pretty sure that he's not having similar thoughts about me as a line forms between his eyebrows.

In fact, his reaction makes me check myself in the mirrored walls surrounding us. Oh *God,* I don't blame him for staring. I quickly run my fingers through my frizzy hair that was blow-dried smooth when I left home. My cheeks are rosy and I have panda eyes from the bit of eye make-up I'm wearing.

As I'm frantically wiping my face, the lift doors close but it stutters and chugs into action so hard that it rocks me back against the wall.

'Whoa,' the stranger says, casting his arms out wide and gripping on to the handrail.

As the movement of the carriage smooths out, the stranger's hold doesn't let up. He's rigid. My camera bag still slung across his shoulder. My unprofessional guess is he's claustrophobic.

I side-eye him. He looks tired in that way people do when they have small children or otherwise carry the world on their shoulders – figuratively, obviously. I know because it's how I've often seen my reflection. I *don't* have kids.

But... and not that I'm *staring*, because that would make what is already one of the most hideously uncomfortable activities in life – riding in a confined space with a stranger – even more awkward... *but* this tired man is really quite attractive in a rugged, sort of unkempt but maybe intentionally messed-up dark hair, masculine kind of way.

This, despite the stiffness in his shoulders and the fact he's holding his breath, either because he's terrified of small confined spaces or because my fish tacos stink.

As I'm wondering whether to explain the stench, the stuttering of the lift car returns and morphs into something more like chugging. With a creak and a loud crack, the lift jolts to a stop. The lights go out for a split second and there's a click before they come back on, dimmer than before.

I glance up to the dial above the door and see that we're at the third floor, yet the doors aren't opening.

'What the—?' The man unfreezes, dropping my camera bag – thankfully padded. He darts forwards, fiercely fingering the OPEN DOOR button. 'Are we stuck? Is the lift stuck?'

He shifts to face me, as if I have the answer.

'I don't know,' I offer unhelpfully. 'Try pressing the numbers.'

We end up both pressing the numbers *1, 2, 3, 4.* Nothing happens.

Even through his thick coat, I can see his chest rising and falling. *He's freaking out.*

'I'm sure it's just a glitch in the mechanics,' I say, trying to sound calm. 'Let's hit the bell.' There isn't one. 'Or the emergency button.' I press it and an alarm rings, though in my unqualified lift-handling opinion, not nearly loud enough. Certainly not loud enough for a hen party with music playing to hear.

Then it goes off. Just like that, the noise stops and as I'm thinking *O-Oh!* the stranger I'm trapped with says, 'I don't have any phone signal. D'you?'

I fumble through my bag on the floor, knowing I won't have but not wanting to seem impolite. 'Not even a bar,' I tell him when I locate my own device.

As I glance up from my crouched position, I notice the man's skin looks grey and clammy. His breathing is faster than Usain Bolt's after a record-breaking sprint.

'It won't be long before someone comes,' I reason. 'Those alarms route through to the emergency services, so the fire brigade will be here soon.' I genuinely have no idea if this is a thing. 'Plus, I'm on my way to a hen party; someone is bound to try to use the lift any minute.'

I take off my thick-knit cardigan and place it on the floor, coming to sit, watching the man and hoping he'll do the same. It might help him relax.

Thankfully, he follows my lead, dropping to his bum opposite me. I lean forwards and hold out my hand. 'I'm Lyra.'

He scrutinises my gesture, then frowns at me but shakes my hand anyway. 'Guy.'

'Nice to meet you, Guy.' I decide to waive the grumpy tone on account of his anxiety.

We fall into an uncomfortable silence. One that simultaneously reminds me of my stinky food box and gives me time to determine that, unluckily, given the smell of fish, this man isn't just handsome, he's really bloody hot. And *familiar.* Oddly familiar, though I can't place him. Maybe I've photographed him before. I surreptitiously glance at his ring finger – not married, or doesn't wear a band.

Sweat beads are forming on his brow and his grey pallor has shifted to rosy cheeks. I want to state the obvious, *take off your coat,* but I don't know Guy, so I refrain.

Instead, I try to distract him. 'Do you live here, or are you visiting?'

'Visiting.'

'Great. Lovely.'

We fall silent again. *Tough crowd.*

Then Guy pulls out the stop on one of his liquor bottles and takes a long swig. *Whoa there, cowboy.*

'Drink?' he asks, holding out the bottle, allowing me to see the tequila label on the front.

I've only ever seen one other person drink tequila like that and not since Cami at university. Not until tonight.

'I'm good, thank you. I'm driving.' I reach for my food box. 'But this is a serendipitous false imprisonment, because nothing goes better with tequila than tacos.' I lift the lid on the food, which has been two-thirds consumed, with four empty taco holders to show for it. 'I have two fish tacos looking for a good home. Would you like them?'

He scrutinises the offering, nose twitching. 'That's the smell.'

Now my cheeks are rosy. 'Yes. My dinner, rather than... *me*.' I titter awkwardly.

'I can't eat your dinner,' he says, simply frowning in the face of my discomfort.

I shrug, trying not to seem like a teenage girl in front of the first boy she ever found cute. 'Fine. But it would benefit us both and the planet.'

He raises one eyebrow, an intersection between mockery and charm.

'I'll otherwise throw them away when we get out of here.' Which I now realise I ought to have done on the walk here. 'I was only bringing them inside to put them in the bin and stop my car from stinking.' I got a new jelly bean freshener yesterday and gave Penelope her annual clean. 'So you'd be supporting sustainability and preventing us from suffering a really smelly...' I check my watch. 'Twenty-four minutes.'

'Twenty-four?' he asks, eyes – striking eyes – widening.

'At worst,' I'm quick to add, 'by my reckoning, we've been stopped for six minutes already and I read once that the *absolute* longest it takes for any lift stall to be rectified is thirty minutes.' I've made that up entirely, but Guy's inhalations are no longer visible from under his coat.

His eyes meet mine and his expression softens in a way that's uncommonly hypnotic.

'I doubt I'll be around long enough to see the demise of the planet,' he tells me, finally breaking away from my stare. 'But I won't say no to a taco.' He reaches into the box and takes the Mexican bite. 'The box says mixed. You ate the meat and veg and left both fish.'

It isn't a question and he doesn't seem overly perturbed as he takes a ginormous mouthful of food.

'I find fish in tortilla ick,' I explain, setting the takeaway down closer to him. 'It's the texture combo. It's my version of long nails being scraped down a blackboard.'

He takes the other half in one more mouthful and chews, watching me until his orifice is clear. 'Why order a mixed box if you don't like fish?'

'Because I couldn't decide between veggie and pork pibil. A mixed box of six was cheaper than two separate boxes of pork and veg. It made economic sense.'

'Yet went against your mission to save the world, two fish tacos at a time.'

Forcing myself to scowl, I tell him, 'A girl can go off a man pretty quickly, you know.'

He scoffs, though character lines draw on one side of his mouth, and something tells me this man is not often in good spirits.

'I'm not complaining,' he says through a mouthful of the second taco. 'Cold fish tacos happen to be my favourite meal.'

'I can never un-see the half-chewed food you just showed me.'

He scoffs again yet takes another bite of fish before replying. 'I bet your parents brought you up to empty your mouth before you speak.'

He's really getting my hackles up. Maybe because I can hear the voice of my mum telling me exactly that. *'Chew your food before you speak, Lyra Clarkson. You're not an animal.'*

'Well, beggars can't be choosers,' I tell him huffily.

He takes another unbelievable swig of tequila. 'Aye. But cheaper for you to just make a decision next time. You're lucky to've fallen into this entrapment so that I can spare the environment your waste.'

'For your information, I'm not very good at making decisions. I'm appalling, in fact.' My mind spins so quickly with every disastrous decision I've made in my twenty-eight years, but I always come back to the same one. The same night. 'They tend to have far-reaching repercussions. Sorry, that was an overshare. It's the stress of our demise.'

He stares for too long before saying, 'It's a box of tacos, Lyra.'

I don't know why but the sound of my name leaving his husky voice causes a figurative puncture in my lungs. There's something about that voice, his face, a feeling of déjà vu. I can't put a finger on it but I think he reminds me of...

'Has anyone ever told you that you look like... Never mind, it's silly.'

He stares at me, as if he's looking beyond my eyes, somewhere deeper. 'Go on,' he croaks.

Guy. 'Guy Walker.'

He continues to bore holes in me, unblinking.

'You know? From the band The Hand Me Downs?'

He doesn't speak but stands, towering above me where I'm still sitting on the lift floor.

He draws down the zip of his coat, but his height and presence are making me nervous. So I do what I tend to do when I'm nervous... talk.

'He was the guitarist. People don't remember him as well as his brother Scott, I guess because he notoriously never did interviews, and he wasn't on social media.' My words are coming faster as his zip comes lower. 'Though he wrote or co-wrote nearly all their songs. Definitely the best ones. He's an incredible songwri—'

Holy Moses! As he slides his coat down his arms, my mouth proverbially, perhaps literally, falls to the floor with the garment. Because beneath it is a torso. A muscly torso, with tattoos stretching across his shoulders and up his neck from his back. And it's... exposed. I mean *exposed.* Like, *naked,* but for a dickie-bow around his neck and matching cuffs at his wrists.

And *bloody hell,* he has the kind of body only people like Glen Powell and Chris Hemsworth and Ryan Gosling and, like, other *really* fit men have. I follow the lines of his lower abs into the waistband of his black trousers.

'I, ah, sorry, I'm babbling. Anyway, sorry, clearly not. You're not, ah, *the* Guy. Guy Walker. Even though your name is Guy – funny coincidence. Because you're a...' *Hen party! Of course!* 'What *are* you? A... *stripper*?'

He slips back down to his hunkers, his proximity suddenly overwhelming in this tiny box, his feet touching mine, his body... His very near *naked* body is very close to me. *Is there a fire under my backside?* It's suddenly insanely hot in here. I subtly fan my face, which does nothing to alleviate the hotness, the heat, the bloody inferno. *And... what was my question?*

'I'm a naked butler,' he tells me, straight-faced, as if this very bizarre scenario that's making my knickers protest beneath what suddenly feels like a primary school teacher's dress is not only real but entirely normal. As if I'm not going to wake up any moment.

And for some reason, *dream me*, who would be much more confident, much more brazen, because she doesn't have real life to face on the other side of these lift doors, says, 'Almost. Not quite.'

But I *am* real and this is *not* a dream. I know because my words bring the kind of colour to my cheeks that means Guy-the-Almost-Naked-Butler is probably thinking he's staring at a cooked red lobster right now.

As if the Gods of anti-mortification are shining down on me, the lift jerks. The abrupt movement knocks us both off balance as the cart recommences its ascent to the fourth floor, saving me from myself.

2

GUY

April 2025

At the Hen Party

'A technical glitch.' That's the explanation the engineer gave Lyra and me when he greeted us on the top floor. 'Sorry,' he'd said, wholly unconvincingly.

Then he looked at my semi-nude form, the two bottles of tequila and empty taco box, winked at Lyra and told us, 'Doesn't look like it was too stressful.'

What would he know? I was on the verge of meltdown and would have had an anxiety attack if it hadn't been for the random musings and non-stop talking of my indecisive, sanctimonious fellow prisoner.

Funny though, now that we've been freed and we're standing at the same door, listening to the Spice Girls playing from inside and waiting to be welcomed to the hen party I have no desire to be at, she's stopped talking.

In fact, she's worrying her lip, holding on to the bag slung across her shoulder. She's staring at the apartment door as it's opened by a red-haired woman wearing a short sparkly dress and skyscraper heels.

'Lyra, hi! You're later than I thought. Did you get lost?'

Nice way to make your guests feel welcome.

'Lift problems,' Lyra says, smiling gently, apologetically. 'It jammed.'

'Oh,' the redhead says.

Then she turns to me, eyeing me from head to toes and back up again like I'm a piece of meat. I guess that *is* what I'm getting paid to be, but it makes me feel like even more of a prat than I already did, if that's possible.

'I assume that's why you're late too?' she asks me, not introducing herself, not even saying hello. 'Could you head to the kitchen? People are having to make their own drinks.'

I run my tongue along my teeth, close to needing to bite it to stop me retorting, but I grin. *Kill them with kindness*, Dave told me. This is my job now.

Position: Naked Twat.

Date of employment: April 2025 to present.

Qualifications: none.

Soft skills: reluctantly sociable recluse.

'I'll get on it,' I say through my drawn-up lips. I hand her the unopened bottle of tequila – the one that's actually full of tequila, as opposed to mine, which has been emptied and refilled with water. 'This is for you. To spice things up.' I hate myself for it but I wink. Because that's my role tonight – cheeky chappy, confident but not cocksure, paid to flirt and get the party started. Paid to disperse with any last trace of dignity I've been clinging on to.

Red takes it and inspects the label. 'Actually, I'm not the bride, just a bridesmaid, but I'm sure this will get the party going.'

Like Lyra, Red has a hint of a north-east accent. It's like nondescript rich girl meets north-east twang. I can't help wondering, if all the guests at this party are uppity, who the hell misjudged so badly that they arranged a naked butler?

She steps back from the door and I gesture for Lyra to head inside before me, oddly less comfortable without her next to me – the near-stranger, who is uncannily familiar, maybe in the way a girl next door is, or something, I'm not sure.

An old Sugababes track is playing now and there are probably two dozen women in clubbing attire – not at all dressed sweetly like Lyra – mingling in the red brick walls of the loft-style apartment.

The entire bottom floor of the duplex is open plan, a great social space, and it's twinkling with tea lights and loads of sparkling *stuff*. Streamers, disco balls, confetti. In the middle of it all, hand over her mouth as she giggles, her eyes on me, is an attractive woman wearing a white dress, veil and tiara that make her look like a Vegas bride. Wild guess, she's Charlotte, the bride-to-be.

I set my bags by the door, cringing internally as I turn my arse to the room, take off my trainers and drop my trousers, leaving my modesty preserved only by a pair of tight-fitting boxers and a short apron. Then I make my way to the kitchen against a soundtrack of cat calls and wolf whistles. A few already drunk hands grope my pecs.

I feel cheap and stupid, rather than flattered by the attention. There've been plenty of headlines written about me in the past and I can imagine what the rags would say about me now: *How the mighty fall. Hard. And never manage to get back up.*

My phone buzzes in my back pocket as I set about locating things in the kitchen to mix cocktails. Dave.

Ur at a party with a group of horny women, let em have their wicked way with you. Or don't. But whatever u do, do it with a smile on ur face and remember it's my reputation at stake.

For him, the message is almost heartfelt. He's never been a man to beat around the bush.

'I look like a fucking muppet, Dave,' I gripe into my phone, sending him a voice note in response.

'Ah, ha way, man, ya can't look that bad. Send me a selfie,' he fires back.

'What, so you can roll it out whenever you need to bribe me into going along with one of your idiotic ideas?' I'm shaking my head as I speak into my phone, as subtly as I can. 'You owe me for this, big fella.'

'Owe ya? Yey were the one who begged me for a job,' Dave replies.

He's got me there.

I was desperate

I type this time.

'And I'm your saviour, fella. Have a good neet. Try not to sleep with any of the hens, especially the bride. I can tell ya from experience, it's not good for business.'

I shove my phone into my apron. I'm not going to sleep with anyone at the hen party.

Then again, maybe that would make this night tolerable because I don't think anything could make it worse.

How did I get here?

But I know exactly how I got here. I had no job. I had no money. Which really goes hand-in-hand with the first problem. I was forced to move back to Newcastle from London because of the second problem. And my old mate and band manager, Dave, was the only person who threw me a lifeline.

So, here I am, semi-naked, utilising the only option I have available.

As I'm mixing cocktails with ingredients that have been bought in for the purpose (dropped off by Dave or one of his staff earlier today), I feel greedy eyes on me. I want to tell them, *It's only good for one night,* but I think that might be the intention. Look, tease, flirt, then go back to their respectable other halves.

Having a group of people staring at me doesn't bother me much. I once had tens of thousands of people staring at me as I performed with the band at festivals, on arena stages, even stadiums at the end. What bothers me is that these people see me for what I am these days: talentless and pointless. Back in the day, crowds sang along to *my* lyrics, they danced to the rhythm of *my* guitar.

What's worse is, I don't want to remember those days. I don't want to think about my time in the band, about Scott and how I let him down, let everyone down.

It was a close shave in the lift. Lyra *knew* it was me, that I *am* the man behind the songs that The Hand Me Downs played. Now, my hair is shaggier, I have a beard rather than gruff, my face is older. But the way she looked at me, it was as if she knew me.

The reason I know she doesn't is because she's sweet. I don't know and never have known sweet girls.

I seek her out now, amongst the increasingly rowdy group of women. When I do, I find her looking my way, a large camera around her neck and held between her hands. She doesn't look away, or smile, or react at all really. It makes me swallow so hard against something building in my throat.

Something that I think could be embarrassment. Mortification even.

She has big dark-brown irises, outlined with thick black, so unusual that in the lift, I lost myself to them for a moment, fascinated.

She has naturally full lips, soft pink beneath clear gloss. Long hair as dark as her irises flows down the back of her pretty dress and thick knitted cardigan.

It's not as if I was *noticing* in the lift but there was very little space and very little else to concentrate on, besides the fact it felt like my life was hanging by a cord. In fact, the most terrifying moment was her reminding me that I was once someone to people.

God, this job could be a disaster. *Will people know who I am? Who I was?*

I raise my cocktail shaker to her: *Want one?*

Lyra shakes her head, then lets her camera dangle from the neck brace and gives me the international gesture for driving.

So, she's here working as a photographer. I guess that explains the mismatch of her outfit to the others in the room.

I finish mixing and pour two cosmopolitan cocktails. This is going to be a fairly inefficient use of my time. Hopefully, most women want Prosecco.

'Lyra!'

My attention is dragged to a woman who looks a lot like Lyra, only with salon-perfected hair and a face full of shimmering make-up. She's waving over my fellow lift captive to where she's holding court on a sofa with four other hens. 'Lyra, do you remember that time when Joshua came to our house for Valentine's Day?' She almost sings the name *Josh-u-ahhh* as if she's been taught to in finishing school.

Lyra looks up from her camera. 'Oh, yeah.' She gives a short laugh, clearly uncomfortable but smiling for – best guess – her sister's benefit.

'So, Joshua came to our house on Valentine's Day. His mum dropped him off in their Bentley and Joshua got out of the back wearing a shirt and chinos and holding a giant stuffed dog. I mean, enormous.'

'Aww,' one of the other women coos. 'Olivia, that's adorable.'

'Oh, he wasn't calling on me,' Olivia says, casting a look across her shoulder to Lyra and beckoning her over. Lyra obliges, making her way across the room as Olivia continues the story and I eavesdrop, multitasking by filling shot glasses with tequila.

'He was coming to see Lyra.'

Gasps ensue from her rapt audience.

'It's true, isn't it, Lyra?'

Lyra nods. I don't really know her but I find myself wanting to get her out of here, away from her sister's performance.

'Mum answered the door but Lyra and I had been watching from our bedroom window. Of course, Mum and Dad loved Joshua, even then. Anyway, Mum called for Lyra to come downstairs, so naturally, I followed. And when we got downstairs, Joshua was staring at *me*. Then he asked, 'Is this your sister?' to Lyra. Didn't he, Lyra?'

She stands by the group but doesn't go to sit. I load ten full shot glasses onto a tray.

'Long story short, it was *me* who ended up with the giant stuffed toy and now, thirteen years later, Joshua and I are both doctors in the same hospital and engaged to be married at Earl's Castle in September.' Olivia holds up her left hand and wiggles her ring finger; a significant rock catches the light and makes for more dazzle than the disco balls.

'How do you feel about that, Lyra?' one of the group asks.

'Pfft,' she says, waving a hand. 'Joshua and I were thirteen or fourteen then; we would never have lasted. Plus, he and Livy are perfect for each other. Both smart, both doctors, both beautiful.'

Olivia beams. She relishes being complimented, I can tell. But I'm far more interested in why she wants to belittle her sister. 'You were *nearly* a doctor. Sort of.'

'I dropped out of medicine at the end of my third year of uni,' Lyra explains, as if she needs to. 'It wasn't for me.'

'I don't blame you,' Red says. 'It's such a stressful job, and the hours we all work are ridiculous. The effort it took to all be in the same room for a few hours tonight was huge.'

'I'd love a job like yours,' another hen says. 'I mean, no one is going to die if you take a bad picture.' This woman looks around the group and reaches for a carrot stick from a platter on a coffee table in front of her. 'Imagine having the time and space to have hobbies!' She waves the carrot around. 'Sure, one day *we'll* all have money but we have to sacrifice a lot for it.'

'We work *so* hard,' Olivia adds, nodding along with the amdram performance of *A Stage Full of Twats.*

'You all deserve the world,' Lyra says, right as I appear at her side with a round of shots. 'It's such a worthy profession.' And I think she's being genuine, which is remarkable, given how they just laid into her, passive aggressively at best, blatantly at worst.

'Shots!' the bride-to-be, Charlotte, yells, appearing from elsewhere in the room and, rightly, taking the first glass.

The second glass is taken by Lyra. She knocks it back unnoticed, not waiting for anyone else.

I lean into her ear. 'Aren't you driving?' I ask, not that it's my business.

I hear and see her sharp intake of breath. She turns her head so quickly, we're almost nose to nose. *Damn,* she smells good. Pretty. Sweet. Like fresh flowers in a meadow. Subtle enough that I missed it beneath the smell of fish in the lift.

'One won't hurt,' she tells me.

Except Lyra doesn't have one. As I'm fondled and ogled, she moves around the room taking pictures. I think, honestly, hiding behind the two cameras she rotates. I notice her have at least two more shots. My guess is, to take the edge off this *It Girl* party.

Around eleven thirty, I extract myself from a woman called Donna. She's a fifty-seven-year-old retired GP from Whitley Bay, recently separated, best friend of the mother of the bride, who traces her gel nails around each of the tattoos on my biceps and chest with eyes hooded like she's desperate enough to slum it for one night. As I'm walking away from her under the pretence of making more drinks, she pinches my arse.

'I think you're onto a sure thing there.' The voice belongs to Lyra, where she's come to lean back against the worktop in the kitchen next to me. She still has her camera around her neck, where it's been all night, more like a part of her than an accessory.

'I'll pass.' I sound as grumpy as I feel – a monkey in a zoo. I'm ready to be done with this night. My enthusiasm for faking it is depleted and, given how drained Lyra seems to be, I don't feel the need to play the cheeky butler for her.

'I thought what happens on a hen is supposed to stay on a hen,' I say, gesturing to her camera.

'That's what I thought! But the bride is a friend of my sister. An old friend of mine, too.'

'She's an old friend? Could've fooled me.'

She looks to her feet and I regret speaking my thoughts aloud. 'Yeah, well, my sister and Charlotte are both resident doctors at the RVI now and I'm… a wedding photographer, much to my family's dismay. So…' She shrugs. 'I was invited in my business capacity, not to help the bride bid goodbye to single life, or herald new beginnings.'

It's none of my business and I don't want to add to anyone's misery, especially this woman who helped me out earlier. Nor my own. So I check my watch. *Thank fuck*, it's eleven-forty-five. I'm off duty at midnight.

'This is a room full of medics, from junior doctors to consultants, so I don't think I'm going to capture too much scandal,' she says, ignoring my observation. 'Although I'm not heading out to the club from here. Who knows what trouble Donna and Jeanette will cause out on the town.'

I scoff. 'It's always the oldies.'

'Horny as hell,' Lyra says, making my lips turn up. It feels alien.

* * *

I step outside onto the pavement, leaving the hens preparing for a nightclub. The cold, salty air is biting and I pull my coat on over my bare chest. Almost silhouetted against the bright lights of the Swing bridge, Lyra is standing alone, staring up to the sky, as if she's asking the stars a question.

She didn't seem drunk upstairs but she's had too many units to drive. I don't know where she lives but I do know she had a pretty rough time tonight, so I ask her, 'D'you need a lift home?'

She startles, her gaze landing on my chest, then moving to my face as I draw up the zip of my coat.

'Ah, no, thank you. I'll just... I'm not actually sure how I'm going to get home, and back for my car in the morning, but this is what happens when I make ill-judged, impromptu decisions.'

'You're not gonna drive.'

'No.' She's staring at my eyes so intently it makes me wonder what she sees. A man barely above rock bottom? 'I'll walk to the taxi rank; it's only two minutes away.'

'Where d'you live?' I ask as she simultaneously asks me, 'Do you wax your chest?'

I rear back from her question, caught off guard, as she slaps a hand across her mouth. I feel the faintest twist of amusement teasing my lips, again. Far from the distant memory of happiness but an improvement on resentment, bitterness, anger or regret.

'Sorry, that's really none of my business. Don't even answer that,' she babbles in a way that makes me fight back a smirk. 'I live in a village near Beamish Museum, so I doubt you're going in my direction.'

She's much shorter than me in her trainers and flustered in a way that's youthful. Lightness against my blackened mood.

She's staring at me, again. Maybe because I'm staring at her, trying to figure her out, for some reason. 'Your eyes twinkle more than the lights of the Millennium bridge,' she tells me, which also tells me, she is, in fact, feeling the effects of alcohol.

'The Millennium bridge doesn't twinkle,' I tell her.

'Okay, lyric police,' she says, dragging me back from whatever hold she just had me in, to reality. To being a lyricist. Or, at least, in a past life.

I want to get off the subject, so I change it. 'Why do you let them treat you like that?'

'Who?' she asks, brown eyes widening.

'Your sister and her friends? Why d'you let them put you down?'

'They don't.' She looks to her feet and I want to nudge her chin up, but I put my hands in my pockets to stop me.

'Really? So, you're telling me you're standing out here feeling good about yourself?'

She glares at me, her light dimmed by my words. *Yeah, I have that effect on people.*

'Didn't think so,' I tell her. 'Why do you let them get away with it?'

She swallows so hard, I know my question has hit home. 'It's complicated.'

'Didn't look it. It looked to me as if they think they're better than you and you don't set them straight.'

'You don't know anything about me,' she gripes indignantly, with surprising fire.

'I know you tried to distract me in that lift because you could see I'm claustrophobic. I know you care about the planet and that you've driven out of your way tonight to be at a hen party you didn't want to be at just to please your sister.'

Her nostrils flare but she doesn't disagree.

'I've met people like them before,' I tell her. 'People who want to put you down to make themselves feel good. They'll keep telling the same stories until you give them something else to talk about. Until *you* change their narrative.'

I'm waiting for her retort as she scowls at me, and I don't

know why but I like her feistiness. Something tells me she doesn't display it often enough.

Before she responds, the door to Phoenix House opens and the sound of animated chatter escapes.

I glance the way of the other hens but my face is turned back to Lyra, her palms holding my cheeks. And she crashes her mouth against mine.

I feel my eyes widen as I wait for my synapses to catch up and send sensible messages to my brain. I meet her focused gaze and, in her look, I think she's asking me to play along, to help her out. To help her write a new song for her sister to sing about her.

I hate bullies as much as I hate people who try to tell you who you are and who you should be. More than that, there's something in Lyra's kiss – warmth, passion, desperation? Fuck knows. But it makes me bring my hands onto her hips and walk her backwards, until her backside meets my parked car.

God, maybe it's just been a while for me because her taste, the feel of her mouth, her body, ignites something in me that I haven't felt for a long time. I grip her hip tighter, bringing my other hand to the base of her neck, fingers gently tugging her hair. Our tongues meet, slick and hot, making my eyes close. And when she groans into my mouth, I forget where we are, rolling my hips against her.

Then the hens are whooping, bringing me back to the pavement, and I hear someone demand, 'Lyra, what on earth?'

But her words spur Lyra on. She slips her arms under my coat and pulls me, hard, against her. *Jesus*, this is as close to fucking as I've been for months.

'Oh, leave the girl to it. Someone ought to enjoy him.' I'm sure that came from Donna. It reminds me of something one of my old bandmates used to say: *It's always the older ones that want to throw their knickers at you.*

Just like that, I'm thrust back to reality. Kissing a kind girl on a pavement so she can piss off her sister.

Sensing the group move away, I open one eye to confirm, then prise myself away from Lyra's touch.

'I guess you're right,' she whispers, eyes still closed as she draws a thumb along her lips in a way that makes me want to feel them on mine again. 'I doubt the next story my sister tells will be about how her fiancé preferred her over me when we were teenagers.'

And *I* guess this is who I am now. All I'm good for.

Lyra gently nudges me away from her and peels herself off the car. 'Sorry, that was... Erm...'

I have no idea what she's going to say, and it doesn't matter. Gone are the days when a woman would be the one wanting to take me back to her place. And I've no business wanting to take this sweet girl anywhere.

'Wrong of me,' she says. 'And unlike me,' she's quick to add. *No kidding.* 'I shouldn't have done it. It's just—'

'It's okay,' I tell her, words finally leaving me as everything that just charged in my body drains. 'It's all part of the job.'

'Of course, right, because you're a...' She gestures from my head to my toes. 'Oh God, are you a hooker? A male gigolo? A prostitute? An escort? What *is* a naked butler?'

In the wake of the charge, my dark mood returns. A *joke* is what I am.

Just when I think tonight really can't possibly get any worse, I remember what I'm driving.

Shaking my head at the utter farce of my life, I pull my keys from my pocket and watch the lights of my outrageous wheels flash twice.

I don't wait to see Lyra's reaction to my car, which we've just been pressed up against. On loan from Dave's daughter whilst she's travelling on a gap year, the Barbie-pink Fiat 500 is ridiculous. Bountiful eyelashes have been stuck onto the headlights and fluffy pink dice hang from the rearview mirror, whilst Dalmatian-print fur covers the seats.

Throwing my backpack onto the passenger seat, I tell her, 'Good luck getting home, Lyra.'

'Wh— I— Is this your *girlfriend's* car?'

Forearms braced on the roof of Barbie, I ask, 'Which is it, gigolo or boyfriend, because I'm pretty sure the two are mutually exclusive?'

I squish my frame into the driver's seat as if I'm Debbie fucking McGee – knees almost touching pecs – and fight with the pedals that are too close together for my size-eleven feet.

The car chugs against me once, then twice, then we seem to call a truce and I pull into the road faster than I even knew a car like this could move. Angry with the entire fucking universe.

The universe that also feels like being ironic because my car radio is stuck on Heart, which is currently playing 'She is Love' by Oasis. Yet, in spite of the irony, I'm rubbing my lips, where I just received one of the best snogs of my life.

I'm lost in a confused reverie, which the presenter pulls me from when the song ends and he says, 'That one was requested by Jackie from Jarrow. Next up, we have a request from Sheila in Byker, who says this song always reminds her of falling in love with her husband. Happy anniversary, Dereck, from your Sheila. Here's "Loving You" by The Hand Me Downs.'

It's as if the sound of the opening riff turns me to stone – my hands still on the wheel, my foot stuck on the accelerator.

I'm cast back to being twenty-two years old and singing that song to my seventeen-year-old brother for the first time in our parents' garage and telling him, 'This'll be the one, kid, I'm telling you.'

In my memory, as I sing the lyrics I've just finished writing for my brother, Trev and Jay strum chords in the sequence I've made up, Scott picks up a tambourine and starts tapping it against his thigh, where he's perched on an old beer barrel. Then he's singing with me.

I remember closing my eyes and seeing a version of us in the future, playing this song to stadiums full of people.

When we made it, years after that day in the garage, it wasn't me singing lead vocals, it was our kid. My younger brother who got all my hand me downs when we were growing up. My younger brother with more talent and charisma in his little finger than I have in my entire body. Our kid, who was the star of the band I named after him.

3
LYRA

April 2025

The Secret Weapon at the Wedding Fayre

'Thanks again for this, Mandy, I owe you one,' I tell my friend as I slip into the passenger seat of her Corsa.

She lowers her shades and looks over me as if she's a paramedic assessing me before we move off in her emergency response vehicle. I wait for her comment but she only hands me a drive-thru cup of coffee.

'White americano, oat milk,' she says. 'You don't look too bad for someone who ditched her car because she drank too many shots of tequila last night.'

I inhale the scent of the coffee, then take a sip, sighing contentedly. 'I need this, but only because I'm tired, and embarrassed, not hungover. I didn't drink enough to be hungover, only enough to make this morning a pain in the arse.'

Mandy zooms away from my very modest, pebble-dashed

mining-village bungalow. It ought to be someone's retirement home but happens to be my first home living away from my parents since my student accommodation at university.

She accelerates so hard, both her car and me are shouting at her as I'm forced back into my seat, my coffee spilling out of the small hole in the lid. She has one speed and it's as fast as her old banger will allow.

'Unload. Vent. Tell me all about it,' she says, reaching for her own coffee cup from the centre console as we reach the carriageway between Beamish and Chester-le-Street. 'You rarely drink, despite my unrelenting peer pressure. Even when you do, it's a sociable glass of wine with dinner, so last night must've been bad.' She sets her coffee back down in the holster. 'It was Livy, wasn't it? No offence, Lyra, but your sister can act like a dick.'

'Hey, she's my sister. You can't call her a dick.'

'I didn't say she *is* a dick, I said she can *act like* a dick.'

I roll my eyes but she's right.

'I can categorically say...' She signals to overtake and flies past a white van, needlessly, since there's no real traffic on the road at seven-thirty on a Saturday morning and the van is travelling at the speed limit. 'That your sister's engagement party was one of the worst experiences of my last year.'

I chuckle. 'It was nice.' It was lavish, so fancy it could have been a wedding, both our parents and Joshua's parents jointly stumping up to mark the occasion.

'I'll admit, the free bar and swanky buffet were great, but the snide remarks and passive-aggressiveness of your sister and her mates who all have washing poles shoved up their—'

'Okay, okay, thank you, I get it.' I take a mouthful of coffee and shrug. 'Yes, they probably drove me to a shot or two. But I also got trapped in a lift, with a naked butler, who was so very, very, *very* wrong for me, yet totally in the right place at the right time.'

'Whoa, now I'm listening.'

I cringe. 'I ended the night snogging his face off, for my sister and all her friends to witness my ultimate demise.'

'Demise? This sounds bloody brilliant!' Mandy is far too animated given the early start and especially given...

'He's like a *prostitute*, Mandy! What was I *thinking*?'

She laughs loudly, her head pressing back into the seat, her eyes closed.

'Eyes on the road, Mandy!'

'Sorry. It's just...' She chuckles. 'This is fantastic. You've finally moved on from that idiot boy next door that you were only dating for your parents' approval and it's with a naked butler. Who, by definition, must be insanely hot, and may or may not have a lot of sex but if he does, contrary to your thoughts, my view is, his training must make him a bloody excellent shag.'

Coffee sprays from my mouth as I laugh. 'I wouldn't know. Thankfully, I stopped myself before getting that far.'

'Why, didn't you have any cash on you?'

'It's not funny, Mandy!'

'Then stop laughing, Lyra!'

I palm my face. 'He was also massively rude and dismissive. Completely... cantankerous. He couldn't bolt from me fast enough.'

'Before or after you called him a prostitute?'

'You're joking but I actually *did*.'

'No!'

'Yes.' I wince, finding solace in my hot caffeine. 'Oh *God*, I just remembered, his car was pink. And had longer eyelashes than an elephant. How humiliating for us both. At least I gave my sister something new to talk about and, thankfully, I'm unlikely to ever see him again.'

We pull off the main road and onto the long driveway that leads across the River Wear and up a steep climb to Earl's Castle, the stunning fourteenth-century building where Mandy and I are selling our worth on stands at a wedding fayre for the full day. After which, I'm going to have to beg Mandy to take me to Newcastle to collect my car, which is probably clamped in Deansgate car park by now.

The thought thrusts me back to *that kiss.* I trace my lips where the butler's were last night. Never have I ever been kissed like that before. It felt closer to fourth base than when I've actually got to fourth base with anyone.

'Did I mention he looked like Guy Walker from The Hand Me Downs, who I crushed on so bad for my entire late teens and early twenties?'

'The hooker?'

I bite my lip to fend off my smirk as I nod.

'Hench, well-versed in the bedroom *and* a rock star look-a-like. I'm turning us around and going to the nearest cash point to buy your foo-foo a treat!'

By the time we pull into the staff car park of the estate grounds, we're both in fits of giggles.

Mandy is five years older than me. She's vivacious and wild in the best of ways. More liberated and comfortable in her own skin than crazy or impulsive. She says what she thinks and does what she wants, though not with a complete disregard for people's feelings. She's kind and fun, outspoken but not rude. She's basically an aspirational human.

Steven, one of the hotel's porters, who has blond-tipped, nineties-boyband-style spiked hair, which doesn't at all match the Regency-era pantaloons he's adorning – because the staff at Earl's Castle all wear period costume – taps on the driver's side window. We take him up on his offer to help us inside with our stuff, which is a lot. Together, we lug banners, cameras and sample wedding albums from the boot and back seats of the car.

Technically, Mandy is my boss. When I dropped out of uni seven years ago, I had no idea what I was going to do. My plans to study documentary photography were kiboshed That Night and the following months became a blur of hospital visits and rehabilitation for my dad.

But once the appointments calmed down, we, as a family, accepted our new normal. Mum and Livy went back to work and Dad accepted that he had disabilities that would forever change life as it had been. *I* was lost, stagnant, inexperienced in anything other than medical care and that was the very last thing I wanted to go back to.

So when Cami mentioned that she had a friend who was running her own business as a wedding photographer and she needed some support on weekends, I thought, *why not?* I get to take pictures for a living and I have flexibility to work around Dad's care.

Mandy and I exchange pleasantries with a few of the other preferred suppliers to Earl's Castle: tailors, seamstresses, decorators, crafters, cake bakers, musicians, magicians, videographers and photographers. Then we set up our stand for the fayre in my favourite room in the castle to photograph weddings.

It's an enormous, three-hundred-guest-capacity room, with vastly high ceilings, intricately plastered walls, and six dazzlingly elaborate crystal chandeliers. Ornately decorated mirrors allow light from the expansive windows to bounce around the pristinely white space. The only colour in the room comes from luxurious midnight-blue drapes that outline the alcoves in which the windows sit.

I love it because it's majestic, charming and bright, yet its simplistic colour allows couples to add personal touches for their celebration. It also gives me freedom to explore stunning lighting, to use different lenses, and make the couples' colour schemes really pop.

The other rooms in the castle are medieval and fun, creepy even, perfect for the murder-mystery nights and medieval banquets held here but really tricky to photograph. Weddings should be bright, shouldn't they? A celebration of love, of new life, of—

'My favourite photographers! Are you ready for a day of selling?'

That's Pearl, one of the family management team who run the hotel on behalf of the owners – whose ownership dates right back to the seventeenth century. Pretty cool, if you're into the history of peerages. I am not. But I do like a romantic venue and I adore Pearl.

She's exactly the kind of person her name suggests – a precious gem. She and her husband Geoff have been managing the castle for nearly thirty years, as Pearl's parents had done before them. And since they reached the twenty-ninth anniversary of their twenty-first birthdays (their words), their kids have been preparing to take over their management business, too.

'Absolutely,' I say.

'With bells on,' Mandy adds.

Geoff appears at Pearl's side, wearing his staple corduroy

trousers and pale checked shirt, clean shaven, grey-white hair neatly combed. 'Thank you for being here for another wedding fayre,' he says. 'Unfortunately, we're sharing some disappointing news today.'

His tone makes me look to Mandy, knowing she won't know any more than I do but wanting some kind of… reassurance? This place is our constant. One of our main sources of income. I see my trepidation reflected.

'The owners of Earl's Castle are considering options for the future management of the hotel. And…' Geoff smiles sadly at his wife. 'That includes the potential for a large hotel management chain to replace our family here.'

Poor Pearl and Geoff. Poor Mandy and me.

'We suffered like everyone else during the pandemic, then with the economy that followed, people haven't been in a position to splurge on weddings the way they did,' Geoff goes on. 'The storm over winter did a fair amount of damage to the castle and the owners need money to deal with the repairs.'

'The problem, in a nutshell,' Pearl says, pressing a hand to Geoff's arm, 'is that we don't have all our slots booked for this wedding season, let alone the level of advanced bookings we've historically seen. And, as you know, weddings are our bread and butter.'

'So,' Geoff says, brighter now, 'what we're asking of you lovely bunch is to put your best foot forward for us for today. Fill the empty slots we have this year and try your best to sell a wedding experience at Earl's Castle.'

'Give us a fighting chance against the big corporates,' Pearl begs.

'We need you all more than ever,' Geoff finishes.

Mandy and I give hugs and words of reassurance that we'll do our utmost to help.

'We know you will,' Pearl says, her signature bright smile in place. 'And Big Dave tells me he's bringing along a secret weapon today, whoever that might be. He promises that bookings will come flooding in.'

She calls him Big Dave, though not to his face, because there are two Daves: Little Dave, who makes handcrafted favours for wedding guests, and Big Dave, who runs an entertainment company with two singers, a band, DJs, a string quartet and a concert harpist.

Big Dave has so many tattoos, they can't be hidden by the shirt and trousers he's wearing today, not unless he also intends to wear gloves to cover his knuckles. But inside, he's less grizzly bear and more teddy bear. Gooey, sort of squishy around the middle, familiar and comforting.

I glance over to where he's still setting up his stand and the small events stage he'll use to showcase his entertainment company to attendees. Running late, by the looks of things. I'm intrigued to know who or what this secret weapon is.

I don't have to wait long before a man in a perfectly tailored black suit slips into my line of sight – back to me as he approaches Dave.

'Decided to show up, did ya?' Dave asks the man.

The guy checks his watch and, not that I mean to look, but my eyes are drawn to the way his jacket tugs against his firm arm. 'It's nine fifty-three,' he grumbles.

'The event starts at ten, matey, and I needed help setting up.'

'Aren't I just the talent?' the man responds, receiving a clip around the ear from Dave.

'Are ya ready to get started?' Dave asks, nodding in the direction of the stage and the standing microphone he's set up there.

'I'm singing? I thought I was just turning up to chat to some brides.'

'The best way to sell the act is to let them hear yer voice.'

He drags a hand through his thick dark hair. 'What am I supposed to sing?'

Dave holds his arms out wide and even I know what he's thinking... 'Michael Bublé, Ed Sheeran, Lonestar, Aerosmith, John Legend. Wedding songs.'

'Christ,' the man says, making me wonder what on earth he *thought* he was doing here. At Earl's Castle. A wedding fayre. Working for Dave's entertainment company.

* * *

Mandy and I look up from our simultaneous sales pitches and smile at each other when we finally hear the familiar *ding ding ding ding ding doo dah* of the beginning of Michael Bublé's 'Everything'. A wedding classic and the song to hopefully put all the brides-to-be in the room in a good mood. Because happy people book weddings.

'So, we're about to hear Dave's secret weapon?'

'Sounds like it,' I tell her, then turn back to my potential client and open a page in one of my wedding albums. 'These are pictures I took in the rose gardens here in May last year. You can see how beautiful the blooms look that time of year.'

Then I still, my next words lost on my tongue as I hear the opening lyrics from 'Everything'. I've heard these lyrics hundreds of times and many times in this very room, but they've never sounded the way they do now. Raw, sandpaper-like, gritty. The song I'm so familiar with is still bright, still beautiful, but it feels deeper, as if the man behind this voice isn't performing for a crowd but for the woman he loves, in their home, in their bedroom.

I love music. Listening to it, moving to it, playing it on my own piano. I'm one of those people who finds music spellbinding, mood shifting and unfortunately in this very moment, like a portal to another time and place.

And as the women in front of my table speak, I don't hear them, because my brain has capacity for only one thing – to find the source of the voice I've heard before, in another time and place. A voice I've fallen for every time I've heard it. Its gravelly rasp. The way his lower register makes my heart thud. The way it makes everything else happening around me fade into nothingness, leaving only his voice and the effect it has on me.

I step out from the table. 'Excuse me one second, ladies, I'll be right back.'

Nervously, jittery, as if *I'm* a bride walking the aisle to meet *my* groom at the altar, I head to the stage.

I come to stop, or rather I'm forced to stop by the gathering crowd around the stage. The suited man, the owner of the voice I hear in my dreams and on playlists in my car, sings. His hands are braced on the microphone and though he's wearing sunglasses, I think his eyes will be shut, because I've seen this man sing before, watching his eyes close as he lives and breathes the music.

The beard he wore last night has been shaved and he's wearing substantially more clothes now, but I'm certain that the naked butler from the hen party, the *hooker* I threw myself at to piss off my sister, is...

Guy Walker.

I slap my hand across my mouth as I gasp. I snogged *Guy Walker.*

Guy Walker is Dave's secret weapon.

And he's working as a *wedding singer?*

The song ends and somehow, through the gathering women, Guy's focus feels as if it's fixed on me. *Oh shit!* I don't wait to confirm, ducking as fast as I can, crawling on my knees between the sea of legs and back to my table.

'Psst, *Mandy*!' I say when I'm next to her.

'Why are you on your hands and knees?' she asks, understandably perplexed.

'That's hard to explain.' I accept the hand she offers to me and come up to stand. 'You know the naked butler from last night?'

'I don't know him but, yeah?'

'Well, he's, he was, he *is*... Oh *God*, he's *Guy Walker*.'

'Who's—? Wait, from The Hand Me Downs?'

'Shh. Yes,' I whisper. 'He's also Dave's secret weapon and he's singing right over there.'

'No way!' She hops up to stand on her seat. From her new vantage point, I imagine she can see across all the sales banners to the man who is now singing 'All of Me' by John Legend. 'For real? Are you sure he doesn't just look— Oh shit, yeah, his name's all over Dave's stand.'

She gets down from the seat and looks at me. 'Well, fuck me gently. You snogged a rock star.'

I get back to my clients but zone in and out of their conversation, still tuning into Guy in the background, feeling... *bizarre*.

It feels so trippy that he's here. That he's a naked butler, a wedding singer. That he's *not* performing to packed-out stadiums. I know he hasn't released music for years, not since his brother died, but *this?* His talent deserves more than *this*.

Then again, he rejected me last night – sort of understandable now, given he's a rock star and all – and really wasn't all that polite about it. Though I did call him a prostitute. *God,* imagine all the women he's slept with who *didn't* pay him.

This is... *mortifying.* Whilst at the same time, I'm kind of tingling all over. Once, I was supposed to meet him and... well, That Night never worked out. Now, seven years later, I'm in the same room as that voice again.

4

GUY

April 2025

Completely Over the Fucking Wedding Fayre

I take a packet of cigarettes from my backpack and wiggle them at Dave, who's mid-conversation with one of the endless stream of clients contracting his entertainment company for their wedding parties. I'm pleased he's making a success of things. I always felt bad for how The Hand Me Downs left his management.

Add it to the long list of things I feel justly guilty about.

Dave nods and I assume I'm dismissed. I must have sung thirty songs already – songs my subconscious seemed to know the tune of, though I kept having to check the lyrics. I don't sing any more and I can feel it in my unexercised throat.

Maybe I should have applied for a job as a bin man because this performance business is not coming easily at all.

Now, Dave has plastered my name all over his banners, which he promised me he wouldn't do, upped his prices and booked me in for weddings two years from now.

All I want to do is scream for everyone to hear, *I'm Not That Man Any More!*

That man would never have been seen dead singing Bublé in a fucking suit. For the record, I own two suits. One doesn't fit any more, since it's from my end-of-school dance back in 2008, which begs the question, why haven't I binned it? The other, which I'm wearing and wishing I wasn't, is another torturous reminder that I watched my brother be buried three years ago.

Honestly, I'd refund every single booking Dave has made this morning if I could, but I can't, because my money is tied up. It isn't mine. Right now, my options are limited.

So, I'm standing outside this posh castle, shades on and a fag between my lips, thankfully, with no way of lighting it. I keep a packet of cigarettes on me all the time – both as a reminder that I could smoke but I chose to give it up, and because it's a nifty get-out-of-jail when I need to take a breather.

Hands in the pockets of my funeral trousers, I walk out to an old oak tree to look out across the estate's park land, coming to rest a shoulder on the solid trunk, thinking... *This. Is. Not. My. Life.*

The truth is, I arrived here on time this morning. I *wanted* to be on time, for Dave's sake, to let him know that I *am* grateful for this lifeline he's thrown me. But at nine twenty-five, sitting in my pink car in the staff car park, I just... *couldn't.* My legs forgot how to move. My arms couldn't remember how to bend. My lungs couldn't draw their next breath. I just... *froze.*

It hasn't happened for a while but I guess something about the hen party last night triggered me. Isn't that the buzz word of the 2020s? Aren't I on trend if I'm triggered and spiralling?

At least I have being fashionable going for me, because when I woke in the night, lying in sheets so wet they could have been wrung out like a sponge from a bath, I felt like shit.

I dreamed of *That Night*. Not the one when I got the phone call I'll never forget. The one where it all started. The one where I was so preoccupied with myself – with chasing after a girl, then wallowing when I couldn't find her – that I took my eyes off my kid brother.

Now, I'm minding my own business, intermittently checking my watch to make sure I don't take the piss out of Dave's generosity, when there's a deep exhalation somewhere near me. Then suddenly, a woman standing in front of the oak tree, staring at the same view as me.

She doesn't realise I'm here.

Her long hair falls down her back in a loose plait, the kind my kid sister would have worn in secondary school. Bex is the youngest of the three of us – her, Scott and me. Seven years younger than me, a year younger than Scott.

Despite living back on their doorsteps, I haven't seen Bex, or my mam, for three years. Not since Scott's funeral. By the time that day ended, we all knew where we stood. My stepdad had made his views abundantly clear to me. His *hate*.

He was the one who voiced what everyone else was thinking. What happened to Scott was on my shoulders.

If I could swap places, bring him back, build a fucking time machine and undo all the shit that went wrong, I would, I'd undo it all. I'd go back and make sure he never joined The Hand Me Downs. I'd make damn sure that I'd never taken my eyes off him on That Night, too focused on pining after a girl to notice his first time taking hard drugs.

The girl with the plait shakes her head, as if she's having a conversation in her mind. She takes her hands from the pockets of her long beige cardigan and folds them around her middle, across her summery, yellow dress. As I watch her, she strikes me as familiar, and when she shifts her stance, I do recognise her profile.

Despite standing still, the surprise makes me lose my balance. My foot shifts, snapping a twig on the grass.

The girl from last night – *that kiss* – gasps as she turns to see me. 'Guy!'

My cigarette falls from my lips onto damp grass. *Damn it,* that's been a pack of twenty for probably eighteen months, since I slipped and smoked my previous packet.

Lyra. Her name doesn't make it out of my mouth. Maybe because, as we stare at each other, a sense of knowing, like a *Sliding Doors* or *Groundhog Day* moment is happening. I feel like I'm supposed to know this woman. It's the same feeling I got when I first saw her in the lift last night. A sense of desire that drove me to get lost in her kiss.

I feel like I'm missing something. Honestly, it could just be due to the number of times I replayed that kiss in my mind last night, the girl I'll never get out of my head for many reasons, including that she called me a gigolo. But when she kissed me, when I kissed her back, it felt as if something shifted in me. I'll be damned if I know what. All I know is, it left me angry, or wired, or fucking afraid. Possibly all three.

'Have we met before?' I ask.

I mean before last night but I realise too late, as I watch her swallow deeply, then cast her gaze to the ground, she's taken my question the wrong way.

'No.' She clears her throat. 'Never.'

Now I *know* I haven't met her before last night because I'm reminded how much like a *nice* girl she seemed. A quiet, sweet, unsure of herself girl. Right up to the point of throwing herself at me. Giving me a kiss that wasn't innocent at all.

Easy ones. Angry ones. Filthy ones. Those are the kind of women I know.

I take out another cigarette and I'm about to apologise when she surprises me for a second time, standing taller, rolling her shoulders back, eyes narrowing in temper. 'You know, I came out here to find you and apologise for my behaviour last night.' She shakes her head again, clearly biting down on her gums, maybe the words she actually wants to say, too. 'But since you don't even remember meeting me...' She inhales so deeply, her chest rises. 'You can bloody well sod off.'

Hold the phone! Where did *that* come from?

'*I* can sod off?' I call after her as she strides huffily off the grass, back in the direction of the castle. 'You called me a gigolo. A *prostitute*!'

She spins to face me. 'I came to apologise!' Now she charges back towards me, until she's only one big stride from pressing her pointed finger into my chest. 'If you remember, I asked you if you were... *you.* And you denied it. You lied to me. To my face. Then pretended to be someone else for the entire party. If anyone is at fault here, it certainly isn't me.'

I scoff. She's kind of cute irate. 'Then why were you coming out here to apologise?'

'Because.' She stomps her foot. 'Because I... I didn't behave well. Like... myself. I...'

'Used me to get at your sister? Don't worry about it. Shit happens. I won't lose sleep over it.'

Except I did. The kiss. The way she made me feel worthless, the size of a peanut, immediately after it.

By the time I got home, there was a chink, I think, in the armour I wear these days. In the safety partition I've learned to put between me and the rest of the world because *no,* I *don't* want to talk about *It,* and *no,* I don't think I'm fine but *no,* I don't think I deserve to feel fine either. My armour that says, *Keep your fucking distance, World.*

A chink.

A chink that made me stare at the empty bottle of tequila I'd been drinking water from all night and wish it was full of the kind of stuff that could drown it all out.

And a disturbed night, of nightmares I don't like to mention, let alone relive.

'I'm sure you won't. But if I'd known that you were... *you,* I never would have presumed I could just...'

'Kiss me?' Kiss me like *that*?

She scowls. 'Yes.'

'So it's okay to kiss random gigolos but not musicians?'

'Yes. *No.* Maybe. I don't know. But it doesn't matter, since you don't remember that happening. I guess that's the problem when you drink a bottle of tequila.'

I feel my brow furrow. So full of assumptions, no real clue what she's talking about. If she'd kissed a man who'd drank a bottle of tequila, she'd have known about the smell on his breath, about the stagger in his feet, the clumsiness of his touch.

'Look, Lyra—' For a second, I'm about to explain my unfortunate phrasing, that I do remember last night, and that I was actually asking whether we've met before then. But then I think, *Who the hell is this woman, shouting in my face, as if my day, my week, my month, the last three fucking years isn't bad enough without her taking an unjustified tantrum?*

Instead, I tell her, 'I've gotta get back inside.'

'Why *are* you here, Guy Walker from The Hand Me Downs?' she asks, her words falling on my back because I just can't be arsed with more agro in my life. 'And don't you know cigarettes kill? Are you the last man on earth still smoking in 2025?'

I can't believe it, even as I'm making the gesture, but I flip her the bird across my shoulder. Instead of explaining that I don't smoke, that she's full of the aspersions of a goody two shoes, I call back to her, 'I take it your sheltered life's never taken you to continental Europe.'

'It has, actually. To Madrid in 2022. And I wasted my only trip out of this country for seven years on seeing *you* playing in concert. Now I really wish I could refund myself all that money.'

I've started heading up the stone steps, back towards the giant wood entrance doors of the castle, but I stop, stilled by her words. *Madrid.*

I close my eyes as an image of Scott comes to me. Him collapsed across a sofa in our hotel room from a concoction of exhaustion and drugs. It had already started then. His addiction had taken hold.

To the outside world, we were at the top of our game.

Reality felt different.

My chest tightens and I open my eyes, reaching for the wall of the steps. I know all of this, these memories that come to me. What's the point of my mind showing me again and again? Playing fucking tricks on me. Punishing me for not being enough. For failing our kid.

Pull yourself together, Guy. Get a hold of yourself.

Thankfully, I do. I push the nightmares away and tell the woman who's to blame for this one. 'I'd refund you myself if I could but if I could, I wouldn't be singing fucking Bublé songs at a wedding fayre in County Durham.'

'Why did you lie to me about who you are?' she asks, her

tone softer now, as if she's remembered who she is and what she isn't – a bad girl. I'd recognise one easily.

I turn to look at her and the honest answer is here, on the tip of my tongue: *Look at me. I'm a broke, failed musician, a shit brother, son, human. Why would I want to admit to being me?* But I go with the easier response, which is, 'I didn't. You made an assumption and I chose not to correct you.'

But I'm not Guy Walker of The Hand Me Downs any more. Last night and today are proof of it. There's hardly a trace left of that lad she flew out to Madrid to see in concert. Barely anything at all. Only a name that reminds people of a man who was someone once.

5

LYRA

May 2025
Charlotte's Wedding Reception

It's been three weeks since Charlotte's hen party. Three weeks since I kissed Guy Walker, rock star and most miserable man alive. Today is Charlotte's big day. Though I'm loathe to admit it, the wedding has been so beautiful, even I'm rooting for the passive-aggressive bride and her groom with an attitude.

'Are you sure you don't mind if I head off?' Mandy asks me.

Whilst the vast marquee on the lawn in front of Earl's Castle is being reset – dining tables being cleared and removed to make space for a buffet, stage and dance floor – the two of us have sneaked off for a ten-minute de-shoe and foot rub.

We've been jointly shooting the wedding since 8 a.m., when the bridal party started getting ready – my sister included, not that she's uttered more than a sentence to me since I embarrassed her in front of her friends by snogging a naked butler.

Add it to the long list of things I do that offend my perfect sibling.

'Not at all,' I tell her, digging my thumb into the base of my aching toes. 'You head off. Have you got any plans?'

'Just spending a few hours with Ginny. We've been like ships in the night since she started her new job working shifts.'

Mandy and I tend to take turns finishing early at weekend weddings during the season. Given the lighting is dimmed and most people are milling around the bar or the dance floor for the evening reception, it's much easier for one photographer to capture sufficient moments to keep the newlyweds happy.

But she'd never leave – nor would I – before the leftovers!

I love weddings. Mostly. I love helping my clients document their memories. Mostly. But without caveat, I bloody love getting a posh three-course meal at this time of night, on account of the chefs always over-making, just in case.

Tonight, we have... 'It's the chicken liver parfait,' I tell Mandy, lifting the cloche from one of the plates left out in the staffroom. I stick two fingers into my mouth and fake-gag. 'That's definitely yours.' I lift another cloche. 'There's a Jerusalem artichoke. I'll take that.'

'Excellent trade in my opinion,' Mandy says.

We're sitting in the staffroom, high up in the eastern turret of the castle. Rightly, the waitstaff tending the wedding get first dibs on all spare food, then Nick, the general manager on duty on Saturday nights, will give Mandy and me a nod if there's enough for us.

Given the rest of the venue is beautiful, the staffroom is something of an anomaly. More like a workman's canteen, with six metal tables and four awfully uncomfortable chairs around each. There's a pixilated television attached to one wall.

Since we're the only two people here, Mandy has kicked back on one painful chair and dragged another opposite to prop up her feet.

I lift another cloche. 'Chicken main.' Another. 'Ooh, the salmon.' Another. 'Or the ox cheek.'

'I'll continue the meat theme and take the ox,' Mandy tells me. 'Just don't tell Ginny; she's trying to encourage us to eat more veggie.'

'My lips are sealed.' I move on to three stacked cold plates. 'Now for the best bit. I hope there are profiteroles.'

'You're a creature of habit.'

'If you want to be happy, eliminate choice from your life. I want to be happy bathing in copious amounts of choux pastry filled with Chantilly cream for the entire wedding season.' I expose a plate of my desired pudding. 'Oh baby, where have you *been* all my life.'

Mandy chuckles. 'Fair enough. But I think you and those profiteroles need to get a room. What else is there?'

'Lemon posset times two.'

She rolls her eyes but holds out a hand.

With the plates covering our tabletop, we both dig in. Even though it's slightly dry and hours old now, the food is still delicious. Better than the batches of soup, lasagne and chilli that I've been making for myself on rotation since moving into my own place for the first time three months ago. It just seems pointless to make fancy meals for one.

'I overheard Juliette earlier,' Mandy says. 'You know, the really gossipy bridesmaid with hair down to her arse cheeks? She was talking about your little foray with the butler at Charlotte's hen.' She switches out her starter plate for her main dish. 'You're a hot topic, girlie.'

I roll my eyes. 'I hope my sister wasn't in earshot. She's still pissed with me about it.'

'Your sister's always pissed off with you about something.'

'I agree, though on this occasion, I was reckless and, you know, out of character.'

Mandy raises her eyebrows. 'You kissed a hot guy at a hen party. Who, unknown to them, happens to be famous.' She chuckles around a forkful of food. 'Wait till they realise you kissed Guy Walker.'

'That's not why— I didn't know that at the time. And that only makes it worse. I was like a horny groupie.'

'I'm sure he's had plenty of groupie gropes in his time.'

I snort-laugh. 'Stop.'

Testament to how hungry I am, we eat our mains in silence. Then it's time for the plate I really want... pudding.

'Oh my God, these profiteroles are so, so, sooooooo good.' I have half a ball of deliciousness in my mouth as I speak.

'Are you eating that or making love to it?' Mandy asks, forking her posset. Jealous, I bet.

I decide to rub it in, Meg Ryan style. I lick the Chantilly cream the way I'd eat a Creme Egg, 'Oh, baby, you're so good.' Eying Mandy, I push the other half choux into my mouth, moaning around the pastry. 'Oh, Profiterole. Yes, just like that. Mmm. Yes, yes, yes!'

Mandy's eyes widen, shocked at the outburst that's so very unlike me. But I'm just getting started. I take a second profiterole, lick the chocolate with near incomprehensible sounds of pleasure, then push the whole thing into my mouth.

As I do, Mandy squeezes her eyes shut and points behind

me. I follow her gesture, turning on the spot, full ball in mouth, and see... Guy Walker. *Oh my God!*

I clamp my mouth shut to hide its contents. But as I do, the choux pops and Chantilly cream bursts like semen from my lips. And it squirts right onto... Guy's face, the lapel of his black suit jacket, and... his crotch. Not the *crotch*!

I thrust a hand over my mouth, trying desperately to chew what's inside, whilst at the same time muttering, 'I. Am. So. Sorry.'

If looks could kill...

I glance around the room, remembering the roll of blue paper holstered to the wall. Rushing to grab some, I tell Guy, 'I didn't realise there was anyone else here. I was just—' *What was I doing? How on earth do I explain my fake profiterogasm?*

'Getting yourself off on dessert?' he offers.

'Urgh. That sounds so bad.' Armed with four large squares of blue roll, I rush to him and start frantically rubbing the cream from his suit. As I'm doing so, Big Dave comes into the room.

'Oh aye? What's gannin' on here, like?' he asks.

'It's not what it looks like.'

'Really? 'Cause it looks like you're cleanin' spunk off our lad's Sergeant Major.'

I guess it does look exactly like that...

I press my lips together tightly, fighting nervous laughter as I feel anger emanate from Guy, like a gasket that's about to blow.

But when Mandy bursts into a loud cackle behind me, and Dave belly-chuckles along with her, I can't help myself. I giggle too. 'Sorry,' I tell Guy, again. But he remains the only person in the room who is *not* seeing the funny side of this charade.

'Well, it looks like I've had all the leftover food I need,' he gripes, his jaw stiff as he speaks directly to me. Then he glances to Dave. 'I'll see you in the marquee, once I've sorted myself out in the toilets.'

As Guy turns to leave, Dave calls after him, 'It looks like you've already sorted yourself out, matey.'

'Fuck off,' Guy mutters, storming out.

The remaining three of us look at each other and I don't know who instigates it, but we all fall back into hysterics.

'Is he always that grumpy?' I ask Dave.

'He's a canny lad. Give 'im a chance.'

I nod to Dave but when he follows Guy out of the room, I tell Mandy, 'It's true what people say; you should never meet your idol because they can only ever disappoint you.'

* * *

The marquee looks just as beautiful after the reset. There are fewer tables but the tall vases of white flowers still sit in the middle of each, with spares decorating the buffet. Emerald-green bows finish off ivory-covered chairs. Crockery and favour boxes have been replaced by a multitude of candles giving off a vanilla scent. What's lovely about a May wedding is that the evening do is set against the backdrop of a dark sky, making everything that shines seem a little more romantic.

Now, at the head of the room, there's a black stage, a stool and a standing microphone. Sitting on the stool, looking – I can appreciate now that he isn't covered in my mishap – suave and undeniably handsome, is Guy Walker.

Guests are starting to file back in as he sings a version of Bruno Mars's 'Just the Way You Are' that is wholly recognisable, yet uniquely stunning.

I momentarily forget my job, pausing in taking pictures of

the guests' re-entry to switch from my Canon camera to my personal Pentax. It's a film camera, which I love to develop in my own dark room. It makes me feel artsy. I like the finish of the pictures, as if they're from another time and place. I also relish the solitude of being in my dark room – just me, my trays, my images and my nanna's old radio.

Holding up the camera to my eye, I adjust the focus and take three pictures of Guy, until I feel as if he's staring right down the lens of my camera, frowning at me.

His expression reminds me of what I should be doing... my job! I switch back to my digital camera and photograph the guests – some new faces and lots of new outfits for the evening bash.

Charlotte has switched from her full bridal gown into a sleek white silk, floor-trailing dress. She's let down her hair and added some even more sparkly jewels around her wrists and in her ears. She looks great as she enters the room on her new husband's arm.

Close behind the happy couple come my sister and Joshua, both dressed in their finery. I have to admit, they look impressive. Smart, expensive, polished and slick. They look good together. I click once, twice, three times at the lady, then I blow a kiss to Livy. She may be monosyllabic with me at the moment but I'd still do anything for her.

In fact, no one from the hen party has really bothered to speak with me much today. Maybe it's the shame of that kiss. Perhaps it's the gingham mid-length orange dress and trainers I'm wearing that's not a patch on the finery being worn today.

The only two people who haven't snubbed me from the hen are the older ladies, Donna and Jeanette, the bride's mum and aunt.

The room is filling with people as Guy sings Al Green's

'Let's Stay Together'. Unbelievably, he can pull this off, too, and, miserable or not, he looks bloody hot doing it. His black suit and tie are now notably Chantilly free.

'Yes! I'm telling you, it's true. More than one person from the hen party has confirmed it.' Three female evening guests have taken up seats at the table right in front of me. They're leaning in towards each other, hands indiscreetly hiding mouths as they gossip. 'She snogged the butler in front of *everyone*. No one *saw* them go home together but by the sound of things, they definitely did.'

Oh God! People are gossiping about me. Me and Guy. And now Guy is here. And Guy is...

'Oh my God, Char!' I trip over the leg of a chair, leaning on a table and sloshing water out of the centre piece as I look up to see another guest, about my age, screaming at the bride. 'Is that really Guy Walker?'

Charlotte glances to Guy, who seems oblivious to the commotion as he continues to sing, then Dave is near her and holding out his hands in a way that makes me think he's telling her, *Happy Wedding Day!*

When Charlotte booked Dave's company, she couldn't have known she'd contracted for Guy Walker to be her wedding singer. She couldn't have known because last year, when she booked this, Guy didn't work for Dave's company.

Charlotte's mouth forms a really big, wide, red-painted O. 'I guess it is,' she says.

I don't know why my legs are walking me in the direction of the commotion but that's where I'm headed.

'Give us one from The Hand Me Downs, Guy,' a man calls towards the stage.

'Sorry, mate, I've got a playlist to stick to,' Guy says.

'No, please, I'd love it!' Charlotte calls to him, making her way onto the dance floor.

Guy looks genuinely... panicked? He's shaking his head. 'I can't. I'm just here to sing the list.'

'Pleeeeeeeease!' another woman calls.

'I can't.' Guy is holding out his arms and looking at Dave, who's stepping onto the stage and saying something into his ear. Guy is saying no, and getting aggravated about it. As if he's terrified of being up there, of singing one of his own songs.

I don't like it. The situation he's being put in, in front of all these people. I don't know what I can do about it but I'm moving towards him and Dave, the stage.

The music has stopped and it's clear for everyone of reasonable hearing in the room that one of the bridesmaids shouts, 'Isn't he the naked butler?'

I watch Guy metaphorically go inside himself. He's shaved today, where he had a thick beard on the night of the hen, but to me, and clearly this bridesmaid, he's recognisable for both performances.

Despite the fact he's cranky and obnoxious, I really feel for the man holding the microphone. As I'm thinking that, the groom charges onto the dance floor, making a beeline for his new wife. 'You snogged the naked butler on your hen night?' he yells at Charlotte.

Ohhhhhhhhh sugar.

'What?' Charlotte asks, appropriately aghast. 'I did no such thing!'

'Really? Then why is every woman at the bar gossiping about you snogging the butler and wondering whether—' He shakes his head, walking in a circle like he's a dog chasing his tail, throwing his arms into the air. 'Did you sleep with him?'

'You slept with Guy Walker?' someone asks Charlotte from behind me.

'I didn't sleep with anyone. Jesus, Mark, it's our *wedding* day!'

'Whoa, mate, I served your missus a drink and that's it.' Guy steps off the stage and stands between the arguing couple.

I recoil before it even happens, as I see Mark rear his fist and slam it into Guy's left eye.

'Guy!' I call as Dave and I run towards him, helping him sit up from the floor.

'Fuck,' Guy is saying, rubbing his cheek around the eye socket.

'That's gonna be a nice shiner, matey,' Dave says. 'It'll not be the first time you've been hit over a lass, though.'

'I'm so sorry, Guy, this is all my fault,' I tell him.

He turns from Dave to look at me and says, 'I wouldn't mind if I'd actually got a shag out of it.'

As I gasp, I think I see, for the first time ever, Guy's lips curve up. It's slight and barely there. Blink and you'd miss it. But it makes me scowl back, playfully. 'You should be so lucky,' I whisper.

'Come on, charmer, you've got a night of entertainment to give this lot yet,' Dave says as we help Guy up to stand.

'I can't even believe you'd think that, for a *second*,' Charlotte is saying behind us.

'Baby, I'm so sorry. I'm just drunk and emotional. People were saying things in the bar and I— I'm so scared of losing you, Char.' The groom is crying, sobbing, like the aunt that drinks far too much gin at the family Christmas party. It would be almost cute if the whole thing wasn't so pathetic. From the angry confrontation to the ape-like aggression, to the mess he is right now.

Fortunately, Charlotte isn't quite so offput as I am by the show. She holds out her arms and welcomes him into an embrace. 'I just married you, didn't I, silly?'

Wow, she's forgiving, much more so than I would be with three hundred or more guests staring at me.

'Wait, if Charlotte didn't snog you, who did?' someone asks Guy, who's now holding ice against his eye at my side.

He looks down to me and I look up to him, and as ridiculous as it is in the circumstances, all I can think is how much I melted into that kiss. How I've never been kissed in a way that completely overwhelmed my senses and took me out of reality.

There's a whirring deep in my abdomen that's very reminiscent from the night of the hen party, and a lot like the night of his concert in Newcastle. The night I was supposed to meet him backstage. The night that changed the trajectory of my life.

'You kissed Guy Walker?' my sister asks, mostly shocked, possibly a little impressed.

She snaps me out of my trance. Guy breaks our eye contact, then hands Dave his ice pack and, like a professional, resumes his position on stage. 'Let's have a special one for Mr and Mrs Reilly, shall we, lads and lasses? Get yourselves on the dance floor.'

My sister glares at me but drags Joshua away to the dance floor. Good.

Dave reacts to a gesture from Guy on stage and I hold my breath, wondering which of his songs he's going to sing. But the backing track for Justin Timberlake's 'Can't Stop That Feeling' comes on, and though I'm disappointed not to hear a track from The Hand Me Downs, I can feel myself grinning from ear to ear as he starts to sing.

Just like that, the wedding is back on. Bodies dance wildly around me, blocking my view of the man on stage.

The grumpy, obnoxious, anti-hero.

The man who got a black eye because of me.

The guy who just saved the wedding.

After snapping shots of people dancing – and gossiping about the commotion – and seeing Guy looking the height of discomfort as he signed autographs during his ten-minute break, I'm standing by the side of the stage. My cameras are packed away and I'm leaning back against the ornate dado rail, resting one aching foot against the wall, promising myself after each song that I'm only going to listen to one more.

And I am. This is my last one.

I remember feeling like this when I saw him in Madrid. Wishing the bubble would never burst and reality wasn't waiting for me back home. That I could turn my one long weekend away with Cami into the life of travel and freedom I yearned for.

Once I returned home from that trip, my world felt even smaller than it had four days earlier and I decided after that day not to bother longing for something more.

'So, *you're* the one he copped off with at that hen party?' Dave asks, coming to rest next to me, hands folded across his middle.

I don't dare look at him. My memory of the night is becoming increasingly clear. I threw myself at Guy in desperation. So desperate to tick off my sister and change the discourse of the evening. My cheeks heat with humiliation.

'I didn't know ya had it in ya, lassie. Cheeky minx.'

Dave is kind and funny, the embodiment of the phrase *cheeky chappy*, which prompts me to say, 'Takes one to know one,' rather than denying the mortifying truth.

He chuckles. 'It's been a long time since anyone took a swing at the lad over a woman. It was always Scotty getting in fights over girls.'

'You knew Guy's brother?' I ask, genuinely curious.

'Knew him? I was the first manager the band had, right at the start, when Scott was still a whipper snapper.'

'You managed The Hand Me Downs? *Wow*.'

'Aye, for three years. Until the record label pushed me out. The lads were too young and caught up in all the hype to see it happening.' He turns to me and smiles. 'Anyhow, I've got a good business gannin now and that champ up there'll come good, I'm sure of it.'

I feel my eyes narrowing because I don't fully understand Dave's intentions, but I don't think he wants me to dig any deeper, either.

'Have ya gotta phone on ya I can borrow for a second, flower?' he asks.

'Ah, yeah, sure.' I take my phone from the pocket of my dress and open it with face ID. 'Here you go.'

Guy finishes his rendition of Jason Mraz's 'I'm Yours' and I finally push off the wall to leave, yawning as I do. 'Well, that's me, Dave.'

He hands me back my phone, the screen locked again. I guess he was looking something up on the internet? Who knows.

'See you next time.'

'Aye. Sweet dreams, flower.'

'You too,' I say, glancing to the stage one last time to see Guy telling the party-goers, 'This is my last song tonight, folks, so let's give it up one more time for the bride and groom.' But he's watching me leave, unsmiling.

I hold up a hand and mouth, *I'm sorry.* I doubt he can make it out.

It's only once I'm in my car, with plenty of photographs captured, driving to my parents' house, that I replay my conversation with Dave. It's not until I pull through the electric gates and onto the pebbled driveway of Mum and Dad's house that something occurs to me. Something that makes me hit the brake on the car too hard, thrusting myself towards the steering wheel.

That Night. The man who came out from backstage to ask me to meet Guy after the show. It could have been Dave. I think maybe it *was* Dave.

I reach for my phone from the passenger seat and use my face to unlock it, about to search the internet for—

But I stop. Because staring back at me is a new contact entry.

GUY WALKER

His mobile number.

And in the notes section:

IN CASE U WANT TO APOLOGISE FOR THAT SHINER.

6

GUY

May 2025
The Girl in My Dreams

It's been a long day, from helping Dave set up for the wedding this morning to psyching myself up for the challenge by working out in the gym for hours, until I had to get dressed and head to Earl's Castle.

I turn the key in my Barbie-pink, long-lashed Fiat to lock it, on account of the battery being dead. Pocketing the key, I loosen my black tie and unbutton the stiff neck of my white shirt, then gently press my increasingly puffy eye. It's definitely going to bruise.

How in God's name have I ended up in this situation?

I bypass the entrance to my building and head down the snicket to the beach. The moon's light is bright enough for me to see where my feet are landing and I know the feeling when my shiny shoes come to rest on the wet sand. The wild, grey ocean roars at me, waves crashing ashore, and I close my eyes to let the sound wash over me. For a moment, I disengage from reality, and for the first time in hours, I feel calm.

I can't hear people calling for me to sing songs I wrote for my brother to perform, or asking for the autograph of a has-been. There's no one gunning for me. No women showering me in cream after a bizarrely enticing fake orgasm over a profiterole.

And there's no beautiful, gentle, kind woman drawing my attention to her for reasons I can't fathom, because I know she's not the sort of woman who needs a train wreck like me. She's not even the kind of woman who would want a failed, broke musician who's fallen into selling his body and singing the cheesiest songs known to man.

But there's something about Lyra that I just can't seem to resist.

I open my eyes as the sound of something like a metal bin lid clatters behind me in the distance, a sound that reminds me of the city.

When I left London, I used half the equity from the sale of my Highgate apartment to pay off my nan's, my mam's and my sister's mortgages.

With the rest of the money, I bought myself a significantly cheaper but, ironically, larger, apartment overlooking Roker Beach. When Scott and I were kids, our grandad used to take us to Whitburn on the bus, to watch Sunderland AFC train. We'd walk from the training ground to the beach, stopping for fish shop chips with lashings of curry sauce, then follow the coast all the way along to Roker.

I didn't know what I was looking for when I left London, but I knew I had to get out. Away from my old life in the south, away from temptations, easy access to bars and pubs, to a life I didn't want to be stuck in any more. Rock bottom.

I'm still not sure what it is that I want or how I go about finding it but six months ago, I got off a train in Sunderland with two suitcases, sporting a beard, hat and sunglasses, masking the man I used to be. I'd thought about showing up on my mam's doorstep, cap in hand, begging for forgiveness. But I don't want to keep disappointing her, hurting her, dredging it all back up.

Instead, I walked, luggage dragging behind me, with no direction or purpose, until I found myself at the coast, looking up at a *For Sale* sign on a beach-front apartment.

Now, inside my building, the corner of an envelope is poking out of my post box in the airy communal foyer. Opening it, I see a couple of flyers for takeaway food – one for Indian and the other Chinese. I roll the ads and pocket them. I'm a single lad who can't be arsed to cook for one, and who's used to London prices. A five-course Thursday special for less than fifteen quid is music to my miserable bachelor ears.

Speaking of money, I recognise the letter that had been poking out of the box as a royalty statement from The Hand Me Downs' old record label.

I open the statement in the stairwell as I make my way up to the fourth floor of the six-storey building. I'm always surprised by how much the songs I've written are still played on a daily basis. To me, they're done, in the past, dead, like my brother.

And the royalties make no difference to me because I don't take them. Since Scott died, nearly all my royalties have been directed to a trust I set up for his kid. My four-year-old nephew, Matty.

I refuse to live off the back of songs my brother's voice made famous. He's the reason those songs are still loved and streamed.

I let him down. And I've destroyed my nephew's life, because he'll never know how awesome his dad was.

So the least I can do, the very least, is make sure Matty is taken care of financially.

Like the other royalty statements I've received since moving in here, I stick this one in a tray on the worktop in my kitchen, then grab a can of sparkling water from my fridge, pull up a stool and sit, staring into my lounge-diner. I have six guitars hanging along the wall. Three are my own – a Fender, a Gibson, and my preferred acoustic by Martin. One was a gift from Noel Grealish when The Hand Me Downs supported his band The Flying Eagles on tour. Another was an exchange with Sam Fassbender, when we swapped guitars at the end of a UK festival back in 2019.

The sixth guitar is an acoustic. A Gibson. It was Scott's. His favourite and his last. He rarely played on stage, concentrating on his vocals, but that wasn't when I most enjoyed hearing him anyway.

As I stare at it now, I don't picture him holding it in concert. I see us, him and me, maybe with the other guys from the band, mucking about in the studio, or in my London apartment after a couple of beers. Plucking, strumming, singing the most ridiculous lyrics. Challenging each other to be the wittiest, the funniest, sometimes the downright filthiest. Always joking and clarting around.

Even at the end, even when he was addicted to hard drugs, when we were goofing around like that together, it was as if nothing had changed. Nothing ever did change between us. He was my best friend.

Maybe that was the problem. I was too busy being the lad Scott wanted to have a laugh with to be a good big brother.

I'd give anything to go back and rewrite our history. To

keep those sessions between us, in a rundown bedroom, in a cheap rented flat, barely making ends meet on market-seller and call-centre wages. No fame. No fortune. No fags, booze, women or drugs.

I trudge through to the ensuite of my master bedroom – there are only two, so it really doesn't matter which is the master but that's the one I sleep in because it looks directly out to sea and if I open the window, the sound of the water can knock me into a sleep that often doesn't come easily.

Switching on the light around the over-sink mirror, I get my first proper look at my eye. It's swollen and red on the bone but the groom didn't cut the skin. Though he hit the right spot, luckily for me, he's clearly not a lad accustomed to fighting. It'll be colourful for a couple of days but I don't look like I've gone a round with Tyson Fury.

All thanks to that random kiss. A kiss that somehow felt like it was meant to be and yet meant nothing at all. So why can't I shake the feeling that I know the girl who rubbed Chantilly cream off my crotch tonight? The woman who leaves me thinking, truly, if looks could kill, I'd be a goner? Yet, the very same lass who takes my picture and makes me feel like I'm coming undone as she fixes her attention on me through a camera lens. The woman who, with everyone else, is all smiles and hope and optimism.

The fact she's different with me should serve as a warning but for some inexplicable reason, it fascinates me.

'Your life is complicated enough, fella,' I tell my bruising reflection.

At best, Lyra thinks I'm selling my body for cash – down and out in every way. At worst, she thinks I'm the man she came to see on stage in Madrid. Neither option is right for a girl whose gingham dress isn't even the brightest thing about her.

When I eventually slip beneath my freshly laundered sheets, I'm depleted. Today has been A LOT. Precisely the thing I promised my therapist I would try to prevent when I left London. In a nutshell, he felt like I'd developed 'coping mechanisms' in order 'to deal with day-to-day life', *not* that day-to-day life for me now comes easy. It doesn't.

I'm drifting to sleep, stuck in the limbo I often get to, between my tired body forcing a system shutdown for a few hours, but a feeling like the world isn't right keeping me awake. It's semi-lucidity. A place where I know I'm in bed, that I'm dreaming even, but I can't tear myself out of the moment.

It's 2018 and The Hand Me Downs are playing a gig, one of our last smaller venues, in Newcastle. We've made a pact to enjoy it. The others are all excited about the sudden, relatively unexplainable leap in streams of our music, but I'm apprehensive about moving on from the humble music jaunts we've been playing for years.

Now, we're getting invited to play on the main stage in iconic festivals. Our upcoming tour is a proper one, actually advertised as a tour, around UK arenas, with dates penned for Europe next year. And with that comes pressure.

It's our last gig with Dave as our manager, since the label said they want us to be under their management. I told them to go fuck themselves, so Dave stood down, refused to manage us if we didn't sign the bigger contract.

He's standing off to the side of the stage, a familiar comfort. Where he's been since the start. Head bobbing to the bassline as we play through one of our crowd pleasers. Our first UK number one. Ironically, called 'Addicted', though I wrote it about being addicted to a girl. Not that I had anyone in mind at the time – a question the press love to ask me. One which I ignore because, though the new label has told me how much they hate it, I don't want to give interviews. I'm not a frontman.

As my fingers find the strings of my Gibson, I sing a backing harmony for my brother, stage lights hot on my skin in the best way. It's a feeling I've come to know well. Sweating on stage, the sound of my own music coming through my ears as the crowd sing back to Scott, my words. I'm doing what I love, high on life, up here with our kid, doing our thing side by side. And I know, the best is still to come.

I'm squinting a little, watching the sea of faces.

Then one...

She's near the front of the stage, her eyes closed, her head dropped back, as if she has all the space in the world and not a care on earth. Her hair is messed up from dancing, trailing the shoulders of her black leather biker jacket. She must be roasting. I know she is because she drags a hand back through those dark locks, bringing her head down just enough for me to catch a wide, dazzling smile. A smile that's brighter than all the stars in the universe.

Though the lyrics have ended, I'm still playing us through to the end of the song. Me on acoustic, Trev on bass, Jay on drums. But it's as if everything happening on stage has stopped.

She just looks so... free. Comfortable. Breezy. She's beautiful. Strikingly so. And I squint harder, wishing I could get a better fix on her, though that isn't why I'm mesmerised. It's something else. Another reason. A pull deep in my abdomen, a sense of missing out on what she feels, a liberty I'd love, as mine is increasingly pulled from me. Decisions being taken out of my hands. Obligations owed to more people than I can count.

The lights are switching for the next track and she's still moving, swaying, as if the music hasn't paused. I want to go straight into the next song, just to keep watching her like this. But

I've lost myself, forgotten where we are in the set as I wonder how I get to her.

I want to talk to her. To know her name. To ask her why and how. What's making her feel like she's where she's supposed to be? Because no one can seem so at ease if that's not how they feel.

I know. It's why I don't give interviews. I'm not the kind of man who can fake it, no matter how hard people are screaming for me to be that way.

'Guy, what's happening?' Scott has appeared in front of me, acting casual, like we do sometimes when one of us messes up, misses a cue, head isn't in the game.

Eyes wide, I switch my focus to my brother. Shit. It's mine. One of the few songs I predominantly sing because as Scott would say, 'You wrote that for yourself, man.'

I didn't. I never do. But he'll claim every now and then that some songs sound better coming from me.

And so, I play us in and start to sing 'You and Me,' eyes finding the girl of my dreams again.

Yeah. It sounds like a bold statement, based on a few minutes of watching someone. But I just... I don't know what it is about this girl... I don't know why but I can't take my eyes off her. And I'm singing the words of my song, that I never wrote with her in mind, as if it was always meant for her.

She stops still on the spot.

She's looking at me.

I'm looking at her.

And I'm singing, 'There's just you and me, forget all these people...'

In my semi-lucid state, lying in my bed in Roker, I know she isn't real, I know she's a vague, sort of blurry, twisted and reformed, seven-year-old memory of That Night.

But what I can't figure out is why the girl in my head looks like the photographer.

Why is the girl in my dreams, who looks free and like no one could ever tell her what to do...? Why is she... pretty dress wearing, plaited hair wearing, Chantilly cream smearing, people pleasing, *Lyra?*

In the darkness of my room, I force my eyes open.

Because I know how that dream ends.

I know That Night was the beginning of the end.

7

LYRA

May 2025

The Angel of the North

'Dad?' I tap gently on my parents' bedroom door. 'Are you ready to come downstairs?'

I stayed over at my parents' house last night, as I do every night my mum is on rota to work or be on call at the hospital. She was the consultant cardiologist on stand-by last night for the Freeman hospital. Dad can do most things himself but some are tricky, like making a decent hot meal safely.

I've been awake for a while, reviewing the photographs I took of Charlotte and Mark's wedding yesterday. Couples expect a first Instagrammable cut almost instantly. My first edit is a simple tidy-up. The bad pictures – the ones with a fault, or poor lighting, closed eyes, duplicates – are the easiest to cull. I can drop thousands in a couple of hours. Which is what I've been doing since waking shortly after five, when Mum got called out to the hospital.

She'd already helped Dad up to bed by the time I arrived

home last night. I was later than usual and I blame one angsty musician with a voice I can't tear myself away from.

Dad appears at the door, nudging it open with a crutch. He uses a stick outdoors – a fancy one with a mallard duck head that Mum bought him – but inside, where he's comfortable, he prefers a crutch.

'Morning,' he says, with his lopsided beam. In my head, I add, *Sweetheart*. After his first stroke, seven years ago, Dad's speech never fully recovered. His second stroke, six months later, made it worse. These days, though he can be difficult to understand for people not overly familiar with his speech, and whilst he's a man of few words, he's as rehabilitated as he'll get.

Despite how long it's been, pride won't let him concede on the constant request from Mum to have a stairlift fitted in their house. He can manage the stairs himself but he's clumsy, so we like to have someone walk down in front of him. I don't mind in the slightest. It's the least I can do for him.

In the lounge, we eat toast, I set him up with his favourite news channel on the television, and I continue to edit my photographs. Intermittently, I check my phone, trying desperately to ignore the fact that Guy hasn't messaged me back.

Honestly, I don't know what possessed me to text him last night. I just found myself sitting on the sofa, with Mum reclined in a chair watching a series that I couldn't get in to. I had Guy's number open on my phone screen, where Dave input it.

I had no business messaging him. Nor did I have any intention of doing so. I don't *know* him. He certainly doesn't want to get to know me. Or anyone, it seems. He's cold and crabby.

But wasn't it my fault that he got hit in the face? Wasn't it me who squirted profiterole innards all over his suit?

So I sent him a message:

> Hi Guy, it's Lyra. I hope your eye isn't too bad. If you need anything – ice pack, boxing lessons, someone to hold you whilst you sob – give me a shout xx

Urgh, why? Why did I even hit send? It was too *familiar.* Was it even—? God, I hope it wasn't... *flirty*?

It was, wasn't it?

Give me a shout!

Kisses!! Plural!!!

I pick up a sofa cushion and cover my face. If Dad wonders what's up with me, he doesn't ask.

Around 10 a.m. Mum returns from the hospital, having fitted an emergency stent into a woman's artery, and as I start to pack my camera back into its case, I realise I must have left one of my lenses at the castle yesterday.

* * *

I know exactly where I left my lens; I can picture it on a table in the corner of the marquee, where Dave and I had been chatting to one side of the stage. Hopefully, one of the staff picked it up for me when they cleared out the glasses and crockery and dumped it where they usually leave the lost and found from weddings – in the hidden passageway between the three main function rooms inside the castle.

I don't know why but as I climb the old stone steps, I check my phone again. He's obviously not going to reply to my message. He's seen it. He saw it at forty-seven minutes past midnight.

I type the access code into the heavy wood side entrance to the building, muttering 'Morning' to the pelican on the crest overhanging the door. Inside the cold, windowless corridor, Pearl is standing with a clipboard and speaking into a phone at her ear. 'I can't believe it either, sweet pea, but it's true. I've got a trusty spreadsheet on my board that tells me every weekend of the season has been booked for at least one wedding and next year is starting to fill up. Oh, I've got to go, Holly, darling, Lyra is here.'

Pearl ends her call and focuses on me. 'Good morning, sunshine. Have you forgotten something?'

'A camera lens and I'll need it for work in the week. I didn't mean to eavesdrop but did I just hear that bookings are up?'

'You did.' Her delight is so infectious, I'm beaming with her, genuinely pleased for the people who have become my friends.

'I'm sure I owe thanks to that one from The Second Handers.'

Through laughter, I tell her, 'The Hand Me Downs.'

'That's it.' She presses a gentle hand to my arm and winks at me as she walks by to head outside. 'He's quite a dish, that new man of yours.'

'Oh, God, no, he's not my anything.' *Nothing* stays secret within Earl's Castle.

'Nonsense, I see the way he watches every move you make.'

He does? If that's true, it's probably because he's on tenterhooks waiting for my next faux pas. Still, my tummy jiggles at the idea.

'We just—' *Kissed when I forced myself on him. Kissed in a way I can't stop thinking about.*

Right before the big old door thuds closed behind Pearl, I hear her singing, 'There was an old lady called Pearl, who managed the castle of an Earl. She thought she was doomed, until business boomed. Now she's chirping like a merle, excited to see her brides twirl.'

She really is a dreamboat.

As I near the secret passage, there's music coming from one of the function rooms. My best guess as to why at this time on a Sunday morning is confirmed when I see staff setting up a three-tiered baby-girl cake. A christening party.

I find my camera lens in a bundle of lost and found belongings. Before I go, I can't resist a look at the tables. One of my favourite parts of photographing events is watching through the lens as a naked room is transformed into something special, beautiful and bespoke.

I can immediately tell this is an expensive bash. Pastel-pink tablecloths adorn the large rounds. Dining chairs are being covered white and finished with velour bows. There are pink trinket favour boxes and two florists are preparing centre pieces – tall pink flower vases, complete with sparkling rainbows, feathers and balloons.

'It's only a song, mate. You wrote it, ya know it off by heart.' I recognise Dave's voice before turning to see him and Guy setting up a stool, microphone and speakers at the head of the room.

'I said no,' Guy says, not taking his focus from setting up the standing mic.

Through my camera, I watch him move, unable to resist taking his picture, using the tables to add line and depth to the image, and the decorative arched window in the background as a frame.

'Guy, people'll keep asking you to play stuff from The Hand Me Downs. That's why bookings've gone through the roof. They *want* Guy Walker.'

Guy rises to full height and turns, so that he and Dave are feet apart and facing each other. His eye is lightly bruised, though not as badly as I was expecting last night. 'That's why I told you not to use my name.' His tone is neutral, unfazed. 'I'm helping you out as a wedding singer because you've got too much business for the three acts you've already got on your books. That's it.'

'You're helping me out because you're broke. Because you're playing fucking Angel of the North to a woman you barely know any more.'

I feel the tension that courses through Guy. I watch him stiffen in every limb, in his jaw. 'She's not just some woman, Dave. She's Matty's mam. And the money isn't for her; it's all for the kid.'

'I'm just saying, ya wouldn't have to do any of this if—'

'Dave.' The low register of Guy's words is ominous and sexy in equal measure. 'How I spend my money or invest my money is none of your business.'

Dave holds out his arms. 'I'm just saying—'

'Don't just say.'

'I will just say because people are booking functions here because they want *you*, *Guy Walker*, famous musician, to play at their weddings and christenings. You can't let them down, or Pearl and Geoff and their livelihood.'

'I couldn't give two shits about these brides and mams with their fucking over-the-top christenings. Who the hell throws a four-course meal for two hundred people for a three-month-old kid anyway?'

'Vicky Burton.'

'What? Like the lass from *Geordie Scenes*?' This information seems to halt the argument.

'The OG.'

'Huh.' Guy pauses, hands on hips, and through my camera, I capture the alluring tease up at the very corner of his mouth. But it's a sight that stills me. Because I've seen it before. I saw it once when he was on stage, looking back at me. It seems surreal, that I'm standing in this room with him now – the wedding photographer and the wedding singer.

If someone would have told me That Night, as I held his gaze, that I would become a wedding photographer with a two-bedroom bungalow in a mining village, five minutes' drive from my parents, getting my kicks by writing articles that will never be published… If someone told me that *he* would become a wedding singer, refusing to acknowledge just how great he is… I'd have scoffed with disbelief.

Yet, here we are. Here *I* am, listening to *him* argue with his boss.

'Look, I'm learning the songs we've agreed. I'll learn requests. But I'm not gettin' out my guitar and I won't, under any circumstances, sing a fucking song from The Hand Me Downs. I don't even know Pearl and Geoff, so why should I give a shit about whether they manage this place or not?'

Dave shrugs. 'Because to people like me, they're a lifeline, matey. This is my livelihood now. I'm not a band manager any more.'

His words strike a chord with Guy. I see it in the way he sucks in his cheeks, visible now without the beard he was sporting a few weeks ago.

He looks... heavy. Laden with burden. He *cares.* And for the first time, I think maybe he isn't just an angry washed-up rock star. He's sad. Though the thought has no rational reason for doing so, it makes my insides feel like a deflating balloon.

'Look out, Lyra,' someone says behind me. I'm startled, turning sharply to find two of the waitstaff right behind me and carrying a round tabletop. 'Coming through.'

'Oh, sorry.' Navigating out of their way, I clumsily kick my shin into the metal leg of a chair and yelp.

It strikes me that I oughtn't to be here. I have no business eavesdropping, or taking pictures of private discourse.

But it's too late because Dave is already heading my way. 'Are ya alreet, flower?'

'Yep.' It comes out all high-pitched because just like when you whack your funny bone, it bloody kills and it is definitely *not* funny. 'I was just, erm, picking something up.' I try to stand and walk away but I'm limping, willing the stinging pain in my shin to dissipate.

'Here, sit down.' Guy has appeared whilst I've had my eyes squeezed shut. He pulls over a chair and encourages me down onto it, then bends to his hunkers in front of me. He smells of the same manly scent he was wearing last night, only in the quiet emptiness of the room, it feels like it's all around me, filling my senses, infiltrating my bloodstream.

I glance to his injured eye. 'Does it hurt?'

'It's not the first time someone's taken a swing at me,' he says, avoiding the question.

'First time ya didn't finish the fight, though,' Dave says.

I can well imagine. Something tells me Guy was brought up to hit back harder at anyone who dared to strike him. Maybe it's his stern attitude, or the tattoo I can see poking above the collar of his white shirt. Or perhaps it's simply in the way he seems like a man who doesn't get pushed around easily.

Something about that is admirable. Enviable.

I have no idea where those thoughts come from but they're stark right now as I watch his dark blue eyes soften.

'Should I get you some ice?' he asks.

I realise his hands are touching me, his thumbs gently rolling across my shin. It's kind and gentle, caring. It's a small touch but it thrusts me back to that kiss.

I shake my head. 'It's going off now.' And I fight against my body's desire to look at his soft, plump lips.

What would have happened if I had gone to his dressing room That Night?

The thought brings me crashing back to real time. That Night was a disaster and I don't need to relive it. Not the freedom I had felt so fleetingly for the very first time in my life. Not the way I abandoned my parents' hopes for me by crashing out of medical school. Not the phone call my dad got from the Dean of Faculty to tell him before I did myself that I'd quit. And not the phone call I got just hours later to tell me that Dad had suffered a stroke.

'I've got to go,' I say, brushing Guy's warm touch from my skin and limp-walking as fast as I can away from the place I don't want to go back to in my head.

8

GUY

Welcome to the Wedding of
Mr & Mrs Naisbett
24 May 2025

It's a freakishly hot Saturday afternoon in May for the bank holiday weekend. I'm sitting on a stool to one side of the ceremony area that's been constructed on the lawn outside Earl's Castle, ready to sing Mrs Naisbett-to-be down the aisle. Currently, all I'm doing is watching Lyra take pictures of the guests as they fill rows of chairs either side of an aisle and in front of an archway of white flowers.

I catch her looking across at me sometimes. I can tell when she's talking about me, as if a guest has asked if I'm *him*, the Guy who was. I can tell because she continues to smile when she seeks me out. Other times, I catch her eye and her smile dissolves into something much cooler. Irritation. Regret. Disdain. All three?

I get it, honestly. I can be a twat. A bookie would give its best odds ever on getting good humour out of me these days.

Not that I've ever had a disposition like Lyra's. I've seen too much. Lived through too many iterations of my mam's boyfriends and husbands. Seen, taken and given too many beatings. Stared death in the eyes one too many times.

All of this is the reason why I never replied to Lyra's message asking me how I was after I got punched by the groom at the Reilly wedding a couple of weeks ago. Which, incidentally, may be another reason Lyra looks at me like she's just drank four-month-old milk. But I was annoyed with Dave for even giving her my number. I don't want to share friendly small-talk messages with her – I have enough friends. Or, at least, I don't want any new ones. And I definitely don't want to lead her on if there's anything more than friendly to her reaching out. She's a nice girl and she doesn't need to be mixed up with me.

Still, it hasn't escaped me that I'm only aware that she looks my way sometimes because I'm so often looking at her.

The bride has chosen 'What a Wonderful World' as the song she wants to walk down the aisle to. My voice is really more Kelly Jones than Louis Armstrong but I've practised. Yup, *me*, I've practised being a wedding singer.

I tend not to rely on people in my life because people have a propensity to let each other down. But I can admit that I was disappointed when Dave helped me bring the gear here this morning, then left because he has stuff to do.

I guess I just want him to know that I *am* grateful for this job. I know I'm a prick sometimes and I seem ungrateful. But I'm not... Ungrateful, that is. He knows my performances well enough that he'd have noticed every missed beat and fumbled lyric, when I sang at the Reilly wedding, at Vicky Burton's christening party, and at the twenty-first birthday bash for a Durham University student last week. So I know, if he'd stayed today, he'd be able to tell that I've practised the entire playlist for right now and the wedding breakfast to follow. Though I'm not the best with emotions, I could have shown him my thanks.

I think maybe that's why I was, sort of, looking forward to coming here today. That and, unexplainably, seeing Lyra.

She takes one more picture of the tall, dark, extremely nervous-looking groom, standing next to his best man, then makes her way towards the back of the aisle. She comes my way, her perfume that reminds me, unsurprisingly, of spring flowers – not that I know what they are beyond daffodils. It's more a feeling, a sense of brightness and light. Like the perfume was chosen to match her personality exactly.

She has one of the sunniest dispositions I've known – with everyone except me. She's my polar opposite. Yet, she's playing on my mind all the damn time. Infiltrating my subconscious thoughts and my dreams. I seem to be dreaming or flashing back to That Night daily, but the edgy girl in the leather jacket, who didn't seem to have a care in the world, is replaced by Lyra.

I'm watching her now as she brings her camera to her eye and I'm vaguely aware that in my peripheral vision, the bridal party has gathered at the stone steps of the castle, ready for the bride's grand entrance. And I have no idea why the thought comes into my mind that I hate every person who ever made Lyra feel like she isn't good enough.

Lyra, who pulls her eyes back from her camera and coughs at me, gesturing towards the bridal party.

Oops.

I press play on the music and start to sing 'What a Wonderful World,' exactly as I've rehearsed. I only watch the bride when I follow Lyra's gaze to look at her. I'm fixated on the prettiest woman at the wedding. And she isn't the one wearing white.

All these mushy songs have gone to my head. I need to get a grip of myself. Maybe I need a shag. That's it. I'm just pent up and my incarcerated testosterone and mind-messing dreams are sending me potty.

* * *

The ceremony was nice. Standard really. The bride and groom smiled in the right places, looked scared shitless in others. The bridesmaids fanned their eyes dramatically and the mothers genuinely cried at the vows, or the fact that they're now family, who knows.

I sang the newlyweds back down the aisle as their friends and family gushed words of happiness – sure, they're getting a five-course meal and free bar for turning up. Now, I'm singing in the corner of the courtyard whilst the guests enjoy a Pimm's reception with chocolate-covered strawberries being served on trays by waiters – the higher-brow, fully-clothed version.

It's not that I don't like weddings. I think the whole concept is fine, if that's what you're into. But when you've seen your mother have as many failed marriages as I have, been passed through as many temporary fathers as I have, it makes a mockery of the institution. I wouldn't bother getting married unless I was sure it meant forever.

I'm singing Ed Sheeran's 'Perfect' when I tune into a conversation nearby by a group of suited male guests.

'How did they afford to get Guy Walker?' one of them asks.

'Do they know him?' another adds.

'Nikki's parents are loaded,' a third replies.

But it's the fourth lad who hits the nail on the head. 'Nah, he's a has-been.' Then he adds, 'He hasn't done anything since Scott killed himself.'

I try to ignore it but with his words, I miss the beat of the next lyric. I get it back on track and cast an eye around the guests to see if they noticed. The only person looking my way is Lyra. She's off to my side, where she's returning to the gathering from getting photographs of the bride and groom. The way she stills, then looks between me and the group of lads, tells me she heard them. She most likely heard the falter in my voice, too. They found another chink in my armour. The biggest one.

For some reason, it brings heat to my neck, that she heard. The kind of flush that makes me look away from her. I need to anyway, since I need to check the iPad at my side for a prompt of the lyrics I've suddenly forgotten.

'He didn't top himself.' I can still hear them above my own voice, as if their words are the loudest thing in the open space. 'He crashed in a Lamborghini or Ferrari or something.'

It was a Porsche 911.

'Out of his mind on crack, though, wasn't he?'

That's what the toxicology report said, too. The one that somehow became public knowledge in a trash tabloid. People make up their own minds as to whether they believe what's printed in those papers but I know, in that case, it was true.

'I heard there was a big fallout after he died, about who really wrote the band's songs.'

That is news to me. People still manage to surprise me, despite all the bull I've heard about my brother and the band.

I close my eyes, pretending I'm into the song I'm singing, trying to block them out, keep my head calm.

Then I hear the tenderness of a female voice. 'Guys, come on, that's a real person you're talking about and his brother is right there. If I can hear you, he can too. Imagine if it was your family.'

I open my eyes, thankful for the sunglasses covering them as I look their way and find the lads surreptitiously glancing at me.

'Now, I just saw them replenish the cocktails over there and it isn't an endless supply, so why don't you head on over, grab yourselves a top-up and let me get a picture of you toasting the bride and groom.'

My jaw stiffens as I wait for the backing music of the next track to kick in. People think that somehow my brother's memory and my pain mean nothing because we were famous once. I couldn't give two shits about those idiots but *her,* Lyra, that she just defended my brother like she did. To her, I'm grateful.

As she looks my way, she smiles gently, apologetically, and I feel my lips twist up the smallest amount.

9

LYRA

May 2025
The Naisbett Wedding Party

This may be the most distracted I've been whilst photographing a wedding. I feel unprofessional. Yet I've had my personal camera in my hands multiple times today, capturing the owner of the voice who has truly made the ceremony, the drinks reception and the wedding breakfast remarkable.

It isn't only the voice, either. Or not alone. There was something in the way he looked when he overheard those idiots slagging his brother earlier. Banter, to them, I'm sure. But Guy looked… hurt. Broken. And the vulnerability I heard in the gentleness of his tone made sense.

No one is infallible.

That even Guy Walker lets people get to him struck such a chord with me and I can't shake it off.

So I've given up for half an hour. I'm taking a break whilst the wedding guests eat dessert, before I'm required back in the room for the speeches.

Sitting outside on a love seat beneath the main steps up to the castle, tucked away from the party but where I still have quite a spectacular view of the Riverside Cricket Ground and surrounding fields down the hill, I take out my phone. In WhatsApp, I find my chat with Cami and listen to her voice note again.

The highlights of the six minutes are exactly as I remember from this morning. She's travelling around South America, filming (alongside a stellar production team) a documentary about drug trafficking. She's six weeks into a six-month long trip. It sounds scary in places, exhilarating in others. But mostly, it sounds like she's doing exactly what she always wanted to do – producing documentaries, travelling the world to fulfil a passion that happens to pay her bills. Living her best life.

It's been three months since our last exchange of voice notes and that feeling of closeness I used to have with her is fading. It was inevitable, I suppose. Cami was always flighty, free-spirited, hungry for experiences, and I've always admired that about her. Been jealous of it at times. For a fleeting moment, for one night, I thought I could be more like that. Pushing back against what I'd been told would be good for me because it wasn't what I wanted. Saying 'Yes' when a guy from a band, of whom my parents would never have approved, asked me to meet him backstage.

I scoff into the warm summer afternoon. One night. The same night that the shock and disappointment of what I'd done led to my dad having a stroke. At least contributed to it.

That's what happens when I make life decisions for myself. It's why my tiny little house is still full of boxed-up belongings.

Because what if I stayed living at Mum and Dad's? What if they need me to go back? What if my phone rings and something tragic has happened because I wasn't there to stop it, I was too busy caring about myself and what I want?

I stare at Cami's voice note again. I'll reply later.

There's a rustle close behind and I look around the edge of the seat to see the culprit.

My heart seems to stutter through its next few beats, surprised, I think, to see Guy appear next to my hideout. A cigarette hangs limply between his lips, nudged to one side of his mouth as he speaks. 'Sorry, I didn't know anyone else was out here.'

I snap out of my reverie and grin. It's a genuine reaction, which is weird, because my smart mind knows to be wary but seemingly the rest of my body thinks it knows best. 'No need to apologise, I was just taking a load off for a few minutes before the speeches.' I stand. 'I can leave.'

A tight vertical line forms between his eyebrows, visible above his sunglasses. 'You don't have to leave.'

Oh.

'You were here first.'

Ohhhh. He'll go if I don't. Couldn't really be less hospitable. 'I'm sure there's enough space for two,' I say.

He nods but doesn't come to sit. Instead, he leans a shoulder into the side of the arbour's trellis and looks out across the view, hands tucked into the pockets of his trousers. He isn't wearing a jacket and, I'm not intentionally noticing, but it's hard to miss that his tucked-in shirt and grey tailored bottoms leave no room enough for a cigarette lighter.

I'm grateful for the gentle breeze that takes the edge off the still, hot air that seems to have my skin heating beneath my summer dress.

Funnily, the air always seems a little more oppressive when Guy is nearby. As if the elements are sending me a warning. Maybe what I'm feeling is awkwardness. But it shouldn't be. It's not like I put myself out there sending him a message to simply check if he was okay after he was hit. It was polite. Caring. Nothing more. I don't think I would have even sent a message if Dave hadn't put in my mind that it might be the right thing to do.

But this afternoon, the air carries with it a heady concoction of smooth vanilla and something deeper, earthy, woody. A scent that could overpower the embarrassment of not receiving a reply to my message.

Silence descends between us. Birds chirp in the nearby trees. There's a faint, distant thrum of traffic as life happens around this spot where time can stand still. In my mind, I can see us as a photograph. Two bodies filling the frame. And the motionless moment is oddly calming, soothing after listening to Cami's message.

'Thank you.' His words are unexpected and I wonder if they're even intended for me, with his eyes still focusing on the horizon. 'For moving those lads on from my earshot.' He turns to me now and I wish I could see behind his shades. 'It's true, what they said, in case you're wondering. Scott was high when he crashed.'

My throat tightens, less at his words, more his tone, his downcast gaze, his rounded shoulders. 'You don't have to tell me.'

He nods. It's a subtle move. Barely there. And I know he won't give me more details. I don't want them. It would feel... invasive. Unless...

'But if you want to talk, I'm a pretty good listener.'

His lips seem to twitch up, then settle back to expressionless. 'I could see that about you. You see good in people.'

'There's usually good to be found.'

He shakes his head. 'Not always.' I wait for more but he doesn't offer it. Instead, he comes to sit next to me on the bench, his forearms resting on his knees, that unlit cigarette still dangling between his lips.

His leg brushes mine as he sits, making me flinch. It's not uncomfortable, just startling. Like someone striking a match down the bare skin of my leg.

'You don't smoke, do you?' I say. More statement than question, I think.

'What makes you say that?'

'I've only seen you with a cigarette hanging between your lips. You aren't carrying a light. You don't smell of smoke and you don't—' I stop myself short.

'Go on.'

'You don't taste like it, either.' Enough heat comes to my cheeks with my words that he could use my face to light his cigarette if he wanted. Because with my words comes the memory of that kiss. His hand on my hip, his thumb stroking the bone. His lips soft, yet keen against mine. The urgent press of his body against mine, my back to the car.

He continues to stare and now the silence between us is far from comfortable. 'About that,' I blurt. 'I'm sorry. For kissing you like that. I mean, I don't even know if you have a... *someone*. And I'm extra sorry for you getting punched over it. I'm not usually impulsive or... or...' I can't find the words to say *affected* by men, a man, without sounding like I still have that teenage crush on him, visceral but untouchable, unplacatable.

Heat turns to fire rising up my neck as I draw attention to blunder after blunder when it comes to him.

He coughs, as if clearing his throat. Obviously feeling awkward. *God,* I should just *stop talking* around this man.

He comes to stand in front of me, looking down over me, and I try desperately not to rake my eyes over his body, to erase from my mind how he looks near naked.

'You said already. Don't worry about it.'

Then he starts walking away. As if we had a complete conversation. We didn't.

He's as dismissive to my face as his lack of response by phone suggests, and I don't know why but it stirs a response in me.

'It might have been polite to reply to my message.'

He about-turns and as he stands to face me, he pinches his unsmoked cigarette and takes it from his mouth. 'Trust me, Lyra, you don't need someone like me in your inbox.'

I hate that my name on his lips makes my insides knit.

'Surely that's my decision,' I say, hearing a lack of conviction in my voice.

'On this occasion, I'm willing to bet I know what's best for you.'

'Yeah, well, I've spent my life surrounded by people claiming to know what's best for me, Guy.' I don't know where that comes from or why I confess it right now, though lingering in the back of my mind is Cami's voice note and I know later, with time, I'll understand the connection. But right now, I'm just *irritated* by the know-it-all in front of me. Who starts walking away, again.

'Then you don't need another one,' he calls back.

* * *

Having brushed off the irritation Guy Walker makes me feel, *again*, I'm back inside at the Naisbett wedding reception, Mandy and I working different angles on the room to photograph the speeches taking place on the top table (me) and the reactions of the guests (Mandy). I've seen a lot of wedding speeches and tonight's are fairly standard. Unremarkable. Funny enough – due to the audience being onside more than the content or timing of the jokes – and not overly long.

The worst thing about the speeches is the drunk uncle I'm unfortunately positioned nearby on Table One.

When I leaned forwards to better position myself for a picture, he told me, 'Lean over me if ya want, love.' I just knew he was looking at my bum as he did.

Then when I bent to my hunkers to change the angle of my shots, he said, 'Save yer feet and sit down on Uncle Steve's lap, love.'

All the while, he was laughing as others around the table went with the joke, visibly uncomfortable but smiling anyway. Truly, I know he doesn't mean anything by it. He's had a few beers, everyone's in good spirits, and this is simply his way of being part of the fun. I don't feel threatened at any point – I think he ought to feel more threatened by the way his wife is boring holes in him with every wisecrack he makes – it's just that I shouldn't have to put up with him. In just the same way he ought to tone down his heckling of the men and women brave enough to be giving speeches today.

As Mandy works the room, she hears a bit of his *banter* and I flick her an eye roll across the space with the next uncouth remark. When I find her and she asks me about the uncle, she's standing by Guy, who is quietly packing away from where he was singing through the wedding breakfast at the back of the room.

He's scowling, eyes narrow, jaw tight. *At me? Jesus, what have I said or done now?*

Thankfully, the two best men wrap up their joint speech and the wedding party is relocated for the reset – some people filtering off to their hotel rooms, some outside for air, others to the bar.

I'm snapping a few more images in the bar because that's where the bride and groom are mingling when Mandy sidles up to me.

'You can head off now, Lyra. I'll do this evening.'

'Are you sure? I'm really not doing anything anyway.'

Mum is home with Dad. There's nothing I have a burning desire to stream. I'm mid-way through a roll of film that I can't develop from my personal camera.

'Absolutely. They had profiteroles today and it's my turn to taste the goodness.'

I chuckle. I can always make up an article about a drunk uncle at a wedding. Or... 'I suppose I could unbox some of my things.' It probably is about time I accepted that I moved out of my parents' home and into my own.

'Settled then,' Mandy says.

'Hey, love, clocking off early, are ya? I'll take ya home.' Uncle Steve. Again. What a delight this man is.

I'm about to politely decline the offer from the pervert drunken uncle when I feel a hand on my back. The touch warm, and despite the circumstances, I know instinctively that it isn't another drunken uncle making a pass at me. I know from the firmness of the palm, from the scent that envelopes me and from my body's willingness to lean into it.

'Are you ready to go?'

I turn into the voice, my shoulder moving against Guy's

firm chest. I open my mouth to speak but words seem to have escaped me as my heart hammers against my ribcage.

He leans into my ear, so close his breath caresses my skin. 'One good turn deserves another,' he whispers.

I think I nod, breathless when his lips gently press to my temple, his hand still holding on to my lower back, which is probably the only thing keeping my legs upright.

A message makes it from somewhere in my nervous system to tell my lips to turn up, my voice box to kick into gear.

'Yes,' I barely manage to tease out of my suddenly parched throat. 'I'm ready.'

He holds out his hand and I look from it to his deadpan expression, wondering why he's helping me out, again. The thought occurs to me now, of all times, that he doesn't have a *someone*, not only because he's a naked butler and all that *could* imply, but because he's holding on to me, leaning into me, in a way I would not be thrilled about if he was my boyfriend.

Of course, he isn't. Except for the purpose of getting me away from Uncle Pervert. Which is great on two counts. The first, obvious. The second being, it saves me from the backlash of his mood swings.

I slip my hand into his and for the briefest moment, as my next breath comes sharply and my heart collides with my full lungs, I see a shift in his expression, a widening of his pupils. Or maybe I imagine it to make my own reaction to our connection feel less ridiculous.

He curls his fingers through mine and as he leads me out of the bar, I catch Mandy raising one eyebrow in my direction. All I can do is shrug. I have no idea what Mr Misery Walker is playing at.

We head out of the function area and into the secret staff passage, where Guy almost walks right into Nick, the general manager, who smells like he bathed in aftershave before coming on shift. Who also runs his gaze greedily over Guy, then scowls on seeing our hands locked together.

I drop Guy's hand – maybe he drops mine – as if we've been caught in the act of *something*.

'Are you coming or going?' Nick asks.

'Leaving,' Guy says. Then, grabbing his backpack from a benchtop in the passageway – already packed and ready to go – he slings it across one shoulder and, without so much as a cursory glance backwards, he calls, 'Have a good one.'

Nick folds his arms across his chest, moving to my side as we both watch the unfathomable man stride out of view. 'He's not gay, then?' Nick asks.

'I don't think so?' I sort of confirm, or question, because nothing about Guy is obvious or expected.

'Bi?' Nick ventures.

'Who knows what he is or isn't, Nick.'

'Which I interpret to mean, there's potential.'

I look his way, amused. 'Did you forget to take your medication again?'

'I took it right before I left for work,' Nick replies. 'It's the little blue one, isn't it?'

10

GUY

May 2025
After the Naisbett Wedding

What was I doing in there?

I could have just told that dick to back off Lyra. It's just he'd been on at her all through the speeches, then after in the bar. I saw it and it made her even more uncomfortable than everyone around the bloke.

She shouldn't have to put up with that shit. She's a nice girl, photographing a wedding.

That's all it was, I try to convince myself as I head to my Barbie car.

But there's a devil on my shoulder that I've heard so many times in recent years. He's telling me I wouldn't have taken the same approach with any other woman.

Lyra's apology from earlier was playing on my mind, *is* playing on my mind. She's ashamed that she kissed me at that hen party – that bit doesn't surprise me. I'm a naked butler, for

Christ's sake. But she apologised as if she'd done something abhorrent.

I guess, what I should have said was, I'm not sorry she kissed me. I kissed her back, no question. As soon as the taste of cherry cola bottles reached my mouth, the silk of her lips pressed to mine, that groan she let out like I was the best meal she'd ever tasted, the bow of her back, the feel of her hips in my hand.

I forgot myself. Who I am. The washed-up musician. The broke naked butler. The brother who wasn't enough. I lost myself in her hold.

So maybe I should have told her the truth, if only to change the narrative playing unfairly in her head.

But I didn't. For the same reason I never replied to her WhatsApp message.

I don't want to lead her on. She's a good girl. From the plait in her hair and her bright summer dresses to her endless smiles and helpful nature.

I see the way she reacts to me, as if I'm still the man she saw on stage in Madrid.

I'm not him.

I open the car door manually, set my backpack on the driver's seat and start unbuttoning my shirt.

There's something that takes over me when I'm around her and it's bad. A vulnerability I could do without. I have no idea why she's infiltrating my dreams. That particular dream, getting mixed up with the girl I let slip from my grasp the same night everything else started to fall through my fingers, too.

I'm sure a therapist could tell me something textbook, like I'm attracted to the warmth of her because I've never had it from women in my life. It doesn't matter. The top and bottom of it is, I should do what's best for her and that can't possibly be me.

I clip my white collar and black bow tie into place around my neck. As I toss my shirt on the back seat and reach for my black trousers and apron, my phone rings. *Must be Dave.*

By the time I dig the mobile from the bottom of my backpack, it's rung off. I'm about to mindlessly redial when I see the caller ID wasn't Dave, it was Bex. My sister.

A message pings through from her.

> I've heard you're back in the north east. Is that true? Call me. Please.

Now I do call Dave and as soon as he answers with 'Hey matey!' I respond with, 'You need to stop giving out my new number.'

There's a bleep of an opening car nearby and I see Lyra slip inside it, something twisting inside me as I watch her pull out of her space. *Did she hear that? If she did, she'll think I was talking about Dave giving my number to her. She's that girl. She gives a shit.*

'If I want to see my sister, I've got her number, I know where she lives. You need to butt out.'

'She wants to invite you to her birthday party. Is that a crime?' Dave replies. It sounds like he's driving. Probably heading here with the all-female band who've been hired for the evening reception tonight.

'Am I on speaker phone?'

'Yes! Hi, Guy!' one of the girls, I think Tiff, the lead singer, calls out.

I shake my head, exasperated. 'My sister needs me at her birthday party like she needs a hole in her head.'

'She loves you.'

His words hit me somewhere deep inside. So deep, I don't want to even register where I feel them.

'She thinks I can still afford good gifts. Stop giving out my number.'

'Even to me?' Tiff asks coyly, laughing.

I don't want to be a shit, so I choose not to reply, hanging up instead before I say into the late spring sunset, 'To anybody.' My head is busy enough with just me in it these days.

11
LYRA

June 2025
On the Corner of Bridgerton and Alice in Wonderland

Last night, after the Naisbett wedding, I unpacked three boxes of my belongings – mainly books, cuttings from magazine articles that have inspired me, photo albums of pictures I've developed myself, old university files and pointless stationery. Stuff I've never needed to keep and don't really have space for in my little bungalow. I also unpacked some parcels of kitchen and home bits I ordered that are, similarly, unnecessary, given I have so far used one bowl, one plate, one knife, fork and spoon, one cup and one glass, since I moved in.

Sitting in the middle of the lounge that looks distinctly unloved and uninhabited, I can truthfully say, this is not what I had in mind for my first home. It was time to have my own space – that was well overdue – but I guess, I just thought that when I eventually had a place of my own, it would feel like a home, more than a cottage I'm squatting in until real life begins.

Whatever I mean by *real life.*

It's my fault, really. Like Mandy keeps telling me, if I unpack and spread my things around the space, it *will* feel like home. As she's pointed out, putting sheets on my bed and setting up my dark room doesn't count as moving in.

I'm sure I can grow to love this place. Ultimately, it was within my budget and five minutes' drive from both my parents and Mandy's shop. Handily, seven minutes' drive from Earl's Castle.

Gosh, my life fits into a tiny radius.

I'm already dressed and waiting for my sister and Mum to pick me up, wearing a navy sundress covered in white daisies, which happens to be one of Mum's favourites but mostly because my sister asked that I, and her other three bridesmaids, wear blue today for our wedding hair trials. Ordinarily, I'd have plaited my long hair because it's thick and gets in the way, especially when I'm trying to peer through a camera lens with my own loose tendrils acting as an unwanted frame. Today, though, as instructed, my hair is uncommonly blow-dried into de-frizz mode, ready for the salon technician to work some magic on me, make me look befitting of my sister's bridal party.

Deciding I still have half an hour, I head to my bedroom and pull out one more box of stuff to unpack. As I open the lid on the brown box, the first thing I notice is the folded-up world map I had on my wall in halls at university. Laying it out on my bed, I see each label I stuck on, every place I told Cami I wanted to travel to, to photograph, experience.

I had wanted to visit every continent. I remember us talking about South America. She's there now and I'm... staring at a map that a girl I knew once had been very excited about. A version of myself that wanted to hire a car and drive across the USA, to backpack the Himalayas and drink tea from a yunomi in Japan.

Alongside a couple of miniskirts, my old leather jacket and the pair of lace-up boots that I used to love and haven't seen since I boxed this stuff up seven years ago, there are four travel guides inside the box – South East Asia, the USA, Australia and New Zealand, and Europe. At the thought of that girl's excitement, the me of now feels heavy.

The memory of Guy asking me if I'd ever visited continental Europe pops into my mind. *Once* since That Night. To see him in Madrid on the band's world tour. He was incredible, the whole weekend was, but that brief break that Cami persuaded me to take was like smelling a cinnamon roll. Seeing it. Reaching out to touch the sticky iced topping. Then being told you can't eat it.

It wasn't worth teasing myself, so I haven't been out of the UK since.

My sister honks her horn outside, announcing her arrival and time to put my reverie to bed. I shall live vicariously through Cami's updates. Which reminds me, I really ought to suck it up and reply to her voice note.

My sister decides not to come into my cottage, nor to comment, despite this being the first time she's seeing it. I slip into the back seat of her car, behind Mum in the front passenger seat, who turns to hand me a drive-thru takeaway coffee, and tells me, 'You look lovely, darling.'

Lovely. Nice. Pretty. Dull.

Though I smile and return the compliment, I stare out the window thinking, at what point did I stop looking *hot* or *sexy*? Does that die with age or am I old before my time?

Part of the reason, even though miniscule, for me taking the plunge on renting my own place, has been Mandy reminding me on a near daily basis that when it comes to my *down there*, use it or lose it.

I'm not *crazy*, I don't actually think that a lack of romantic life can cause my orifices to seal shut or anything, but it *has* been a while. I look to the sky. *Understatement.*

The thing is, I've never truly been with anyone who *excites* me. I've had boyfriends but I've had nothing close to the bond, the passion, or the orgasms Mandy talks about with her wife. Frankly, my own wandering down there is better than dating another of Mum's colleagues' sons – usually a doctor, dentist, architect. And, yes, they've been *lovely, nice, handsome and... dull.*

I've been on dates with a couple of guys from dating apps, even Henry who worked the residents' bar at Earl's Castle. None of them stuck. Even if they had, *imagine* me having taken them home to Mum and Dad's house, in my bedroom I've had since I was a girl, asking them to sit down to dinner and seek Mum's seal of approval. *How to make passion die.*

So I guess it hasn't mattered much whether I look *pretty* or sexy or hot before now. And, even though I don't have the excuse of living with my folks any more, I'm not sure why it's bothering me so much today.

Maybe unpacking my box and seeing that brief flirt with being my own person at university has got me riled.

I try to get over myself, making all the right noises to keep up the flow of conversation – or my sister's monologuing – as we drive to our destination.

We're in the salon in Durham City Centre, which is closed to ordinary business since it's Sunday, and open especially for Livy, Mum, and my sister's other three bridesmaids, Charlotte, Elsie and Janie. Beyond the windows, it's a beautiful sunny day and I resent not being able to be outdoors in the fresh air rather than in this stuffy, hot space.

Thankfully, the glasses of fizz we're served are cool and I accept mine, briefly use it to toast my sister, and gulp it down as if it's the best form of rehydration. Certainly, it's going to be medicinal for the next couple of hours. I know this because the gossip amongst the bridesmaids has already begun, about one of their lawyer friends sleeping with one of their doctor friends, who is already married to one of their fund broker friends.

Mum dips in and out of the conversations, adding the 'wiser lady's perspective' here and there. At some point, she glances my way when I'm lost in thought, remembering nights Cami and I spent dreaming up an interrailing trip around Europe. I quickly flash her a beam, not knowing how long she's been watching me.

'Are you okay, darling? You don't seem yourself today,' she says.

'Mmm, yes, fine. Just a bit tired. It was a long day yesterday at the castle.' I don't tell her that actually I left early, my fingers entwined with Guy's. 'I've also been unpacking. I'm trying to sort the house.'

She purses her lips and I brace myself. 'It's a wonder you haven't done that yet.' It's an airy statement, rather than disapproving. More conversational. But she doesn't say much about my moving out from home. I'd checked and checked and checked again that she'd be okay supporting Dad without me and each time, I received a response like, 'We'll be fine.' *Fine.*

'I guess I've been busy,' I tell her. Which is partly true. I have still managed to write my humorous – to me – tales of wedding guests to fit pictures I've taken. I've had time enough to set up my dark room and dig out old film that I haven't yet developed.

Now, she asks, 'How is the job?'

And I do genuinely smile now because I *am* amused. She has a habit of asking about my *job* then asking my sister about her *career*.

'Great!' I gush. Even if it wasn't true, the same word would leave my mouth, but as it happens, 'We're really busy. Fully booked all wedding season and I have a load of family summer shoots midweek, too.'

'That's excellent,' she says, as her focus shifts back to Livy. The overachiever. The wife-to-be. The good child, who never strayed or disappointed, never caused our family to be damaged irreparably by her choices.

Remarkably, I'm grateful when it's my turn for hair and make-up because I'm relocated to another area in the salon, away from the tittering. Moreover, my glass of numbing liquid is topped up.

My hair is combed – detangling I hadn't realised was necessary tugs painfully at the roots – then curled and partially pinned up. More make-up than I even know what to do with is applied to my face, until my cheeks feel sticky and my eyebrows spikey.

I like the woman working on me, though. Her name is Hannah and she's thirty-one. She tells me about her kids. We laugh about trash TV. I mention that I work at Earl's Castle and she asks if it's true that Guy Walker is singing at weddings there now.

For some reason, my cheeks heat as I tell her how incredible he *still* is and even better listening to him close-up. I leave out that his moods swing more than orangutans and he refuses to play his own music.

She and I share a family-sized bag of chocolate. All-in-all, it's a much more comfortable way to pass an hour than sitting talking with my family and supposed old friends.

My sister is finished first and whilst I'm still turned sideways to face Hannah, my chin held in her hand as she paints my lips, I see Livy stand from her padded seat.

'What do you think, ladies?' she asks.

She looks stunning, truly. Her hair is pinned into a loose chignon, with her natural, glossy blonde waves tumbling down, as if by perfect accident. A gold vine has been threaded through her bridal do. Whilst she has on more make-up than usual, every beautiful feature of my sister's is enhanced, augmented, bedazzling.

I wait for something akin to jealousy to come and smack me in the face, *proverbially*. There've been so many times that I've thought, if I were just a little more Livy and a little less me, I don't know... good things would happen.

I wait. I'm *waiting*.

Surprisingly, the pang doesn't come and I realise, I'm happy for her to be happy but I'm not desperate to walk down the aisle, or to be exhausted from climbing a defined path in a highly respectable career, even knowing those things would please my parents endlessly.

My phone pings as everyone – including me – is gushing over Livy's bridal look. I reach for it from my backpack.

CAMI

You should come here. You'd love it!

And accompanying her words is a selfie of her, cleverly positioned to look like she's being kissed on the cheek by an iguana.

I fire a quick reply:

I miss you! Can't wait to meet the new guy. I'll reply properly to your voice note. Currently getting a bridesmaid hair trial for Livy's wedding.

Good luck! Miss you too!! PS you'd photograph the shit out of this place x

As I slip my phone back into my bag, the pang of want finally comes, and it isn't anything to do with my sister's wedding. I'm not convinced it's directly related to South America, either. I think it's for a version of myself that I can't quite capture in mind any more. One that felt free-spirited and empowered to make my own life choices.

Did she ever truly exist?

For some reason, I find myself tracing my lips, thinking about that kiss with Guy that was so spontaneous and outrageous and completely unlike me.

'No, no, don't touch your lipstick,' Hannah says, tugging my hand away from my face. 'I'm all done. Are you ready to see yourself?'

I inhale deeply. 'Sure.'

She turns me in the rotating seat to face the mirror and my *God*...

I look...

Like a cross between a girl from *Bridgerton* and the Red Queen. My hair has been curled into tight ringlets and partially pinned. My eye shadow is blue – *blue???* – and my lips are bright red.

I have nothing against *Bridgerton* or *Alice in Wonderland* but this is 2025, I am twenty-eight years old, and this look is hideous.

All I can say is... 'Blue?'

Hannah smiles sweetly. 'To match the dresses.'

My sister and mum don't seem to register my horror. Probably because I'm trying to internalise it.

'You look lovely, darling,' Mum says.

'Do you love it?' Livy asks.

Notably, the other bridesmaids stay silent and I don't dare glance in their direction. I look ridiculous. *How did this girl end up kissing a rock star?*

'Do *you* like it?' I ask my sister, rather than saying, *I absolutely hate the way I look.*

'It's great!'

'That's what matters. Is there a top-up of fizz?'

Whilst I'm waiting for more numbing liquid and the others get back to chatting around me, I take a selfie and send it to Cami. She replies in an instant:

Is the wedding fancy dress? X

Now, I really miss her.

I turn back to look at myself in the mirror and another thought occurs to me. Whilst I'm dressed like someone out of the Regency period who has been hit in the face with two heavy blue balls, Guy will be there at my sister's September wedding at Earl's Castle, singing my sister's playlist.

It shouldn't matter. He's just a man. A really moody and dismissive one, too.

But it *does* matter.

12

GUY

June 2025

It's Not a Crime to Smile

'Stop being a big girl's blouse!' Dave tells me.

We're holding opposite ends of a hefty floral-patterned sofa belonging to Dave's parents. We're helping them move from their bungalow in Seaham to an assisted living flat in what seems to be quite a nice mini village, set around a green, about five minutes along the road. This is the final big piece of furniture. We've been at it for a couple of hours now, both sweating as we do the heavy lifting in twenty-odd degree heat.

Betty, one of the new neighbours, brought us tea and homemade scones at eleven. Since then, Dave's mam and dad have been in Betty and Fred's place, resting their respective false hips and knees whilst we graft. Not that I mind. Martha and Rob are class, honestly. Dave's lucky to have them.

Especially since... 'I'm not being a big girl's anything. That's Lyra and my sister you've given my number to and now you're asking about putting the band in touch.'

We make it to Martha and Rob's new living room and I drop my end of the sofa in place just before Dave, letting him see how pissed off I am.

'Ha way, man, you'll put my back out!' he gripes.

'I haven't spoken to any of the band. And I don't want to. There's nothing left between us. Trev was just as complicit for being a passive witness, and Jay? I'll never speak to Jay again.'

Dave rises to full height and we're both panting, hands on hips, facing each other as if we're having a stand-off. We are. Sort of.

'D'ya not think it's time now, though, Guy, eh? Let bygones be bygones.' He speaks calmly and for some reason, that makes the words he speaks hit me harder. 'Wouldn't ya like to get the band back in one place and see how you'd get on without Scotty? You as frontman.'

It's as if all the energy drains from me and I'm no longer trying to catch my breath, I'm holding it. 'There is no band without Scott.' My words feel like they catch spikes on the way out. 'Even if— I'm not a frontman. I never was.'

'I hate to be the one to point out the obvious but you're the only man singing at these weddings and the crowd are lapping it up.'

'Literally an hour ago, you told me I had to cheer the hell up and sing what the guests ask me to sing,' I tell him, though a part of me that I massively resent is a tiny bit buzzed by his compliment. And I don't know why, but my mind goes to Lyra, again.

Lyra who came to see me perform in Madrid once at the top of my game.

'I'm just a has-been singing Ed Sheeran's wedding classics,' I say. 'I'm Adam Sandler.'

'Oh no, you're much more handsome than Adam Sandler.'

Martha's voice comes from the small kitchen behind us, then she and Rob shuffle-walk into the lounge.

'He's the one who shouts for a laugh, isn't he?' Rob asks. Meaning Adam Sandler, as opposed to me, which he confirms when he says, '*Happy Gilmore*. Don't find him funny either. He's not got a lot going for him, that lad.'

Dave and I smirk together, friends again, I guess. 'Except a bank balance the four of us'll never have put together, Dad,' Dave says.

'Aye, well...' He plonks down onto the sofa we just placed. 'Money isn't everything, son. Yer mother and me have barely had two pence to rub together all our lives but we've had a good life, Martha, haven't we?'

Martha rolls her eyes but she's smiling and *this,* if I could freeze *this* frame, is one of the things I love about Dave's folks.

'He's soppy when he wants to be,' Martha says. She takes hold of my chin in her hand, wiggles my head and tells me, 'It's not a crime to smile, young man. It suits you.'

'Leave the lad alone, Martha,' Rob says.

Fifteen minutes later, a brew and a KitKat Chunky consumed in payment for our efforts, Dave and I are back in his van, windows down and enjoying the sea salt breeze, fabricated by the drive on this otherwise still day.

'Did ya message her back, then?' Dave asks.

'My sister? Not yet.' I'm not convinced I will.

He signals and takes a right at a roundabout. The smell of fish and chips drifts into the van, making me close my eyes. It's a smell that always reminds me of my grandad.

I look to the few wisps of cloud in the sky. I'd bet he and Scott are sitting up there munching on fish, chips, mushy peas and curry sauce every night for dinner.

'*She'll* keep on at ya until ya do. So ya might as well grow a pair and get on with it. But I meant have ya been messaging Lyra?'

I come back to look out of the side window at a family of two-point-four children making their way down to the beach front, the youngest boy carrying a kite, the eldest a bag of beach toys. The mam telling the boys to walk nice by the road, the dad limping under the weight of a cooler and two deck chairs. *A very average family*.

What I would have given to be average at that age.

'She doesn't need me messaging her,' I reply. I bet Lyra had that kind of upbringing. Loving, complete. *Average*. 'Can I ask you something?'

Dave looks at me and even through his sunglasses, I know his expression is saying, *Duh*.

'Do you remember that last gig in Newcastle, with you as manager?'

'Well, aye, since I was fired right after it.'

I wince behind my sunglasses. Technically, he resigned but only because I refused to let him go and put our record deal on the line. 'Do you remember that I asked you to get a girl from the crowd to come backstage to meet me?'

Again, he looks at me like *duh*. 'I was always gettin' girls to come backstage.'

'Not for me, you weren't.'

He inclines his head, conceding. Later, as the band got famous and I realised getting girls to come back almost went along with the job, *yeah*, I asked a few more times, but not Dave, and not That Night.

'Aye, I remember, vaguely.'

'Well—' I stop myself, knowing how crazy I'm about to sound. Wondering if years of smoking and drinking too much might have messed with my brain.

'Well?' Dave presses.

'Nah, forget it, it's mad.' *But what if it isn't?* 'Okay, here it is. Was it Lyra? The girl. Was she Lyra?'

Dave pulls out of a junction and when he straightens the van, he looks at me. 'How the hell would I remember that?'

Yep. Booze and nicotine sent me potty.

He checks his watch, hand still on the wheel. 'Fancy a Greggs? I reckon we can squeeze in a drive-through pasty, since you're getting showered at my gaff.'

'I used to love a Greggs,' I say, my mouth filling with saliva. 'Do they still do a steak and bean pasty?'

'What d'ya think I'm getting?' He turns us full circle at a roundabout, so that we're driving in the opposite direction. 'Do me a favour though, matey, don't tell Kylie. She's got us on a couple's diet.'

I reach over and pat his beer belly. 'Looks like it's working out well for you.'

'Keep yer hands to y'self. Or yer photographer girl. But leave my gut alone.'

My playfulness is short-lived and replaced with something between dizziness and nausea, panic and excitement. I find myself swallowing down the ball of mixed emotions, my foot tapping, fingers scratching my head. Why? Because I'm going to see Lyra in... I check my watch... a couple of hours?

I don't even know her.

Though I see her in my dreams most nights.

Haunting. Terrifying.

Beautiful and real.

I catch Dave in my peripheral vision, chuckling and shaking his head.

What is *happening* to me?

13

LYRA

Congratulations
Mr & Mrs Bailey
6 June 2025

I'm starting to get used to seeing Guy, usually alongside Dave, at Earl's Castle. Brides have got the memo now, it isn't a surprise that the entertainment they booked a year ago has turned out to be a rock star. Or, ex-rock star? Can you be an *ex*-rock star?

Even my sister has moved beyond her grump with me and decided she's excited that the naked butler is also going to be a famous wedding singer for her big day in September.

Guy has become as familiar as the waitstaff, the bar staff, the porters and the DJs. Yet, I'm taking group shots of the crystal-adorned bride tossing her bouquet on the steps outside the castle when I see his bright-pink Fiat 500 with its super-long lashes coming flying up the main drive. I'm so distracted, by both the car and the way all my internal organs seem to have donned their headphones and started a silent disco in my torso, that I miss the moment the bride's aunty catches the handtied calla lilies.

'To my third attempt,' the aunt calls out, waving the now slightly dishevelled flowers above her head.

That picture, I do manage to capture. But my fingers are unsteady on the shutter button, even as the campest car, driven by the grumpiest, most severe, incredible singer, even better lyricist, I have ever met, moves out of view.

'That's great,' I tell the group of women around the steps. 'Thank you. Now go and enjoy your dessert.'

It feels like I finally exhale when I'm standing alone, regaining my composure. I realise I've been waiting to see that flamboyant car and the man inside it since he brushed the small of my back and pressed his lips to my temple last weekend.

It's like that sickly, nervous, excited, excessively giddy feeling I remember from being a teenager with a crush.

Not that I'm crushing on Guy, *obviously*. He's moody and obnoxious. He hates that I have his phone number. And I have no idea *why* he's here, at this castle, performing everyone's songs except his own, for ordinary people having ordinary weddings.

Conversely, I don't mind the knot in my tummy when I see him, or the energy I felt this morning, knowing that he'd be here today. My typical Saturday has become less mundane.

There's no harm in looking, as Mandy keeps telling me every time I refute that I'm the least bit bothered by Guy's presence at my day job. I'm just looking, I'm not buying.

In any event, nothing about that man suggests he's for sale. He's a closed book. A locked safe.

I walk the long way back into the castle – for fresh air, as opposed to giving myself extra time before bumping into Guy

– through the courtyard and past the reception desk. I wave a hand to the receptionist. As I slip through the archway into the long corridor towards the central staircase, I become flanked on each side by six feet tall knights in armour – the metal, sort of creepy kind, as opposed to real people.

Heading up the central staircase to the first floor – slightly uneven and turning like a horseshoe – I flick through my pictures from the bouquet toss, hoping I got some good ones to make up for missing the actual in-flight moment and catch.

I'm still reviewing the images when I reach the top of the staircase and walk smack bang into something firm, unmoving and delectable smelling.

'Yikes, sorry, I—' Recoiling, I look up into the midnight-blue eyes of Guy. Dangerously close to stumbling back down to the ground floor, I reach out to the first thing I can to steady myself. It just so happens, that's his hard chest. The feel of his heat through his shirt thrusts me back to his bare chest just last week, when I watched him undress by his car before leaving the castle wearing only his butler bow tie.

The same moment he declared to someone on the end of his phone that they should *not* give out his number to strangers. Presumably, *me*.

And *that* memory has me swallowing down a lump of discomfort. 'I wasn't watching where I was going.'

He nods once, frowning – *surprise, surprise*.

Side-stepping him, I notice Dave waiting with their equipment, ready to set up in the room at change-over.

'Hiya, flower. Alreet?' he says, glancing up from where he's fiddling with nozzles on a sound box.

'Great, thanks,' I tell him, walking backwards towards the function room. 'It's a fun crowd today. You guys will have to roll out all the goodies.'

And by goodies, I mean Guy needs to get his Abba, Queen and Mark Ronson on because the guests are big drinkers and with big drinkers, dancing shoes usually follow.

My gaze unwittingly flicks to Guy and I find him staring – maybe glaring – back at me, his hand held to his chest where I just felt fire against my palm.

'No profiterole stains today, I promise,' I tell him, holding up my hands to show they're mess free.

'Whit-woo, *Guy*! You look and smell divine.' As Nick drifts through the corridor, the duty manager leading a line of wait-staff holding bottles of champagne ready to pour drinks for the speeches, I slip out of the corridor and back into the party.

Internalising as I do my wholehearted agreement with Nick's statement.

'You're back,' Mandy says as I sidle up to her by the top table. 'I'm reliably informed that the father of the bride is nervous as heck, so he'll be making a short speech. Father of the groom hasn't been invited to speak. The groom has pulled a short speech from ChatGPT and there's only one best man, who's already on thin ice with the mother of the groom.'

'So it could be wrapped up quickly,' I say, fiddling with the settings on my camera in anticipation, as champagne flutes are being filled and dirty dessert plates collected from around the twelve round tables in the room.

The theme of the day is ivory. *Everything* is ivory. Thank goodness for the groom's nanna on Table One, wearing a bold lime green and purple two piece, though she long since ditched her wide-brimmed hat to a corner table.

She's also decided to ditch etiquette, drinking from her toast glass before the MC – Uncle George, apparently – has announced the groom's opening gambit. I snap her photograph, Mandy and I chuckling together as we watch the scene play out. I capture another, as Uncle George's wife chastises Nanna, who rolls her eyes in return.

'Gotta love families,' Mandy whispers.

'You can't choose them,' I tell her.

'Tell you who you can choose... Men who look at you the way Guy Walker looks at *you*.'

I dart my focus to her. 'Like he's going to kill me, you mean?'

'Or devour you.'

I shake my head, brows scrunched together, but there's an annoyingly mischievous grin threatening my lips.

* * *

Mandy's predictions were spot on. The speeches were through in quick time. Cake cut. Pictures taken – the bride refused to be fed cake but honestly, I can't blame her; the corset in her dress looks like it's stealing the life from her torso, let alone making an extra space for what I'm told is lemon sponge with raspberry cream filling.

Sadly, despite getting to the staff room slightly earlier than planned, there aren't many spare meals today and the waitstaff have already commandeered most of the dishes. I settle for a watermelon and feta starter plate and a couple of chocolate dipped strawberry canapés.

Tonight, the new Mr and Mrs Bailey have requested that both Mandy and I stick around because they want as many shots as possible of the party. Apparently, their first date was at a concert of The Hand Me Downs, so they're especially giddy that the wedding singer they booked two years in advance has turned out to be the band's singer-songwriter.

I didn't have the heart to tell them at their pre-wedding

picture day that the man they're swooning over is highly unlikely to play *anything* he's written himself.

When Mandy and I make our way back to the function room, the castle's staff are already making quick work of the room transformation, whilst the guests mill around in the separate bar area, spilling out into the corridors, where I can guarantee at least one middle-aged dad will pretend to fondle the todger of an armour-clad statue of a knight.

I'm standing to one side of what will become the dance floor as two porters roll up a portion of the carpet. With one hand under my chin to catch any drips, I delve into my final, big, fat, juicy, chocolate-dipped berry.

A groan of sheer indulgence escapes me as strawberry juice wets my lips. I lick my skin clean before taking the final delicious mouthful. *God, it's good.*

My moment of bliss is interrupted by the clatter of metal hitting the now-exposed wood floor. Glancing to the source of the sound, I find Dave laughing hard and Guy telling him, *con* expletive, to... ah... get lost.

'Coming through,' one of the staff says as he and a colleague carry a round table top out of the room.

I'm wondering where Mandy got to when Pearl appears, sweating and panting as if she's been partaking in the reshuffle of the room. She's fit as a fiddle, for her age, but she doesn't need to be lugging tables around.

Taking my camera from around my neck and setting it aside, I ask, 'What can I do to help?'

'Oh, Lyra,' Pearl says, catching her breath with a hand on her hip. 'Would you mind? We're short-staffed tonight. There are two more table bases down in the dungeon that need to come up.'

'I'm on it,' I tell her.

'It's a two-person job, love.' Then she turns towards Dave and Guy, who are now back in professional mode and setting up their stage and speakers for the night. 'Dave, you couldn't spare that young man to help Lyra with a quick job, could you?'

Guy looks our way, pointing to himself – *Me?*

Pearl nods. 'Thanks, love.'

Dave pats Guy on the shoulder, confirming he's free to help, which I'm sure he's thrilled about.

I don't *know* what he's thinking but I can make an educated guess.

I'm not sure what to say, beyond, 'It's this way,' to which he replies, 'Following you.'

We traverse the secret staff passages of the castle and make our way down the awkward turning stone steps to the dungeon in silence.

It doesn't work out terribly well for me, because I think about the last time we walked the staff passages together, the way he'd nuzzled into my hair and whispered into my ear, breath hot on the skin of my neck as he slipped my hand into his.

But as we reach the heavy wood door of the dungeon and I hold it open for him to walk in ahead of me, I remember how he quickly dropped my hand again once we were out of the view of that drunk uncle. He couldn't wait to be clear of me.

'After you,' I tell him, trying not to inhale the deep smell of pine and cinnamon as he passes by me.

Cold emanates from the dark depths of the dungeon, chilling my legs beneath my summer button-down dress. He hesitates on the threshold of the abyss.

'Is there a light?' he asks.

Big. Baby.

Reaching inside, I flick the switch and dull lighting illuminates the space. The dungeon acts as an overflow for the wine cellar, so along the walls are two rows of dusty bottles of red wine, port and mead. Deeper into the void, there are table bottoms stacked against both sides of the space.

'We need two square bases,' I say, following Guy deeper into the dungeon. An involuntary shiver escapes me. Even Casper would be a little spooked in here.

Guy doesn't reply, or maybe he does and I don't hear over the boom of the heavy door closing.

'Shit! What was that?' Guy asks, both of us turning to the entrance of the dungeon.

'I guess the door shut.' I'm sure my thoughts are a match for his expression – I don't like it either – but I won't appear like some kind of damsel in distress.

Instead, I go ahead of him and start manoeuvring the two frames we need from the stack. 'Here, you take this one.'

As he reaches to take it from me, his fingers graze mine and whilst I don't believe in those silly descriptions in love stories about bolts of electricity and lightning striking when the girl and the boy meet, there is something about his touch that feels as if it penetrates my skin, travels my bloodstream and makes the hairs on my arms stand up.

For a split second, no more, I think his tense expression means he caught whatever I did, too. Then he casts his eyes back to the closed door, our only exit, and I remember, his tense expression has nothing to do with our contact and everything to do with his claustrophobia.

'Don't worry, it has to be physically locked by someone, I'm sure.' I start lugging the surprisingly heavy table stand towards the exit. 'It's one of those metal bar locks, from memory.'

Only... when I push against the old timber, the door doesn't budge. I nudge harder, giving it a rattle, trying not to panic because I can only imagine how Guy is feeling right now, but... yeah, kind of panicking.

'Is it jammed?' Guy frets. 'Let me try.'

I'm mildly offended that he thinks I'm incapable of opening a door but honestly, willing to let him try. I'm not claustrophobic but the thought of spiders, rodents, bats, ghosts, poltergeists... Those things I'm not keen on.

'It's not budging.' He turns to me, fear widening his pupils, obvious even in the dim light. 'It's locked.'

'It can't be locked.'

But we both push again together. Again and again, banging into the door and watching it barely move a millimetre.

'I think it's locked,' I say eventually.

'You don't say,' he retorts sarcastically.

'Hey! I didn't lock it!'

He takes a deep breath in through his nose, eyes closed. 'Sorry,' he says, all heartfelt and special. *Not.*

We try banging on the door and calling out, to no avail.

'Someone will come. They know where we are and they need the tables. Any second, someone will come down, you'll see.'

And I believe it. Of course they will... won't they?

14

GUY

June 2025

Giant Arachnids

Well, this is *fucking* brilliant.

Not only am I stuck in a confined space but one that likely has a bat infestation or giant arachnids in the shadows just waiting to climb out and entrap me in a web of stickiness that I can't unravel from.

I'm also trapped in here with a beautiful, smart, sort of well to do girl. Every time she lays her eyes on me, or her hands, my body reacts without my brain's instruction. My heart rate sky rockets, my temperature soars, and there's a tingling sensation in every nerve ending throughout my body.

I forget how to do the most basic of things, like turn my lips up into a smile or even fucking speak. Nothing comes out. I'm left staring at her in awe. This good girl. This sweet girl. This girl who really ought to do what's best for herself and stay away from me.

I know she notices. She takes my silence as slander, my

expressions of conflict and confusion as an insult. I know because her very presence in a room seems to lift everyone else. Yet, with me, she's damning, cutting. Deservedly so. Markedly so. And it's weird how much I like that. As if I have an in that nobody else does.

Now we're imprisoned in this bastard dungeon together. I have no idea whether it's the thought that I'm locked in with the woman whose simple groaning around the juiciest of strawberries makes my member feel like it's been hardwired into an electric pylon. Or that I'm stuck with a stranger who seems so familiar to me, it's terrifying.

So it's like the elevator all over again, except with bigger, darker demons. An even bigger phobia.

I stare at the rows of wine bottles lining the stone walls of the space and wait for it... The yearning to pick up a bottle, pop the cork, and drain it to get me through this situation.

'Are you okay?' Lyra asks me, thankfully, stemming my spiral.

'Am *I* okay? Are *you* okay? This place is the stuff of nightmares.'

I should know. Nightmares are my specialist subject.

'So long as any rodents are old enough to be wearing false teeth, I'll be fine.'

I chuckle. And immediately marvel that I've managed to have a socially appropriate response around this woman. Her surprise speaks volumes.

We get no reply to another round of banging and shouting on the dungeon door. The rational side of my mind believes Lyra; someone will come. It's only a matter of minutes, maybe even seconds, because they know we're here and I'm sure that if I don't get back out there, Dave won't replace me on that stage. I've heard the man on karaoke. He'd empty the room faster than a skunk farting.

To distract myself, I start setting up one of the table frames Lyra and I were carrying.

'What are you doing?' she asks.

I plonk the tabletop onto the frame, patting the surface that will keep us both much cleaner than the grubby stone floor.

She hesitates, then hops onto the table and I take a seat next to her, my thigh unintentionally grazing hers as I do. It's there again, that hit of something like adrenaline or, dare I say it, desire. It feels like I'm sinking into a warm bath. The immediate heat of the contact spanning out through my limbs and making me feel hot, then soothing me, calming me as I slide deeper.

'Can I ask you something?' she says.

'Something tells me you'll ask regardless of whether I say yes or no.'

Damn that pouting mouth. Those soft, plump lips that have touched mine before. She could ask me anything right now and I'd answer.

'I'm assuming that was intended to be a derogatory comment,' she says.

'Take it as you will,' I reply, surprising myself with the light-heartedness in my own voice. She's looking at me and I'm looking at those lips and I ought not to be. So I tell her, 'Smart people ask questions, but be careful; sometimes curiosity kills the cat.'

'I take it I'm the cat in this situation?' She smirks and it looks good on her. It's not the cute smile she reserves for her clients. It's cheeky, mischievous, sexy. 'When we first met, I asked you if you were Guy Walker. Why did you deny it?'

Something about the situation or that I know her better now makes me feel like I can't lie, but I try to adopt the approach I did in the lift that night. I attempt to avoid the truth.

'You didn't ask me if I'm Guy Walker, you said I reminded you of him.'

'You're avoiding the question.'

I consider the stone wall opposite us and notice how the pointing between the stones is cracked. I'm still focused on the wall as I admit, 'You were asking me about Guy Walker the musician. The guitarist from The Hand Me Downs.' I exhale, trying to get my next words right, in a way that answers her question but doesn't lead to any more. 'More often than not, I don't feel like him. He's someone from my past.'

I sense her eyes on me and whilst I don't want to look back, I'm drawn to her like a bug to fructose.

It takes her so long to respond, I'm wondering what she'll say. Whether she'll ask me how I can divide myself, compartmentalise myself into two different versions of the same man, or tell me that I still am *him* because I sing at fucking weddings.

She asks neither of those things. She watches me for a while, probably a nanosecond but long enough that I have to look away, feeling as if she's reading every thought I've ever had.

'Is that why you won't sing your own songs?'

She is smart. Too smart. And I'm curious about her, too. I don't want to answer her question and expose myself any more, but maybe there's a trade-off that's worth it.

'If I give you a response, I get to ask *you* something, and you have to answer truthfully. Deal?'

There's something like trepidation in her eyes, the way her

dark pupils widen against her brown irises, widening into flecks of hazel and gold. She has incredible eyes.

'Okay.'

'I didn't write those songs to be sung by me; I wrote them all with my brother's voice in my ears. Now that he isn't here to sing them, the words have lost their purpose.' I laugh to cover the threat of emotion but even I don't buy in to the sound. 'It took me three years of therapy to come up with that response and you've dragged it from me in a matter of weeks.'

I expect her to say something along the same lines as my therapist did in London, that Scott would want me to sing those words in his stead or in his honour. That life goes on and I have to find some way of coping without Scott in it. That music can live on and can keep him with me.

She surprises me again because she doesn't take that tack. 'You didn't write all the songs for Scott. My favourites are all songs that you performed.' She swallows, and even in the dim lights, I swear that flush that's so fucking cute on her skin is back.

'Go on then, what was your favourite song?' I don't know why I care or why I ask, except that it feels like safer ground than delving into my therapy sessions.

The question seems to hang in the air and for some reason, I have a charged sense of expectation.

'"You and Me",' she says, looking at me in a way that feels like a triage.

My next breath shudders because I already knew she was going to say that. I knew before she said it and it's crazy because I know that the girl from That Night wasn't Lyra. That girl wasn't wearing a floaty dress and didn't have long plaits in her hair. She wasn't cute and restrained; she was edgy, free.

But the song I was singing when my eyes met hers that night was 'You and Me'.

'What?' she asks.

I'm about to tell her that I know how crazy it sounds but every time I see her, I have an overwhelming sense of knowing, as if we've met before, but that would lead to me saying I dream about her every night and have dreamt about her every night since she kissed me up against my Barbie-pink car and woke me up for the first time in three years.

I swallow deeply, finally shifting the tightness. 'My turn.' Clearing my throat, I try to disguise the desire that's washed over me. 'Why do you let your sister and her friends speak to you the way they do, putting you down?'

She raises her legs and suddenly finds her toes the most interesting thing in the room.

'Honestly, I let them down.' She bends and flexes her toes, still not diverting her attention as she shrugs. 'I guess their...'

'Passive aggressiveness?'

Finally, she glances up to me but it's brief, then she's all about her feet again. 'I think it's their way of reminding me... and I don't feel like I can retort, truthfully.'

'Am I allowed to ask what you did that was so bad?'

'The crux of it?' She looks at me now and those usually bright eyes are filled with something so close to sadness, it punctures my heart. 'I was studying medicine at Newcastle University, exactly the way I was supposed to. Following in my family's footsteps. I was miserable doing it and, at the time, I convinced myself that I just didn't *want* it enough. It took three long years but after my third-year exams, I quit.

'As if throwing Mum and Dad's time and money back at them wasn't bad enough, that night, whilst I was out at—' She stops herself short and I wonder what the blank is – a bar? A club? Some lad's bed? 'Well, I was having the time of my life for a few hours, then I got a call from my sister. The Dean of Faculty knew my dad and had shared my news before I ever got a chance to.'

Her hand is gripping the edge of the table between us and I have an unexpected urge to reach for it, to soothe her skin until her fingers relax. Tentatively, I slide my own hand from my thigh, down to the tabletop, and I'm reaching for her. But before I make contact, she shifts her hands into her lap, fingers interlaced.

Good for her. For me. For us.

See, she's smart.

'That was shitty of the Dean,' I tell her, recovering from my near blunder.

She scoffs. 'In some ways, I guess he saved me from back-tracking. I'd tried to speak to my parents about dropping out and each time, they persuaded me to stay, assuring me that one day, I'd look back and be grateful.' She shakes her head. 'I was grateful for the opportunities I'd been afforded, I really was. I just...'

'Felt like a square peg in a round hole?' I offer, not understanding her story but able to empathise, I guess.

She fixes her gaze on mine. 'Exactly that.' Her lips twist into the kind of sad smile I've only seen on her once, shortly before she kissed me. The thought knocks my next breath out of rhythm. I'm aching to reach out and hold her face in my palms, to run my thumb along the edge of her soft lips.

'I spent my third year on placement, with real patients. I wanted to help people. I still do. But I couldn't hack being around so much pain and suffering every day. The bad seemed to outweigh the good and it was slowly draining the life from me.' She shrugs. 'Then I met karma.'

I have an urge to hold her and tell her she only deserves the good. But I don't.

'For what it's worth, I don't think that gives your sister and her friends a right to belittle you the way they do.'

She inhales deeply. 'Well, that's not how the story ends, unfortunately.' Her eyelids hold their next blink. 'That same night, my dad had a stroke. From the stress of it all. *That's* the reason my family are the way they are with me. It's the reason I don't push back and the reason I don't have a right to.'

She looks at me now and her eyes are full of a sadness I wish I could take away for her. 'Dad could have died that night, whilst I was high on my newfound freedom. Dreaming of studying documentary photography and travelling the world with a camera and notebook and pen.'

So that's what she wants. 'The wedding photography, is that… your penance?' I realise how shitty that sounds as soon as the words leave my mouth. I quickly follow up. 'I'm sorry, I just mean…'

She chuckles and I feel as if I've been let off the hook. I'm starting to get the sense that Lyra's pretty good at letting people off lightly, though I know there's a feistier side to her; I've witnessed it.

'It's okay,' she says. 'And no, not exactly. I enjoy photographing weddings and families, making people happy. It's not what I dreamed of doing with my life but I like what I do and it means I can be around to help when Dad needs me. I'm no doctor, of course, but I'm… content.'

Content. That sounds both aspirational and depressing.

She rubs her index fingers against the corners of her eyes and I check she isn't crying – that's the last thing I want. Though, I did tell her, curiosity kills the cat.

I am 100 per cent curious about this woman.

'You're probably thinking I'm some whiny little rich girl, aren't you? Fallen from grace.'

'That's not what I'm thinking, at all,' I tell her. I'm thinking and feeling a thousand things, so I take a pause to decide how to respond. 'Everyone's story's different. Yours sounds difficult and repressive. No one should be forced to feel guilty for being who they are.'

I can't imagine that anyone who knows this woman would want her to be anything less than who she can be and who she wants to be.

'Can I be objective, though?' I ask, receiving a subtle, apprehensive nod in response. 'I can also see that your family love you and want the best for you. They haven't gone the right way about it and from what I've seen, they still aren't going the right way about it, but maybe this isn't about you not being a doctor. Maybe they... don't think you're reaching your potential.'

Her eyes narrow to slits and I know I've overstepped. 'My *potential* is supporting my dad. Helping Mum balance work and life. Being there for my sister when she needs me.'

She slips down from the tabletop, hands on hips, and I hold up my hands in apology. 'I'm sorry, I overstepped. I'm no good with words and—'

'You're one of the best lyricists I've ever come across!' Her words would be kind on paper but there's fire in her expression and in her tone.

'All I meant was, I know what it looks like when a family doesn't love you, believe me, and, whilst I think your sister can be a twat, I don't think—'

'You can't call her a twat!'

'Sorry, again, that's your prerogative.' I'm about to continue making my case when Lyra slaps a hand across her mouth and that twinkle I've seen in her eyes, that sparkles and dances in the dimmest of light, it's back.

The sweetest sound of laughter replaces her irritation. 'She can be a bit of a twat.'

I shouldn't smile. I know I'm going to say or do the wrong thing again, but damn it, she drags my lips up.

Who'd have thought it? I'm trapped in this dungeon, with no way out, and my tortured soul has been repressed by a woman who is my opposite in every way. From the way she loves and is loved, to her willingness to put others before even her own happiness. She's the sun to my storm cloud and she should be repelled by me, yet everything inside me is fuelled by her warmth. And I... *Damn it*, I want *more*.

Against all my better judgement, I take a step towards her. Unexpectedly, she makes a move closer to me, where her rays are stronger, fire to my ice, and all I can think about is how gentle her kiss was the first night I met her. How she feels like someone I've known all my life. Someone I don't deserve, someone I'll hurt or fuck up somehow, yet a woman I seem incapable of taking a step back from.

I edge closer still, hearing her inhale, smelling or imagining the sweetness of strawberries on her breath.

Walk away.

I can't.

Her glance from my eyes to my lips is the final undoing of any self-restraint I have.

One of us makes a move that presses our stomachs together and my hand reaches for her face—

'Lyra? Are you down here?'

The door to the dungeon is pulled open and light from the corridor beyond puts us under spotlight. *Almost* caught in the act. *Or saved from it.*

Lyra's eyes widen, I think a match for my own, as if our bubble has been pierced by reality.

'Mandy, finally!' Lyra says, spinning away from me.

Finally. Right.

Go, Lyra, go back to helping people.

I follow Mandy and Lyra out of the dungeon, carrying both table frames we came down for. Considering the door as I go, I conclude that the only way we got stuck in there is for someone to have locked us in from the outside by placing the metal bar across the frame.

It's not until I peer back into the black void that I realise the yearning to pick up alcohol and drink never did come. She took me to places in my mind that I hate going. I was locked in a dark, confined space. Yet, there was no part of me that wanted to drink as I sat on that table next to her.

***

Back upstairs, despite only being MIA for twenty minutes, the wedding reception is reset. Dave is set up and ready for me to take the stage.

The two table frames I carried are set up in the corner of the room but seem to have no purpose whatsoever and when I locate Lyra, her hands are planted on her hips as she gives Pearl what-for, albeit playfully.

Did we get pranked?

There's no time for me to overthink because Dave is thrusting a microphone into my hand and telling me, 'They asked for you to start with Lonestar's "Amazed". They're ready for their first dance.'

Of all the songs, in all the world, why do brides love this one? It's so cringeworthy.

From the middle of the stage, I say, 'Ladies and gentlemen, please welcome to the dance floor for their first dance as husband and wife, Mr and Mrs Bailey.'

I sing the lyrics as if I'm interested but through the entire song and the Take That track that follows, I watch the only thing I'm actually interested in. I see every picture she takes, noting what interests her, wondering what she sees through her lens that makes it a moment to capture.

I watch the way she smiles at the newlyweds as they dance together. How she beams as the youngest bridesmaid gives her best ballet moves for a doting audience. How the loose summer dress she's wearing still affords me an occasional glimpse of what lies beneath, the way her hips twist and turn, the flatness of her stomach and pertness of her breasts.

More than once, I think she feels my gawping and though I look away each time she catches me, I know she sees. She couldn't miss that I've been fixed on her.

Would we have kissed in the dungeon if Mandy hadn't come?

Lyra had a lucky escape.

I should return the kindness she shows everyone else and leave well alone.

Once I've sung for an hour, Dave gives me the signal and when I get to the end of Westlife's 'World of Our Own', I announce a short break.

A couple of people ask me if I'll sing something from The Hand Me Downs as I step down from the stage, but I give my usual line about the playlist. I speak quietly, to avoid the protests of the bride and groom because Dave has already forewarned me that they have some romantic connection to one of the band's gigs.

I'm making a beeline for the rear entrance of the room to

hide outside on the same bench I disappear to every night I sing here, tucked away from view on the lawn.

'Guy?' The sweet voice of the young bridesmaid makes me stop and I turn back to the room, looking down to her.

She's maybe eight or nine years old. The ringlets in her hair now less than perfect since she's danced her heart out for the last hour. She lifts up an Earl's Castle notepad and pen, the kind that get left in hotel rooms by the old-fashioned landline phones.

'Please can I have your autograph?'

I want to say no, *you don't want that, sweetheart*. But she's looking at me with the kind of expression I can't refuse. Her mam is standing behind her now, hands on her daughter's shoulders, and giving me the kind of expression that comes with a warning – DO NOT DISAPPOINT MY DAUGHTER.

Still, I'd really like to say no – I'm not that man any more.

But someone else appears behind them and when I glance her way, Lyra's expression isn't threatening or expectant; it's intrigued, I think. *Will he sign?*

I nod and make my way back to the girl, crouching down in front of her. 'What's your name?'

She grins from ear to ear. 'Anabell. Ah, nu, ah, be, eh, lu, lu.'

Taking her pen, I spell out her name and sign mine. The way I used to, without hesitation, as if it was just yesterday that I'd sign hundreds of posters for promotions, t-shirts, caps and banners after concerts. For a nanosecond, I forget.

A sharp flash brings me back from wherever my mind wanders to and I see Lyra, with a different camera to her usual one, taking a picture of the moment.

I scowl at her. *No*. Then hand the notepad and pen back to the girl, give her the kind of response I used to give on autopilot to fans, and head outside, into the cool fresh air, taking a cigarette from my inside pocket and placing it between my lips as I head to the solitude of my seat.

Crossing the gravel between the castle and the lawn, I hear voices on the balcony behind me, frantically calling out for 'Nanna!'

'Has anyone seen Nanna?' a woman asks.

I continue walking.

I'm in such a blind from the last hour and a half. From feeling like I've been cracked over the head with an emotional mallet. I'm starting to hallucinate. Just like the lone man in the desert seeing an oasis, I smell the sweet solace of not just nicotine but the specific brand I used to smoke.

I'm glad I don't smoke any more, or drink or take drugs. I've worked hard to get here, for myself, and for Scott. I have what my therapist describes as an addictive personality and the lifestyle I had in the band legitimised it.

But damn, that smell is still a welcome one.

It's so strong, it makes me take my unlit stick from my mouth and check I didn't accidentally take a lighter to it in my emotional fog.

I didn't.

Now, almost at my hideaway, I see a plume of smoke rising into the dark night.

Stronger than my yearning for that old habit is my irritation that someone has nabbed my spot.

As I tuck around the corner of the seat, I see an elderly lady, resting back into the bench, her ankles crossed beneath her green and purple dress, feet swinging back and forth like someone seventy years her junior. She takes her next drag like she really needs it.

Just as I decide to leave this woman in peace, she says, 'Oh, hiya, love,' in that way people from the north east can, as if they've known you forever, so you can't turn on your too-shiny shoe heel to walk away.

She glances to the cigarette between my lips and starts reaching into her small purple handbag. 'I've got a light,' she tells me.

'I'm good, thanks. I don't smoke.'

She considers this, taking in the picture of me in front of her, presumably pondering whether I'm being sarcastic. Then, she takes her cigarette between two fingers, removes it from her lips and turns her head to blow her smoke in the opposite direction to me.

'I had a friend who packed in that way,' she says. 'Joyce from along the road. She was always trying to quit. She had the patches, the gum, even tried one of those hypnotherapists who she met at the bingo one night. None of it worked.'

She shuffles along the seat and lifts her handbag onto her lap, leaving a space for me that I feel obliged to fill, coming to sit next to her.

'Eventually, someone told her that what she missed was the physical act of it. Doing the action with her hands and what-not.' She waves her fingers that are still holding her near-finished cigarette. 'So she tried what you're doing. Whenever she wanted a drag, she'd put a cigarette between her fingers and pretend to smoke it. Aye, she was one of the good ones, our Joyce. Lovely woman.'

'I'm going to take a punt here but are *you* the Nanna people are looking for back at the party?'

She hisses her next breath through her teeth, head shaking. 'Can't a woman have two minutes' peace?'

'I hear you. Your secret's safe with me.'

We fall into silence and in the distance, I can hear another call for 'Nanna', as if this woman isn't capable of looking after herself. She seems just fine to me.

'They're all squabbling amongst themselves about who let me have too much whiskey.' Her head's shaking again. 'Do I look drunk to you?'

I turn her way. Her eyes do look a little glassy but I get the sense that might not only be from alcohol.

'Not in the slightest.' I'm not sure why but I offer her my right hand as I tell her, 'I'm Guy.'

'So they tell me,' she says, accepting my hand. 'You've got a musician's hands.'

By that, I assume she means no labourer's callouses. I've also lost the hardened tips of my fingers that I had when I played guitar every day.

'My father was a musician. He used to play piano and sing in the clubs. He was good. All the locals loved him. They'd always ask for one more tune.'

I smile. Genuinely feeling like this woman is a pretty cool nanna. 'Shall I just call you Nanna?'

'Most people do, love. But I'm actually Mary. Mary Winnifred. People call me Winnie, though.'

'Winnie.'

'I haven't had too much whiskey. They're only on at us because none of them want to look after us and they think I'm too bloody old to look after myself since my Billy died last year.'

'Was Billy your husband?'

'Sixty years. We spent our entire lives together. He was a hard man to live with. Drank too much. Smoked too much. Ate far too much lard. Never lifted a finger around the house.' She looks away but not before I notice her eyes glaze over even more. 'But d'ya know what he'd do if he was here, Guy?'

'What would he do?'

'He'd say, Winnie, you only live once. Get yourself another whiskey, darlin'. Hop on my feet and I'll turn you round that dance floor.'

She reaches into her purse, takes out a crumpled tissue, and sounds like an elephant blowing its nose as she corrects herself.

'Nanna?' we hear being called again.

I don't know what's happening to me of late. Maybe it's all that therapy or getting older. Or being trapped in small spaces with a woman who wants to help everyone.

Standing, I hold out my hand. 'Come on, Winnie. I might not be a replacement for your Billy but I'd be honoured if you'd let me turn you around the dance floor tonight.'

15

LYRA

June 2025

The Moment My Crush Graduates

I'm all set to apologise to Guy when I see him come back through the rear exit of the function room. He was clearly unhappy about me taking a personal picture of him signing the girl's notebook. It felt kind and sort of pivotal. As if a snippet of Guy Walker from The Hand Me Downs was in the room. But the way he glared at me when my flash went off told me an entirely different story.

I've been hovering by the stage, taking pictures of the party, but mostly waiting for his return. I felt like we crossed some kind of invisible line in the dungeon – when *Pearl* locked us in the dungeon. I'm not sure what game she was playing but I'll admit, as unexpected as it was, Guy and I shared a moment down there. Though I'm no expert when it comes to men, I think, if we hadn't been interrupted...

I stop dead in my approach to Guy when I see he's holding

the hand of a woman I think is the missing Nanna that the groom's family have been frantically searching for.

Nanna looks anything but perturbed, though, as she lets the wedding singer lead her into the room.

Guy gestures to the dance floor and Nanna walks into the middle of the empty space, holding out her arms as if to say, *I'm here, stop your needless worrying.*

Meanwhile, Guy says something to Dave, pointing to his ear. Then Dave is fitting a sound pack and an ear microphone to Guy, who slips out of his suit jacket. This leaves him standing in black trousers that hug his thighs and bum deliciously and though they need no holding up, black braces are clipped to the trousers, drawing my attention to the very firm torso beneath his white shirt.

'Jaw up, hunny,' Mandy says, appearing at my side.

'I have no idea what you're talking about,' I tell her, unable to hide my amusement.

When I turn back to the dance floor, I recognise the backing track that begins to play. Guy makes his way to Nanna, who is patiently waiting in the middle of the space.

As he sings the opening lyrics to the Stereophonics' 'Step on My Old Size Nines', he takes hold of Nanna. With one hand on her back and the other holding her hand, he lifts her until she places her feet on top of his, and he moves them both around the floor, singing to her with the kind of gravelly voice Kelly Jones would be proud of.

Step by step, Nanna's smile grows. Little by little, every woman in the room seems to melt, every man wishes he'd had the same idea, and I... feel like an ice-cream in a fish and chip shop. He's more than a rock star, more than a miserable singer with a mesmerising voice. He's *human*. A *good* human.

As he twirls Nanna into the second chorus, the bride and

groom lead their guests to dance, and when the track stops, I don't hear what Nanna whispers into Guy's ear before she presses her lips to his cheek, but I do hear the most unexpected and bellowing laugh. Guy folds over his knees.

I have no idea why I'm chuckling with him, a lump in my throat. Why, when he glances my way and that laughter turns into a beaming smile, I'm grinning right back at him.

* * *

From the moment Guy turned Nanna around the dance floor, the wedding party cranked up another gear. Guy sang with more energy than he has since the start of the season. Every wedding guest has partied like tomorrow will never come.

Even Dave was swinging his bum and bumping hips with Mandy and me. The whole evening has been electric and now, whilst the reception rages on courtesy of one of Dave's DJs, Mandy, Guy, Pearl, Geoff and Dave are heading to the much quieter residents' bar for a night cap.

I'm packing up my cameras as they pass by me in the staff corridor.

'Come on, girlie,' Mandy calls, breaking her animated conversation with Dave momentarily.

I'm going to tell her that I can't follow but she's back to giving Dave grief about something, both of them bantering hard. I zip my cases and jump when I feel the presence of someone behind me.

'You're coming, aren't you?' Guy asks.

I spin to face him, a little too quickly. He's so close to me, I lose my balance and he steadies me, grabbing hold of my elbows.

He's still wearing his shirt and braces, though the sleeves

of his shirt are rolled up now and his black tie has been discarded. His hair is mussed up, like he's been performing for hours because, well, he has. And I watched all of it, eyes glued to him, ears unable to focus on anything other than the voice I love.

Now, on top of it all, that woody, peppery scent that's becoming a drug to me is mixed with something incredibly masculine, and it's all-consuming. *He's* all-consuming.

Because of that, I want desperately to go for a drink with the group, to learn more about this man, to cling on to the buzz of the night for just half an hour more. But...

'I can't.'

'Why? Sorry, don't answer that.'

I give a short laugh at his awkwardness. The man who had an entire room eating out of the palm of his hand not long ago. 'It's okay. I have to get home. Or, home to my parents' house.'

'Your dad?'

I nod. 'My mum is on call; she's a cardiologist. I usually stay over in case she gets called out and Dad needs anything.'

He's expressionless, deadpan. Yet I feel as if he's searching into the depths of me. I want to know what's going through his mind.

'Plus, the bar doesn't have hot chocolate,' I say, to plug the silence.

'Then I guess I'll see you next week?'

'Unless you want to hang out in my parents' house with me and drink a thousand-calories-a-mug hot chocolate?' I think I mean it as an invitation. God, no, of course I don't.

Come to my parents' house for hot chocolate? Am I sixteen?

Guy opens his mouth to respond but I cut him off, not needing to hear an excuse. 'See you next week,' I tell him, hoping the heat of embarrassment hasn't made it to my cheeks.

I've given him the out.

So why isn't he moving?

He's still so close to me that his scent is coating me like velvet – warm, smooth, luxurious. I'm not an impulsive person, generally. I've trained myself not to be as an adult. And I never have the kind of urge I do now, to take hold of Guy's braces, pull his body to mine and beg him to utterly ravage me.

His face shifts ever so slightly closer to mine and there isn't a muscle in my body not twisted and tightened with expectation. *Want.*

'Goodnight, Lyra.'

'Goodnight,' I barely manage, watching him follow the others in the direction of the bar.

'Guy?'

He turns to face me but continues walking backwards, away from me. 'Lyra.'

'I'm sorry about taking your picture earlier, when the bridesmaid—'

'Don't worry about it.' He shrugs. 'I guess it reminded me that I used to be able to sing once.'

'I never saw you strut moves the way you did with Nanna tonight, though,' I tease, grateful that he's not angry about the picture I'm actually looking forward to seeing developed.

'What can I say? If I could've chosen myself a grandmother, she would've been just like Nanna Winnie.'

* * *

I wanted to stay so badly. I waved goodbye to the group in the residents' bar as they were being served a tray of drinks. I couldn't help noticing that Guy was drinking a pint of squash, which seemed odd because he'd had pints of beer lined up on the stage all night, which party guests had bought for him following his adorable moment with Nanna Winnie.

Worse than the feeling of FOMO I had driving home is that I've pulled onto the driveway of my parents' house and the lights are out. Not even the blue flickering light of the TV is dancing around their bedroom curtains. Mum and Dad are sleeping. I know Mum is home because she would have messaged me if she'd been called to the hospital already.

So I'm missing out on all fronts, and my mind keeps drifting to that brain fuzz I get whenever Guy is in my remote vicinity. He is moody, still. Yo-yos make fewer one-eighties than his personalities. But the more time I spend with him, the more there seems to be about him that I want to discover. He intrigues me, sparks something in me, and for my sins, he turns me on like no man has ever. Those *braces.*

The distraction of having Mum around tonight would have been good. Instead, I pad quietly upstairs to my old room and switch into bed shorts and a lazy t-shirt that slops off one shoulder. Comfy clothes to match the cosy hot chocolate I decide to make. I bought Dad a velvetiser last Christmas and we joke that I bought a present for myself, though drinking hot chocolate with my dad in the evenings, snuggling up against his side, is one of my favourite things to do.

I set myself up at the bench seat table in the kitchen and open my laptop. As I plug my camera into the computer, I plan to work on edits, but I find myself skipping to the pictures of Guy twirling a very happy lady around on his *large* feet.

I know before I start typing that the story I write tonight

will be about Nanna Winnie. Or a version of her I invent to indulge my hobby.

Less than a paragraph in to the article that will never be published, my mobile vibrates with the name of a caller I don't expect.

'Guy?' I ask, despite answering a call from his saved number.

'Are you awake?' His voice is quiet and I don't hear the background noise of the bar at the castle, or any noise, in fact.

'Ah, yeah, why?'

'I really fancied that hot chocolate.'

Everything beneath my ribcage starts thumping to be let out. I mean, *technically*, I invited him. But I didn't *invite* him.

'Lyra? Are you there?'

I swallow a feeling that could be excitement, or nervousness, or Norovirus. 'Ah, yeah. I'm here.'

'Let me in?'

I'm so discombobulated that I practically fall from the bench seat at the table, shushing myself as I come to stand, and tiptoeing across the creaky floorboards to the front door.

Is this for real? Am I living in one of my fictitious articles right now?

I'm caught so unaware that I completely forget I'm wearing my bedclothes.

Until I open the door and standing in front of me, still roguishly handsome in his shirt and braces, is Guy.

His eyes rake from my head to my toes, before he says, 'Hi.'

I know from my very brief medical training that two things are happening right now. One, my sympathetic nervous system is working overdrive. Two, my motor neurons are malfunctioning big time. *Hello? Motor neurons? Want to do your job and make me speak?*

'H— Wh— How do you know where my parents live? What are you doing here?'

He slips his hands into the pockets of his trousers and I try my very best not to notice the way the material stretches across his crotch, so much so, I end up looking to the stars in the night's sky and I think I hear him snicker.

'Mandy gave me the address and before you say something whip-smart about privacy or whatever, *you* got *my* number from Dave, so it's quid pro quo.'

Now I look at him, worrying my lip with embarrassment. He knows I have his number because I messaged him. He never replied.

Yet here he is, on my parents' doorstep at 11 p.m.

'As to the other question, you invited me for hot chocolate. I think?' His lips curve up slowly, confidently. 'You were right, the bar doesn't serve it and after we spoke...' His smile fades into straight lips. 'It was all I could think about.'

I step back from the door, welcoming him inside. 'Mandy must have told you about my velvetiser.'

He chuckles, short and quiet, then steps inside, into me, a full head taller than me but his chest close to mine, so close I don't think I'm imagining the quick, shallow rise and fall of his upper torso.

'My parents are sleeping so we need to be quiet.'

'I can be quiet,' he says. Then his lips part and it feels like his tongue meets the soft flesh in slow motion, whilst I'm unable to look away.

'The kitchen's through here.' My words are barely audible.

I use the short distance from the hallway to the kitchen to get a grip of myself. To dampen my body's betrayal of my rational mind.

But it's hard to be rational when *he's* here. I'm not saying this is a move, but this *is* a *something*.

'Were you working?' he asks on seeing my laptop open on the table.

'Oh, ah, not really, no.'

He frowns as he takes a spot on the bench seat opposite mine and I take back out cocoa powder and milk.

'It's kind of nerdy. In fact, I'm not even going to tell you.' I hold up my two hot chocolate ingredients. 'Do you actually want hot chocolate? I could find something stronger – wine, beer?'

'Hot chocolate is the reason I'm here.' He grins and it's a short-bed-shorts-melting kind of smile. 'Plus, I don't drink.'

Now it's my turn to raise a brow. 'You don't drink alcohol?'

He shakes his head.

'But you always have pints lined up on the stage.'

'Dave disappears those surreptitiously for me.'

Huh. 'But the tequila, in the lift and at the hen party?'

'My bottle was filled with water. People expect the naked butler to bring the party. Drinking water doesn't appear as fun, does it?'

I'm staring at him, rudely so, trying to think of all the times I've seen him near alcohol but, with the exception of the tequila bottle, I haven't seen him drink it.

'You're quite the enigma, aren't you?'

'Enigma?' He shakes his head. 'Closed book, maybe.'

The velvetiser completes its cycle and I pour Guy's drink into one of my comfort mugs – an old Newcastle Uni one that's more small bowl than drinking vessel.

I give it my signature touch, drizzling a smidge of salted caramel around the rim and shaving my favourite dark chocolate on top.

When I put the finished article in front of him, Guy looks from the mug, across the table to me, where I've slipped back onto my bench, one knee tugged up to my chest.

'Are you trying to keep me up all night?'

'You knocked on *my* door,' I counter, my brain not engaging before the flirtatious words leave my mouth. I can see he's taken by surprise and I feel shockingly forward.

I'm relieved when he tells me, '*You* kissed *me* first.'

I pick up my own drink between two hands, more for the distraction than the warmth emanating from the mug. I'm suddenly hot enough. 'Are you going to dine out on that forever?'

His laughter breaks the... whatever it is that's passing between us, and I'm pleased it does because the way he looks, the way he's looking *at* me, has me hotter than any cocoa. The kind of temperature that makes a girl dizzy.

Raising his drink, he slurps as he sips. The sort of uncouth sound that would make my mum wince but that I hear as enjoyment. 'God, that's good.'

'I hate to say I told you so but...'

'You told me so?'

I hold my arms out in response – if the shoe fits. 'Why are you really here, Guy?'

He brings his forearms to the table and twists his hot chocolate between his hands. 'I had a good night.' He glances up to me. 'It's been a long time since I had a good night, and I think it started when I got locked in a dungeon with you, so I guess... I wanted it to end with you, too.'

He renders me utterly speechless. Because I'm flattered and there are jiggly beans dancing in my tummy over his words. But also because I didn't do anything, I don't think. If he had a good night, it's down to the kindness he showed other people. I think I'm sad for him, for the rock star, the musician, Guy Walker, and it surprises me.

I find myself wanting to know everything about him that isn't obvious. All the bits in between the chart-topping era and now. All the parts before.

I hear the creak of a bed above our heads, a sound that makes us both shift our attention to the ceiling.

'Let's take these into the extension; it's almost soundproofed to the rest of the house,' I tell him.

He follows me into the extension, originally constructed to be a playroom when Livy and I were kids. Over the years, it became the room one of us was sent to when we fought. In secondary school, it became the music room, which was home to all the instruments Mum and Dad forced Livy and me to take up. Dotted around the room are boxes containing my old violin, a cello and a clarinet. My upstanding piano, which I actually was good at because I enjoyed it.

When I was an older teen, right up until I left home recently, this room became my hideaway. I'm the only person who really comes in here, to hide away with my vast stash of old vinyl records and the bulky second-hand player I bought, which has nineties-style tape cassette and triple rotating CD options. I'm sure it was cool when it was new on the market.

Guy follows me inside. It's cold, so I switch on the old electric heater. 'We'll be roasting in ten minutes. Would you like a throw in the meantime?' I gesture to a stack of folded blankets on the ottoman between two leather sofas.

'I'll be fine with my warm sugar overdose. Thank you, by the way.'

'You're welcome,' I say as we face each other, both wondering where we should sit, I think. *I* am wondering where I should sit. On the same sofa as him? On the sofa adjacent?

I decide to let him make the call, tucking myself into the corner of one sofa and pulling a throw over my bare legs.

His focus flicks between the seating options. Eventually, he chickens out, setting down his drink on a coffee table and walking around the room.

'Who plays?' he asks, motioning to the boxed instruments.

'You're looking at the band-camp geek. Though my repertoire mostly extends to three-note nursery rhymes. I'm very proficient with the triangle and the tambourine, though.'

I'm finding myself funny but there's something about my words that seems to jar with him, right before he gives me the kind of smile that doesn't light him up.

'I could play the piano well,' I tell him.

'Could?' he says, trailing his fingers along the old Yamaha, probably collecting dust on the tip.

'I haven't played for a long time. I always think going back to an instrument you know well is like riding a bike, though. It either clicks, or it doesn't. Most instruments never did for me. Piano was the exception. I could get lost in here for hours.'

He nods. 'It was always guitar for me.'

'I would have loved to play the guitar but it wasn't encouraged at my school. It's what all the bad boys played,' I tease.

'Why do you think I played? Absolute babe magnet when I was a teenager.'

I splurt my next mouthful of creamy cocoa.

'It cancelled out the acne,' he says, then tentatively tinkers with the keys on the piano, which is slightly out of tune. 'I taught myself to play piano a bit. It helped me write but I was never good enough to perform on it. I always thought if you could crack the nut of the piano, you could teach yourself to play just about any instrument.'

'Well, I tried to teach myself guitar when I was at university, and I can assure you, it's not as translatable as you think.'

'Maybe you didn't give it enough time.'

'Probably right. How about you? Do you still play often?'

He glances my way, creases forming at the side of his eyes, then he quickly moves away from the instruments without answering my question. He moves to one of two long shelves that are packed full of my LPs.

I watch him run a finger along the collection, slow enough to read the spines, wondering how it would feel to have those fingers run lazy lines across my skin.

'Oasis. Stereophonics. U2. Arctic Monkeys. The Killers.' He reads the titles as he works along the row, then slides the next one out and tucks it under his arm, obscuring it from my view.

He continues scrolling. 'Kings of Leon. This is their best album. Florence & the Machine. Billie Eilish.' He takes out the next one and tucks it under his arm with the other, so that I can't see either. 'Sam Fender. The Goo Goo Dolls. This is a wicked shelf. Who's the music lover?' He moves towards the big old LP player which sits central to the long wall in the room, flanked on either side by shelves of vinyl. 'Does this work?'

'It does. And the music is mine. My own place isn't big enough to house all this stuff.'

I watch him navigate the music player as if he's used it every day of his life, despite it being far from intuitive. It was one of the things I liked about it when I bought it ten years ago. It's needlessly complex but the sound is beautiful.

He slips the two albums from under his arm and holds one up. 'The Cab? Tell me about them.'

'American pop-rock band. My friend Cami bought me that one. I found a song called "Bad" when we were in our first year of uni and I played it on repeat, incessantly. Then Cami came over here one day and when she realised I had an unhealthy obsession with vinyl, she bought me that one.'

He reads the track list, then sets 'Bad' playing. My body instantly sinks into the sofa, my head hanging back against the cushions as the music takes me back a decade. I remember how much I wanted what the band was singing about – a crazy love, the kind that kept a bad girl up all night.

I can feel Guy watching me as I smile up at the ceiling and explain. 'It was the start of me wanting to pull away, I think.' I shift my body to look at him. 'Do you ever hear a song and think, that's exactly the song I needed to hear? As if it validates something you're thinking or feeling?' I scoff. 'Does that even make sense?'

He doesn't speak, he just watches me, listening to the music, or me, or both; I'm not sure. He leans back against the tall table holding the LP player.

'I was so fed up of being the good girl. Being everything that everyone had told me I was supposed to be and should *want* to be. I don't know how I managed another two years of studying medicine, to be honest.'

I wait for Guy to say something but he's silently listening. At end of the track, he holds up the other LP he slipped from my shelf. 'This one?'

'Ah. American rock band, Lifehouse. I bought that album. The lead singer-songwriter, Jason Wade, has a gorgeous voice. Not as distinctive as—' I stop myself short of saying *yours.* I don't even know why; maybe he'd be flattered to know there's not a voice on the planet I prefer listening to more than his. There's also a high likelihood he'd find it a bit creepy. 'Some singers,' I say instead. 'But he's a good lyricist, too. His songs are pretty.'

'Which one should I listen to?'

'Hmm. Since you have that particular album in your hand, I'd say "Falling In".'

Guy sets the song playing and I feel my body stiffen at the lyrics. As Jason Wade sings about falling in love, I'm hoping Guy doesn't think I've picked it to make some kind of play. That would be mortifying.

He watches the floor as he absorbs the lyrics and I see his cheekbones rise. 'Cheesy rock?'

I fight my grin, biting down on my lip, so pleased he doesn't think I'm trying to be mushy, or worse, that I'm trying to send him a message that I'm in love with him.

'Who did you have a crush on?' he asks, smirking.

Now I can't help my laughter because he's caught me out. 'I had a very brief crush on the bartender in the student union. Until I realised he had a girlfriend back home in Hampshire and was pretty receptive to any undergrad crushing on him.'

'He was fit, though?' Guy teases.

'In a teen-crush kind of way, yeah.'

'Pecs and spice-boy hair?'

'The spikier, the better. There was also something that felt almost exotic about him being from southern England.'

Guy laughs and it's a sound I'd love to record and play on repeat. It's a close second to the sound of his singing voice. 'When I was a lad, anything outside a twenty-mile radius was exotic.' His words seem to sober him and I'd love to know the reason why but in the style I'm becoming accustomed to, he's partially opened a door – not even a door, a window – into his life, and rather than expand, or let himself go wherever his words are taking him, he turns his back, moving to the second shelf of LPs.

I cringe as he works his way along the shelf to a bundle of LPs he'll most certainly recognise. Seven in a row. Each of them an album from The Hand Me Downs.

I'm up off the sofa, hot chocolate abandoned on the floor, rushing to stop him. Until I'm right behind him and I think, *Why?* Why stop him from knowing that I loved, I *love*, his music? His lyrics, the compositions, the way he played, the way he sounded.

The room is much warmer now, most of which I think is coming from the heater, rather than my blushes.

Guy traces the edges of the records with his fingers, then chooses one – the band's final album. I think he's going to take it off the shelf. Instead, he presses the corner, rocking it out slightly, then pushing it back in.

When he turns, he isn't surprised that there's just inches separating our bodies. Or, if he is, he doesn't show it.

A wave of urgent want comes over me. I'm close enough to see every character line in his face, the teasing half-moons either side of his kissable lips, the crease above his cupid's bow.

I've made the plunge before; I won't do it again. Just because he turned up on my doorstep, just because he wanted to end his good night with me, doesn't mean he wants to kiss me.

I inch forwards, my arm reaching around him, feeling as if I'm moving in slow motion. The opportunity is here, if he wants it. But he's only watching me, as if he's memorising every cell in my face. By the time I take hold of my favourite album of his band, he hasn't kissed me, so I pull away, LP in hand.

'This is my favourite,' I tell him.

He considers the cover. I think he's going to stop me from putting it on but I shift to switch out the record on the player.

'My favourite track that Scott used to sing is this one,' I say.

The song 'Addicted' starts to play – Guy's riff, the drums, then Scott's voice.

Guy stiffens and I watch his Adam's apple move up and down in his taut throat. 'I haven't listened to this for a long time,' he eventually croaks.

We listen to his brother, facing each other, staring at each other, everything still, despite the upbeat track.

We stand in the stillness for so long, my urge to touch him increases with every note. For three long minutes, I will him to just *kiss me*.

Then the track changes and with the first strike of a chord, the first note he sings, I'm thrust back to That Night. To the song he sang to me, before Dave asked me to go backstage.

Before Madrid, when I watched a man entirely out of my grasp singing to thousands of people, and marvelled at how his life had exploded, whilst mine had become so incredibly small in the same space of time.

But he's here now, unbelievably, and his voice coming through the speakers brings with it the rise of goosebumps on my skin.

I know he doesn't, couldn't possibly, remember the same moment in Newcastle. But I wish he did, and though I'm too practical, too logical to think that the way he's looking at me now is the way he looked at me from the stage then, his pupils dilate and the irrational part of my brain could be fooled.

His gaze penetrates me in the same way it did in that music hall. I want it back, him back, and before everything went completely pear-shaped, That Night.

My body gravitates towards his, weight draining from my legs, and when he reaches out to me, my entire insides turn faster than a vinyl on a record player. Adrenaline courses through me as he twists my hair around and through his fingers.

He takes a breath, then his lips part and he sings his own lyrics, 'What is it about you, that makes me feel so alive?'

If it weren't for the shift of his outstretched hand from my hair to my face, I could believe I'm completely liquified. His voice. His words. *Him* right here. Not angry or stubborn, but something else entirely.

And it's... really overwhelming. Terrifying, all of a sudden.

I take a step back, intending to break our contact, but he shifts forwards, keeping the same foot of distance between us.

Then he sings, 'There's just you and me, forget all these people. Because it makes no sense, but I can't tear my eyes away from you.'

I'm undone.

My inhibitions have left the building.

I'm twenty-one years old again and mesmerised by this man.

I reach across the distance between us and grab his braces, intending to tug him against me.

Only, his braces are elasticated and stretch towards me, his body unmoving.

I chuckle. 'That didn't go to plan.'

He shakes his head, a sexy-as-sin lopsided grin playing tantalisingly on his lips that I *need* on me. 'No, it didn't.'

Then he sobers, and I tug the braces a little harder, smiling as they finally reach their full give, nudging him towards me, until—

'What is happening in here?'

'Mum!'

I let go of the braces and turn on the spot to see my mum, hands on hips, chastising me like I'm a thirteen-year-old girl who snuck her first crush into the house after hours.

The elastic slaps back against Guy's chest and he screams as it lands. 'Jesus!'

I shift to stand next to him. Hands by my sides, proving I'm not touching him. Nothing is happening.

'We were just listening to music,' I tell Mum. 'With hot chocolate.'

To be clear, there's no underage drinking going on here, unless there's a plus twenty-eight years age restriction on high-sugar cocoa-based drinks these days.

'And you are?' Mum asks Guy, her tone utterly admonishing.

His hands slowly trail his torso and come to rest on his nipples. The skin of his neck is fiercely red. *Oh God, I've really hurt his nips.*

He whimpers before telling Mum, 'I'm Guy. I work with Lyra.'

Mum seems to straighten. 'Oh. You're the wedding singer.' Then she glares at me. 'And naked *servant*?'

'Butler,' Guy corrects her, still rubbing his nipples.

Suddenly, the whole situation hits me and bursts from my lips as a snigger.

Mum is boring holes in me and, in a flash, every single time she told me off as a girl dances like a storyboard through my mind.

I feel Guy going too and when I look at him, fighting his amusement, rubbing his bruised pecs, it's the final straw. I'm gone. Laughter escapes me, then him.

'We'll talk about this later. Turn the music down; your dad is sleeping. I have to go to the hospital.'

I do hear her, every word, but it doesn't stop me creasing, nor does it stop Guy from doubling over as soon as she's gone from view.

'I'm so sorry,' I tell him, barely able to get the words out.

'Next time, just tell me you're not into me, would you?'

Maybe laughter makes me brave. 'I don't tell lies.'

We're standing facing each other again and his laughter fades back into that too-attractive-for-his-own-good half-smile. And I think we're going to slip back to where we left off. But I'm left bereft as he moves to the coffee table, drains his hot chocolate, then tells me, 'I should go, let you get some sleep.'

Oh.

'Absolutely.' I've no idea why I now feign a yawn because I'm about as wired as I've ever been. 'I'll show you out.'

Though he actually leads the way through the house, away from my hideaway, back to the front door, and I don't know which emotion I feel strongest – disappointment, relief, or mortification.

16

GUY

June 2025

Summer Solstice

It's just before midnight as I make my way out of Lyra's parents' house. It's as dark outside as the sky gets this time of year. The day of the summer solstice. The longest day of the year.

It's felt like it, too. I've lived as many emotions today as I've let myself feel for... I can't remember how long.

Helping Dave's mum this morning, having my cheeks pulled and my hair ruffled as if I was part of a family. It was... I don't know. Nice?

Locked in that dungeon with Lyra and talking about things with her that I hate thinking about, let alone verbalising. It was draining, but it also felt like a relief that the words were falling out of me in a way I used to write into lyrics.

Dancing with Nanna Winnie and the way her smile encased some part of me that I've shut down since Scott died. No, long before then – since I was a rejected kid, not loved by his dad, cast aside by his mam whenever it suited her not to have a kid around.

All the while, through the entire day, the constant in the back of my mind has been the question, *What will Lyra think?* I have no idea why. It's crazy. When I sang my words into her ear before, it was as if I'd written them for her.

What is it about her?

She put on Scott's song and my instinct was to do exactly what I'd do if it came on the radio – turn it off. To do what I've done in bars – walk out.

But I couldn't. I listened to my brother sing for the first time since he died. Because of Lyra. The woman I can't get out of my head.

Then it came on, the song from my dreams, and I believed, in that moment between us, that she'd been the girl with the short hair, the tiny skirt and leather boots, a camera around her neck, arms out from her sides as if she was flying like an eagle. I felt like I was in my dreams, back there, That Night.

And I wanted... No, I *needed*... to kiss her. The girl I was supposed to meet.

Then her mum came and I got the worst nipple bruises of my life. Worse than when Scott used to twist them as we fought.

The disdain the woman showed in her expression when she looked at me. The disappointment on her face when she looked at her daughter. It told me that it was a good thing I'd been stopped short of kissing Lyra. Helpful, kind, smart and from an entirely different class to my dragged-up existence.

I'm not the right man for her.

But goddammit, as I'm walking out of her house now, I can feel her behind me, doubting herself, wondering why I didn't kiss her. Because there was something there. There *is* something there and if I, numb from pain, addiction, fear of feeling anything again, know there's something between us, then she must too.

At the front door, she turns to me and whispers, because her dad's asleep upstairs, 'Let me get the door.'

She flicks the latch and pulls down the handle, opening the door and stepping back against it to let me slip out into the darkness.

But my insides are contorting the way they do every time I drive to Earl's Castle knowing she'll be there. It's an ache, a twist, a feeling that's so discombobulating and... *new*, that I feel like I'm on a small boat on a choppy sea. I'm sick with whatever this pull is, her magnetic draw. Despite myself and my better judgement, the rest of my body is begging me to stay in the light with her.

Or just with her anywhere, because even in the darkness of the dungeon tonight, sitting next to her made it bearable. More than bearable. I wasn't afraid or anxious.

I was just me. Sitting next to her on a flimsy old tabletop. The rest of the world shut out. I wanted to kiss her then, too.

But now, with her looking at me expectantly, remembering the look on her mam's face, I take a deep breath and give myself a chance to do the right thing because I'm not the rock star who sang those songs any more. I'm also not the man who wants to get it wrong any more. And if I'm going to get something right, shouldn't it be now, here, in this moment, with a woman whose heart seems to radiate goodness? Shouldn't I get something right for her?

'Well, if you ever need a celebratory hot chocolate again...' she says, and though she's smiling, it's not like her smile from earlier. I see it in her eyes, and she's killing me. Even when she casts her gaze down to her bare feet, I still feel it, whatever it is that she's projecting, and I don't want to be the man to make her feel sad.

So, I'm torn. My hands balled into fists by my sides because I want to reach out to her, to take her face in my palms like I did in her music room, and press my lips to hers. Not because anyone is watching. Because they aren't. Because it's just her and me and this tightly wound knot in my stomach.

My next breath takes me by surprise. It's short and sharp, a demand from my lungs to take in oxygen. To breathe.

'Goodnight, Lyra.'

As I speak her name, she looks up to me through her lashes and she's going to undo my final resolve. So I turn away and walk to my camp-as-Christmas car, the tiny pink sanctity with enormous eyelashes.

I manipulate myself into the driver's seat and start the engine, flicking on the headlamps, putting Lyra in the spotlight. A star.

I watch her close the door and through the stained glass of the window, I see her press her back to it, arms on her head, gaze to the ceiling.

Clunking the car into reverse, I back out of the driveway.

Lyra turns out the lights inside and with it, the lightness I've felt today.

And all I can think is, *Fuck it*, I want it back.

Grinding the gear box into first, I pull back up to the house, kill the engine and head to the door.

I raise my knuckles to rap on the glass but they don't make it because Lyra opens the door and she's looking at me through hooded eyes.

I'll be damned if I can walk away without—

I step up to the door, finally holding her face in my palm,

my other hand sliding into her hair. When she raises her chin towards me, I bring my lips down to meet the soft skin of hers.

She's my longest day of the year. My favourite day of the year. And she's pulling me in like gravity. A force I can't see, one that's hard to explain, but it's real, it exists, and I'm powerless to stop it.

It's slow at first, tentative. I let our mouths connect, the tip of my nose gently nudging hers, silently asking her if this is okay, painstakingly waiting for her response.

Her lips part and I tease the space with my tongue, waiting for her to be the one to give me a signal, to give me more, to tell me to stop holding back.

She moans in response, the sound vibrating against my skin, and it's the request I want. I deepen our kiss, tightening my grip on her hair because, damn it, I can't get enough of her.

I'm not sure which of us leads but we're walking into the house, her back meeting the wall of the hallway, her hands on the skin above my hips, fingers digging into my muscles, tugging me into her. Our tongues meet, the rich, creamy taste of chocolate still in her mouth.

It's not going further than this. I'm not in the headspace to know what I want, except to know that I don't want to hurt her. But when she drags my lip between her teeth, my body's reaction is instinctive; the hard length of me presses against her in those tiny fucking bed shorts and it's my turn to groan.

In response, she tugs my shirt free from my trousers and I'm trying to say no, we shouldn't, but the feel of her fingertips on my skin, her nails drawing up the responsive sides of my body, take over every sensible thought I have. Instead, our fingers entwine and I take her hands above her head, pressing them into the wall, my body flush to hers.

It's messy. It's fast. The need I have for her, the unfathomable familiarity, the curiosity, the outright awe and want I've been trying to repress for weeks, it's all combining into a perfect storm. Strong, undeniable, unbeatable.

I don't know who makes the first move and my rational mind is telling me to stop as I take hold of her thighs and lift her legs around me.

As we reconnect with the wall, we also collide with a sideboard, knocking a heavy old clock to the floor with an insanely loud clatter in the otherwise quiet house.

We still. The darkness in Lyra's eyes and the wideness of her pupils both recede. Her lust, our lust, turn down a notch.

There's a loud noise upstairs, above our heads, as if something's been dropped in a bedroom, too. Lyra's breath hitches, her fingertips coming to her mouth, and I lower her legs from around my waist, resting my forehead against hers.

This is a good thing. Necessary. We got carried away. *I* got carried away.

'I need to check on my dad,' she whispers.

I want to kiss her one last time, just briefly, to tell her it's okay, but for some reason, I don't. Maybe it would be too intimate and honestly, I have zero clue what the fuck just happened. How I just lost myself in her like that, all sense gone.

She licks her lips, her teeth worrying the same spot as she casts her beautiful eyes down to the hallway floor. I take hold of her chin, encouraging her to look at me and softly pulling her lip free from her own bite. The confusion she wears is an exact reflection of mine. And the plumpness of her lips makes me want to kiss her all over again.

I force myself to tell her, 'Goodnight, Lyra.'

Then I take a step back from her, back towards the open

door and the cool of the night, a contrast against my body that's still a smouldering fire.

She nods. 'Guy.'

I watch her walk up the staircase to check on her dad before I close the door and head back to my borrowed car for a second time.

Borrowed because I'm a skint has-been, who has no business messing with a nice girl's head.

***

She's just a girl, I try to convince myself for the entire drive home to Roker. It's not like I haven't kissed a girl before. Show me a musician who got famous in his twenties and *didn't* enjoy the girls who threw themselves at him.

The dizziness I'm feeling, the tingling sensation in the wake of Lyra's touch, that's just because I haven't been with anyone for a while. I haven't wanted to be. No one has turned my head.

In any event, this wasn't even second base, it was... nothing. No big deal.

But for the whole drive home, that nice girl, and the way that kiss didn't feel *nice* at all, is all I can think about.

I don't know if I'm energised by yesterday, completely wired, or emotionally depleted. What I do know is, I'm not ready for sleep. On reflection, that could simply be a sugar high. In fact, I'm sure it is. No need to spiral over a sugar high. Not unless it turns into ten hot chocolates a day. Quite possible for me.

It's also quite possible that I'm becoming addicted to seeing Lyra and whatever feeling it is that she ignites in me when I do.

Urghhhhhh. Stop. Fucking. Overthinking.

Inside my apartment, I drop my keys onto the kitchen bench and stand by them, hands in the pockets of my trousers, the only light in the room coming from the wall light I must have forgotten to turn off yesterday on my small balcony overlooking the sea.

The space feels emptier than ever and no matter how much convincing I've tried in the car, I want to turn around and go back to Lyra, to finish what we shouldn't have started. I shouldn't have gone there in the first place but as I sat in the residents' bar in Earl's Castle, listening to my friend tell jokes I've heard before, watching others laugh around him as they all enjoyed a drink, all I wanted was to go to Lyra.

Maybe I thought if I saw her, I could get to the bottom of why I can't stop thinking about her, but it backfired, because all it did was make me want her in every possible way.

I rub my hands over my face, pausing on my lips. *Jesus, that kiss.*

But I'm so broken. Parts of me might never recover.

Then, why? I ask the air above me. *Why send her my way?*

Temptation I can't explain.

Gravity.

I untie the laces of my polished shoes and slip them off, casting my socks on top of them, padding barefoot to my lounge wall and the six guitars that hang in stands, untouched since the day I put them there.

The furthest away is Scott's Gibson. I go to it first and watch my hand move towards it, as if it's someone else's body I see. At the last moment, my fingers bend, curling away from the instrument, not daring to touch where my brother used to play.

The next guitar is my own Gibson. I do let my fingers skirt

over the smooth body. Then my Fender. My softened skin skims the harsh strings of the electric guitar. Then my favourite, my Martin.

One by one, I pluck each string over the sound hole. Despite being out of tune, the noise from it, the feel of it, forces my eyes to close. Unwittingly, I unhook it for the first time in forever, remembering the weight of it, the way my hand bends around the neck.

I bring it to the sofa and tweak the tuning pegs until the sound of the open chords is flawless.

It's been a while but Lyra's words from her hideaway come back to me; picking up an instrument you know so well is like riding a bike. I'm thinking about her and I guess that's why my fingers start to strum what she told me is her favourite song.

As I fall into the rhythm, lyrics start to spill out of me, not because I mean to sing but because my muscles have memory. I sit on my sofa and for the first time since my brother died, I play a song from The Hand Me Downs. I sing my own words.

I can ignore it as much as I want but every part of me knows that this is something to do with Lyra. She's the reason I'm crossing an invisible barrier.

She's under my skin, she's in my head *all* the damn time, and she's got me playing again. A version of myself I used to know.

* * *

There's a hammering on the front door of the apartment and whatever dream I'm having shifts to a memory of a council flat in Jarrow.

Mam is still in bed, there's shit all over the lounge floor – food wrappers, takeaway cartons, empty crushed cans of cheap lager.

My sister is a baby, screaming in her cot. Scott is carrying a dinosaur, one he never went anywhere without, as he totters towards the door. It's his dad, my stepdad, at the door. 'Open the fucking door, Tracy,' he's yelling.

I stir on my sofa, a grown man, still half in a daze as I shift my guitar from my lap onto the other side of the sofa. The banging on the door comes again and as I clumsily make my way in the direction of the sound, I realise I'm still wearing my shirt and braces from last night.

I fell asleep on the sofa.

'Guy, lad, what're ya deein'?'

Dave.

Yawning, I open the door. He's wearing oversized gym gear, a cap covering his shaved and balding head. In one hand, he's holding a protein shake, which I'd laugh at if I wasn't still coming round – it's his first day of training with me; he doesn't need a protein shake – and in the other, he's holding up his phone, the screen facing me.

'You're viral, mate,' he says.

Instinctively, my hands reach for my neck, checking for swollen glands. 'I feel fine,' I croak.

'Not that kind of viral, ya numpty. You're gannin' viral on social media.'

My head aches from lack of sleep. 'What?' I ask, walking away, assuming he'll let himself into my apartment whilst I move in the direction of, 'Coffee?'

'I thought we were gannin' to the gym? Don't have too much to drink, ya said. Be at my place bright and early, ya said.'

I grunt, moving around my small kitchen, as he finally accepts that we'll have a coffee first. By my reckoning, I've had four hours' sleep, at best. Christ, playing my Martin into the early hours, no sleep, it's like I've regressed to the good old days. Except, I wouldn't have been drinking hot chocolate and coffee back then.

'Are you still in yesterday's clothes?' Dave asks.

I turn to him, milk carton in hand. 'No, mate, I wear braces to bed.'

Then I follow his gaze to my sofa. He double-takes at the sight of my guitar and I don't know why but I feel as if I've been caught in the act. Of what, I don't know. It just feels like I've been doing something… taboo.

'Big night with the old girl, was it?'

I lean back against the worktop and stare at my Martin, not giving Dave a response, because, yeah, as ridiculous as it sounds, it was a big night. I'm not sure what any of last night means but today, I feel like something happened, or shifted. I'm thrust back to that kiss in Lyra's parents' place. Holding her thighs around me, our bodies colliding, her fingers clawing at my back.

Jesus. I turn to face the cupboards, trying to clear my mind and hide the part of my anatomy that just woke up.

'I thought ya were gannin' to see Lyra,' Dave says.

'What gave you that impression?' I ask, feigning nonchalance and focusing on my task in hand, because I'm not ready for questions I can't answer.

We fall into silence whilst I finish making our drinks, then slide a full mug across the worktop to Dave, holding mine in my hands as I stand facing him where he's perched on a stool.

He inclines his head in the direction of my sofa. 'Are ya playing again? Is it time for me to call the lads?'

'Stop pushing, Dave. I've told you, I'm done with all that. Playing a few chords on my old guitar means nothing, except that I couldn't sleep.'

He slides his phone in my direction. It takes me a moment to recognise what I'm seeing play out on his screen. *Me.* Singing 'Step on My Old Size Nines' by the Stereophonics. A warm, slightly drunk Nanna Winnie moving around the dance floor on my feet.

'Four hundred thousand people and counting are begging for ya to play again, matey,' Dave says.

I'm not stupid. I'm not on social media myself but I know what going viral means. I hate that it's given me even the smallest buzz to know people are listening to me sing.

I nudge the phone back to Dave. 'Did anyone ask that woman whether she wanted to have her face splashed all over the internet?'

'Correction,' Dave says, ignoring my question. 'Four hundred and fifty thousand now.'

I need to get out of here and burn off whatever kinetic energy is bouncing around in my system. I've taken one mouthful of coffee and my body feels like I've sunk ten espressos.

'I'll get changed; let's go.'

Outside, Dave tells me to get in his van because, in his words, he's 'not being embarrassed by the hairdresser car'.

'You loaned it to me,' I tell him, conceding and climbing into the passenger side of the van, gym bag and coffee in hand.

'Aye, and it's good for *you*, but I'm butch.'

'Butch?' I chuckle. 'Does Kylie tell you that when she's cracking the whip?'

When he tells me to shut up, I only laugh harder.

'If ya want a better car, ya know what ya could do? Get off yer arse, write some new music, and sell out an arena.'

'Just like that?'

We drive the rest of the way to the gym in silence, each having the hump with the other.

The gym is owned by an old school friend of mine. Ex-army. Rough around the edges. Covered in tattoos. Shaved head. The type of burly bloke you'd expect to run this kind of establishment. The aircon is hit and miss, so usually it's hot and stuffy inside what looks like a large garage. There's zero finesse about the gym or Gaz but the building has all the equipment I need. The lads who lift in here are canny enough, and Gaz is like a marshmallow when you get past the aesthetics.

I like that there's no pretence and there's nobody in here who gives a damn about who I am, or was. I'm just another man in a sweaty gym, working out.

'Alreet, Guy, lad?' Gaz asks when I walk through the front door that's been propped open by a red brick. I guess the aircon is on the blink, again.

'Hiya, mate. You remember Dave?' I gesture behind me, where Dave is bringing up the rear, still grumpy.

Gaz leans across the front desk that looks like a counter from a corner shop and shakes Dave's hand. 'Just paying for a session, are ya, mate?'

While they deal with the cash and spend another five minutes procrastinating, on Dave's part, I warm up on the treadmill. Finally, with space to myself, it hits me. *Lyra*. That kiss. What I would have liked to have done with her if we hadn't been interrupted. That pull she has that's making me want more, even if I can't put my finger on why. Whatever it is, she made me pick up my Martin last night, as if I needed to play through it.

It's how it all started for me. I took to guitar in school as easily as breathing and I needed it like air. It was the only reason I went to school. One of the only teachers I'd listen to was my music teacher. I'd sit in that classroom for hours, strumming, picking, *hiding*.

I hadn't missed it until last night.

'Penny for 'em?' Dave asks. He got onto the treadmill next to mine without me noticing. He's walking on a barely there incline and he's as red as a cooked lobster, panting between guzzles of water.

I smirk. 'Kylie's right, you need this.'

'Not you an' all.' He sets down his water bottle in the machine's holster. 'So, did ya really fall asleep with the old girl last night? Ya didn't pay Lyra a visit?'

I could tell him but I haven't worked out what I was doing there myself yet, so I stick with, 'I was tired.'

He nods, gathering enough puff to ask, 'And the guitar? You taking it back up?'

I'm going to give him some smart-alec quip but something, some*one*, stops me in my tracks when he walks through the gym door. I watch him move in the wall of mirrors in front of me and the way he looks our way tells me he knew Dave and I would be here.

'What's he doing here?' I grind out.

Dave meets my eyes through our reflections. 'Who?'

'Don't give me *who*. Trev.'

'Trev's here?' Dave looks across one shoulder then the other, when all he'd have to do is look in the mirror at Gaz on the desk, who's taking a fiver from my old bandmate.

I hit the emergency stop on the treadmill and by the time I roll off the machine with the slowing belt, Trev is warily making his way over.

What kind of game is Dave playing?

It's a good thing it's Trev and not Jay because I don't immediately want to punch Trev in the face. But I'm still blindsided by his being here. I don't know how I feel about it but I do know that I'm pissed off with Dave for setting me up.

I fold my arms across my chest, rooted to the spot. The last time I saw Trev was Scott's wake. I was a mess, he was a mess, and we ended up sitting on a wall outside the pub, away from everyone else, both of us finding solace in the bottom of a beer bottle. The tears we'd been fending off in front of others fell silently between us as we smoked and drank.

He was my oldest friend. The only person I thought had even a small insight into how cut-up I was inside. I couldn't bear to see him again after that day.

I can't bear to see him now, because with every step closer he takes, it's all coming back to me. Like bullets, memories are striking me one by one, making me bleed.

The funeral, the police turning up to my apartment in the early hours of the morning, Trev standing behind me as we both, drunk, tried to comprehend what the officer was saying.

Scott was dead.

Trev reaches me, uncertain too, I think. I'm waiting for the chips to fall, for maybe anger to land, but surprisingly, all I feel is sadness. As if I lost more than my brother in the midst of everything that passed. Trev was my best friend and looking at him now, I think I could miss him, if I let myself.

Equally, I am mad; I'm mad at Dave. 'You planned this,' I say, stating the obvious.

Dave holds up a hand from where he's folded forwarded, the other hand on his knee as he tries to catch his breath. 'Mate, I can't breathe.'

'That's a cop out,' I gripe.

'How're ya doing?' Trev asks, ignoring our old band manager and his borderline cardiac arrest.

I don't know if I can do this, pretend like nothing happened, as if the world didn't fall down around me, the earth being pulled from under my feet.

But, unexpectedly, I want to try.

Trev was only as complicit as me; less so, because it wasn't his brother we failed. Jay, that would be a different story entirely.

'I've been better,' I tell him. 'Been worse.'

He nods, as if he gets exactly what I'm saying, and I think I believe him when he tells me, 'Me, too.'

I'm grateful for the distraction of the gym. Given it's something I do to get my head straight, it's helpful to be exercising when I'm being paid a visit from Ghosts of Rock Bands Past.

Dave is taking a fake call outside, which Trev and I know to be fake since Dave is blowing out of his arse so badly, he wouldn't be able to hold a conversation.

His absence leaves Trev and me alone, switching in for each other as we do reps on the lat pull down machine.

'Kylie's on his back,' I tell Trev, nodding in the direction of outside and Dave. 'She's told him he's gonna either have a coronary or give himself diabetes if he doesn't cut back.'

Trev chuckles as he comes to rest on the machine, me standing by, waiting to switch in for a turn. 'Gotta love Kylie,' he says, wiping his forehead with his arm. 'No holds barred.'

'She's brutal but she calls it how she sees it.' Only as I speak does it occur to me that Trev still sees them. I don't know why he wouldn't, since he's back living in the north east these days, but it feels too close for comfort somehow, as if the past is sitting on my shoulder.

Dave and Kylie have been together since they were kids, getting on for thirty years. I knew her first, when she used to babysit me. In the early, fun days of the band, Kylie was a permanent fixture at our practices and pub gigs.

'How about you, Trev? Are you with anyone? Married?'

He stands from the machine and I replace him.

'Not married, yet. I'm with someone, though. Natalie Judd. Ya remember her?'

'Tally?' I ask, surprised. 'Kiss, cuddle or torture behind the bike sheds Tally?'

He chuckles. 'She'll laugh at that. Aye, ten months now, and we've got a baby on the way.'

I drop the weights, hearing them clatter and holding up a hand in apology to Gaz.

'You're gonna be a dad?' I'm astonished. Not at Trev being a dad as much as the acknowledgement that we aren't boys ourselves any more. I stand and fold him into a sweaty hug. 'Congratulations, man.'

He thumps my back, unspeaking, and I mirror the gesture. Somewhere in the hold, it stops being about congratulations but something more.

'I've missed you, mate,' Trev says, and our patting arms still, until we're having a hug that's as camp as the car I drive. So camp, it's making my eyes sting, forcing me to put an end to it before things get *really* humiliating.

'A dad,' I say, shaking my head. 'You excited?'

'Nah, I'm nervous as hell.' We laugh together, despite the truth in his words. 'I just don't want to make a mess of it, ya know?'

I nod. I do get it, or I can imagine how he feels, but I'm not the man to ask. I felt paternal over my brother and look how that panned out.

'How about you?' Trev asks. 'Are ya with anyone?'

As I'm saying no, I think of the one girl who has truly

turned my head since the girl at the gig That Night. I tell Trev I'm not seeing anyone and it's true, but I can't stop thinking about that girl. That woman. Who kisses me like I've never been kissed, who gets my blood pumping just knowing I'm going to be in the same room as her.

A woman who is so far out of my league, it'd be like Sunderland playing football against Manchester City.

'Not seeing that old bird from the video that's going viral, then?'

'Nanna Winnie?'

'You rolled out your best husky tones and sang "Step on My Old Size Nines"; you had to be trying to get into her bloomers, weren't you?'

I laugh so hard that when Dave finally returns, I'm folded forwards, Trev bent over next to me, and I think it's a cathartic release.

17

LYRA

June 2025
Why Hasn't He Called?

'Earth to Lyra,' Mandy says.

I'm leaning on the counter in our store, staring at the high street beyond. 'Sorry? Do you need me?'

'What's going on with you today? Is everything okay?'

I sigh. 'I don't want to be *that* girl, Mandy, but why hasn't he called, or even messaged?' I turn around to face her, where she's setting up the studio for a baby photoshoot – shaggy rug on the floor, a moses basket, teddy bears, pink love heart confetti, and a bubble machine. 'It wasn't just a kiss, it was...' Subconsciously, my hand has travelled to my neck, where his mouth was four days ago. The insides of my thighs twitch, remembering the feeling of being wrapped around his waist, held up by his arms and rendered completely senseless.

She stops setting up the lights for her shoot. 'I've got to admit, I'm surprised. When I gave him your parents' address, I was so happy for you. I've never seen you like this about a lad as long as I've known you.' She shakes her head. 'If he doesn't call, do I have permission to cut off his balls and sell them to all these crazy TikTokers who're in love with him?'

I chuckle. 'You'd probably get a good price with two and a half million people competing.'

She sobers. 'Jokes aside, babes, it's only Tuesday. He might still get in touch. Also, he's a man. Men are totally useless when it comes to romance.'

'I thought you've never *been* with a man.'

'True. But my point is, if he doesn't get in touch, his loss. You're a catch, Lyra. He'd be punching anyway.'

I watch my friend get back to work, all the while thinking, *Am I?* What I've known for most of my twenties is suddenly screamingly obvious – my life is completely mundane. This can't be all there is. *Can it?*

Mandy fixes her camera to a tripod. Staring down the lens, she asks me, 'Have you thought about messaging him?'

'Me?' I ask, incredulous.

Mandy shrugs, still fixing her set up. 'Shy bairns get nowt, hunny.'

And forward bairns get burnt.

* * *

By the time the Hump in the Week comes, I've stopped waiting for a message from Guy. I had the kiss of my life. Correction – two pretty amazing kisses, though the first was nothing like Saturday night's kiss. Saturday was hot, steamy, knicker-meltingly good. There was a moment when I wondered where we were going to go – the sofa? The back of my car on the driveway? Because I was there, in it, desperate for more, completely lust-fuelled, and there was no going back.

Until it ended abruptly. Now, four days have passed and it's clear Guy didn't have the same reaction I did. Maybe in the moment. Surely, he did, because I couldn't make up the fire that ignited between us. But now, afterwards, I guess he's thinking he had a lucky save. I'm not the kind of girl who's going to beat herself up for no good reason but in this situation, the evidence speaks volumes. He isn't interested.

Honestly, I'm gutted. I don't know what it is about him – the voice, the lyrics, sure. But it's more than that; it's the way he looks at me, the way he looks when he's thinking. Those moments when I catch him lost in thought and he isn't just grumpy, he's sad. And I want to be the person who picks him up. Cliché, I know, but true. I admire that he's fallen from the top and he's still going, grinding on the hamster wheel of life and making ends meet.

There's no denying there's an aesthetic perspective that's more than a bit appealing. On a hotness scale, he's a nine out of ten, near perfection. Only getting marked down because it doesn't belong to me.

And, I don't know, maybe there's something about him that reminds me of my university days, before the proverbial shit hit the fan. When I aspired to see the world one day, take pictures and turn them into sellable work.

'Penny for your thoughts?' Mum asks as I'm standing at the kitchen bench in my parents' house, chopping vegetables to make a hot pot, which, I have pointed out, is an odd choice for the time of year and the freakishly hot weather we're experiencing.

'Hmm?' I ask, holding my knife aloft.

Mum's eyes widen but with good humour as she stares at my weapon.

'Sorry.' I slip the knife onto my chopping board. 'Actually, I was thinking about taking a holiday. Do you remember my map I used to have with all the stickers on it marking places I wanted to visit? I found it.'

Mum frowns. 'Was it amongst your old medical papers?'

My old medical papers. From the degree I never finished. Mum gets back to slicing onions, her disappointment loud yet unspoken.

Just like that, I'm reminded why I'm here, making dinner in my parents' house when I moved out months ago.

Because I created a situation and this is the bed I need to lie in. Mum can't be here all the time, so I am, to take care of things, to make reparations for what I caused, and I'm just... *tired*. And for some reason, Mum's onions are having a stronger effect on my eyes than usual. My nose is running and my eyes watering and I know it's just the onions but I think I'm sad, too.

'I made you a hair appointment for next Saturday morning,' Mum says, snapping me out of my pathetic, sulfuric-acid-induced reverie. 'Just for a trim.' She scrapes her onions into a pan and starts to fry them off. 'Olivia wants you to keep your hair in nice condition for the wedding.'

'I'm capable of making a hair appointment when I need one, Mum. Plus, I have an early wedding next Saturday.'

Huffily, I drop my cubes of root veggies into a casserole dish.

'You have the first appointment at 9 a.m.' She looks to the heavens as if *she's* exasperated by me being mothered. 'It's only a trim, Lyra. It wouldn't kill you to be more enthusiastic about your sister's wedding.'

I could lie and tell her I am enthused. Or I could be honest and tell her I'm fed up with hearing about it and receiving directions to organise something or collect something because they think I have time on my hands.

Instead, I avoid the argument and simply say, 'Sorry.' It isn't worth the aggravation.

Mum scrapes her softened onions from the frying pan into the casserole dish with my veg. I pour boiled water from the kettle on top and slip the dish into the preheated oven.

'Now,' Mum says. 'I'd like to talk about that man you had over here on Saturday night.'

Here we go.

'Don't give me that look, Lyra.' She wags a finger at me. The same action I've seen many times in my twenty-eight years. 'If you want to have fun with someone like that, please do it in your house and don't tell me about it. When you're ready to bring home someone who doesn't take his clothes off for a living, you may bring him to lunch.' She starts walking out of the kitchen, turning for one parting shot. 'I'd suggest you take all the protection you can. You've no idea where a man like that has been.'

I fight back my amusement as I tell her, 'He says he only sleeps with the pretty hens.'

'Lyra.' Her tone is a warning.

'Mum,' I reply, in much the same way.

But as I watch her go, I'm wondering if maybe Guy does sleep around. Maybe that's why he came here on Saturday night and why he hasn't bothered to call or message.

Suddenly, I'm not laughing inwardly any more. I'm not even amused.

Mum's walking away, and I want her to. I should let her go, let *it* go, the animosity or whatever it is that drips from her, just like I always do. Hands braced on the worktop, I take a deep breath.

Nope. Something has snapped inside me and I'm powerless to stop it as I follow Mum into the lounge, where Dad is sitting watching TV in his armchair.

'Why do you do that?' I ask her. 'Why do you act like we're so much better than other people?'

She's just sat down on the sofa and turns her head slowly, shocked. 'Excuse me?'

'What if I do like him? Then what? He's not good enough for me? He's actually a musician. A brilliant one.'

'So fantastic, in fact, he's taking his clothes off for a living. Fornicating with women at parties. Singing karaoke to someone else's wedding playlist?'

'Stop it, Mum. Just stop it! You don't get to dictate who I like. What do you want for me? To have a neurosurgeon as a husband, whom I never see and have nothing in common with? To spend my life photographing other people's happy endings, whilst I spend my evenings alone, making hotpots to leave in the oven for my husband, who's devoted to work rather than me, to eat alone in our fancy kitchen when he comes home?'

I've gone too far, I know it. I've called out Mum's life, Dad's life, and that isn't what I intended to do. I'm grateful for everything I had growing up, and their stifling opinions aside, Guy is right; I've always known I'm loved.

My cage feels too small lately and I don't know why now. Maybe it's been moving out, or finding my box of stuff from university. Maybe it's the reminders I seem to have at every corner recently of that time I decided to live the life I wanted for myself. Perhaps I'm wound up anyway this week because the very man Mum has just called out is messing with my head in every possible way.

'Lyra, I don't want you to sit at home, as much as I don't want you dating a dead-end man who briefly used to be someone. I see people from every walk of life in my job and I treat them all the same but I don't necessarily want them for my daughter.'

She picks up the TV remote and changes the channel, which pisses me off for two reasons. First, Dad was watching that. Second, it's downright rude and dismissive, and it makes me dig my fingernails into my palms with rage I don't normally feel.

'Sweetheart, contrary to your belief that I want you to be a wilting flower in a house with potted plants and a vegetable patch, it's your lack of ambition that disappoints me.' She sets down the remote on the arm of the sofa and looks at me now. Not looks, *fixes* on me, as if she's willing me to be better. 'It always has been.'

I stare back at her, then find my feet, avoiding the pull I feel to look at my dad and see if his expression is also one of disappointment.

The fire I had a minute ago is being put out by water. I feel it filling my eyes. A burning sensation replaced by clouded vision.

18
LYRA

July 2025
The Morning of the Thorp Wedding

'Are you sure you want to do this?'

I consider my reflection where I'm sitting in the hairdresser's comfy leather chair, wrapped in one of the salon's black cloaks. Beneath the cloak, I'm wearing smart khaki cargo trousers that sit low on my hips and a tight-fitting sleeveless crew neck – both of which I found in one of my boxes of old clothes as I continue to unpack, snail's pace, into my own home.

Though it's the same salon that my sister is using for her wedding day, Mum couldn't get me booked with the same stylist because she's on location for a wedding today, as it happens, which is perfect, because she can't talk me out of what I'm about to do.

Am I sure? 'Yes, let's do it.'

The hairdresser pulls my hair into a ponytail, ties it in a

band, then cuts off about twelve inches, bagging it for a wig charity I've chosen to donate to in an attempt to cancel out my bad karma for being a shitty sister.

'No going back now, Lyra,' she tells me. And I smile because, as silly as it seems, I feel like I'm reclaiming something that used to belong to me.

Nearly two hours later, I see a younger version of myself in the mirror. A more confident, sexier version of me that I haven't seen for a long time. I'm not sure where she went or why I want her back now but there's something that feels a lot like excited anticipation running through my veins.

I take a selfie of my jagged above-shoulder cut and send it to Cami, who, despite the early hour in Brazil, replies with:

> Now all you need is a flight and I've got my BFF back.

As I'm busy biting down on my lip and wondering if I would dare just up sticks and fly out to Brazil to meet her – knowing that one haircut and a few highlights doesn't negate all my obligations here – I catch the time on my phone.

'Sugar! I'm going to be late for the wedding.'

* * *

I'm not late for the wedding, though I'm not as early as I usually am. There's still plenty of time for Mandy and me to divide and conquer once she gets over her initial shock at my new look.

I photograph the bridal party as they get dressed and make their final preparations. Mandy snaps the groomsmen.

It's an outdoor ceremony, which is going to be hot in the

midday heat because, believe it or not, the north east of England is experiencing a heatwave. It's practically sub-tropical out here.

By out here, I mean on the perfectly groomed lawn of Earl's Castle, which has been set with white seats tied with bells – yes, bells – and in place of an altar is a trellis decorated in pink flowers and more bells – yes, bells.

Bells, because the wedding has a theme…

'Cows?' Mandy asks when we reconnect right before the ceremony. We're standing in the aisle to capture the entrance of the hundred or so guests.

In the background to all our pictures are the groom's prized dairy cows, each adorned with a bell – noisy as hell – and a pink bow around its neck.

'He's a cow farmer,' I explain.

'Weirdo, if you ask me. Who loves their cows enough to host them as wedding guests?'

I chuckle, trying to mask it behind my camera. 'The best part is, the bride is terrified of them. The bridesmaids were breaking their necks to tell me.'

'No! Why on earth has she agreed to this?'

We both hit our shutter buttons.

'To be fair,' I say, glancing further across the lawn to the wedding set-up, 'the barn theme looks good, especially in today's weather.'

The reception is taking place under an open-sided marquee, with hay bales as seats, set around real wood fire pits to be lit later, when the temperature drops. Large candles have been dug into the ground and picnic baskets are full of blankets and cushions. The entertainment for the evening is a country band and two hogs are already roasting on spits.

Thankfully, I won't need to see Guy. Or pretend to him that I'm not hurt that he kissed me in the heart-stopping way he did, then ghosted me. I won't need to pretend to myself that there isn't still a part of me wishing he'd call or message.

Against the cosy theme of the wedding is the backdrop of the magnificent castle, in a way that feels very old England.

It's sweet, even though something tells me the bride, in her sequin-embellished dress, would have preferred a luxury indoor castle wedding over the cows. One of which is currently taking a dump on the castle lawn, much to the amusement of the guests.

I'm covering my own laughter with my hand, Mandy rocking into my shoulder in absolute hysterics, when the fun is zapped right from me.

Because making their way to a discreet set-up I haven't even noticed to one side of the ceremony chairs are Dave and Guy.

My internal organs leap into my throat, and my heart starts hammering against my ribcage, begging me to let it go free because I have tried to forget that kiss over the last two weeks of complete radio silence. Yet here I am, watching him take up a seat and a microphone, rocked by his presence, irate with myself for even giving a damn about him when he clearly couldn't care less about me.

The problem is, I can't get him out of my head.

I realise I'm staring when Dave clocks me, holding up a hand in greeting. He leans down to Guy's ear and whispers something that makes him jerk his head in my direction, and I guess he's shocked to be face to face with the girl he kissed *like that* and never messaged. He's probably used to walking away and never seeing us again, girls like me.

I wait for him to seem ashamed, remorseful even, but all he does is watch me from behind his sunglasses, mouth softly open.

Damn him for looking as good in his trousers, shirt and braces as he did two weeks ago.

I tear my focus from him and back to my job because he doesn't deserve my attention when he gives me none of his.

If only my treasonous body would agree.

Thankfully, guests move between us, getting in the way of the view, reminding me why I'm here. But they don't stop the sound of Guy's voice reaching me as he begins to sing 'I Don't Want to Miss a Thing' by Aerosmith.

Kill me. Kill. Me. Now.

Any kind of death would be easier than this slow and beautiful form of torture.

Once the guests are seated, Mandy and I are standing next to each other, waiting for the bride to make her entrance. The groom, his best man and the ring-bearing dairy cow with the biggest pink bow are standing in position by the registrar. The groom is mopping his brow, again. A hangover, a three-piece suit and a bundle of nerves in near thirty-degree heat are not a good look on him.

'If he keeps sweating like that, he's going to smell worse than those cows before the wedding breakfast,' Mandy says.

'Stop,' I whisper, though I'm entertained by her sheer abhorrence of the cows and the cow farmer.

'I was drunk on his whisky breath taking his picture earlier,' she adds.

'I bet he's regretting that now,' I tell her, watching him dab his forehead again, looking decidedly pale next to his red face of a few moments ago.

'God, speaking of regrets,' Mandy says, leaning in to my ear again. 'D'you feel naked? Because that lad hasn't *stopped* undressing you with his eyes since he arrived.'

'What are you talking about?' I ask, raising my camera as the bride's choice of music begins to play.

It's Christina Perry's 'A Thousand Years'. The one from *Twilight*. It's a gorgeous song but how Guy is going to fare with it, I don't know.

'Guy Walker is what I'm talking about. Caged animals have drooled less over their breakfast steaks.'

Her words aren't the reason I shift the focus of my lens to him. The sound of his gritty voice singing 'A Thousand Years' as if he'd written it for himself is why I turn to him and capture the moment. Through my lens, I watch him watching me as he sings, and I see the phones of numerous guests being held up to video him, too.

The bride is making her entrance and I'm fixating on the wedding singer, as are half the guests.

Mandy digs her elbow into my side. 'Earth to Lyra.'

'Sugar, sorry. I'll get the groom,' I tell her.

I reposition myself to get a better view of the farmer. It's a happy coincidence that I have Guy on my horizon, too. But I manage to snap the moment the groom sees his bride for the first time. That first look.

And it's... *not* good. The little colour left is rapidly draining from the groom's face. He wipes sweat from his temples again, this time using the sleeve of his jacket in haste.

By the time the bride reaches him, he barely manages to raise his lips. The guests are seated and the registrar begins to speak but I'm glued to the groom like a new episode of *Nobody Wants This* as he stands opposite his bride. I take their picture again and through my Canon lens, I watch him sway. It's subtle but there, an unsteady movement. He's disoriented.

I whip my camera over my neck and set it aside, running and sliding down to the grass just in time to catch the groom as his legs give out and he passes out in my lap, knocking me back against the ground as he does, his head slamming into my chest.

The bride screams and the guests are rowdy. 'It's okay, he's just passed out,' I tell his wife-to-be, already shifting out from under him, peeling his jacket off and balling it to use as a pillow under his head.

'What can I do?' Guy is by my side, crouched down.

I glance up to him, forced to set aside my irritation because someone needs me. 'Raise his legs in the air.'

He nods and takes the instruction.

'Can we get a cold flannel and some water?' I calmly ask one of the staff.

Ten minutes later, the groom gives the crowd an even bigger surprise. As he sits on a chair, beneath the shade of the castle, he tells his bride, 'I can't do this.'

She strokes his hair, then his face. ''Course ya can, babe. You'll feel better once you've had some more water.'

'I mean, I don't want to do this. I don't want to get married.'

There's a first time for everything.

This is the first time I've seen a bride jilted at the altar.

And in front of all those cows.

* * *

Pearl and Geoff are with the bride and groom inside, each of them in separate rooms.

Geoff has announced to the guests that the wedding won't

proceed, so now they're milling around drinking the free booze and talking animatedly because, why not?

The hotel staff are already dismantling the ceremony area and I'm aimlessly hanging around in the staff car park, wondering what to do with my day now that I have a rare summer Saturday back.

Mandy is on the phone to her wife and if my eavesdropping is accurate, she's being talked into a day of shopping and cocktails. The shopping, I know, will be a blow for Mandy. Day drinking, less so.

Dave is also hovering near his van and sounds like he's on the phone to his wife, too. I'm leaning back against my car, face tilted towards the sun that's dazzling in the cloudless sky, even through my sunglasses. My things are already packed away and I'm ready to leave once I've said goodbye to Mandy.

'You were great out there today,' Guy says, his voice interrupting my moment of bliss.

I shift my attention to him. 'He passed out; it was hardly brain surgery.'

Though the memory of the groom crashing down on top of me reminds me of the clatter of his head against my chest, and I rub the sore spot subconsciously.

Guy watches me. 'Everyone else was up in arms. I was ready to ship the lad off to the morgue. But you were cool as cucumber.'

A family trait, I guess, though I decide to keep that to myself.

'Is that all you have to say to me?' My words drip with animosity.

He pushes his hands into the pockets of his trousers. The trousers he wore when he liquified my knickers on my parents' doorstep. But his focus is on his feet as I watch him swallow hard. 'You cut your hair,' he says.

'Top marks for observation,' I say with a good helping of sarcasm. 'I had a moment of playing the anti-bridesmaid in the hairdresser's.'

It's subtle but I see the corner of his lips twitch. 'Are your family still on your back because you had a male gigolo in the house?'

Now it's my turn to smirk. 'Something like that.'

'Can't say I blame them.'

I can feel the resolve that I've built up over the last fortnight dissolving in his presence. I watch his gaze fall to the slither of skin that's exposed between my cargo pants and my vest, and something about the way he looks has me hotter than the midday sun.

He swallows so deeply that I see the movement in the sinews of his neck. Whatever feelings I just caught, I think they registered with him too.

'Do you always kiss a man the way you kissed me at that hen party, then walk off into the sunset never to see him again? Never even ask for his number?'

Me?! 'That kiss was uninvited,' I tell him, insinuating that the kiss we shared two weeks ago was very much mutual.

'That doesn't mean it wasn't welcome.'

Now it's my turn to swallow, staring at his lips, his hair, remembering the feel of his roots under my fingers as I tugged. Remembering with an ache between my legs the feel of his excitement pressed against me. God, I'm pathetic.

'What about you? Do you always kiss a girl like you're going to take her to bed, then disappear into the night?'

He opens his mouth and I can't *wait* to see what cock and bull excuse he comes up with but—

'Guy, mate, ya need to head home and get yer swimmers because I've been roped into a beach barbeque with the missus and her friends.' Dave's words save me. 'I've seen them all after a glass of wine and I refuse to be the only man there.'

He appears, as if popping up from nowhere, making sure I still don't get a resolution to my question. Mandy is off the phone, too, and comes our way.

'D'ya fancy it, lasses? A beach barbie?' Dave asks. 'The more the merrier.'

'Sorry, I'm being roped into shopping and cocktails with Ginny. I don't often get a weekend off in the sunshine,' Mandy says.

In the background, a small group of wedding guests – two men sweating in suits, three women wearing fascinators, a flower girl and a page boy – approach Guy and ask for his autograph. I notice his lack of hesitation, the way he signs their napkins and wedding invitations like it's second nature to him. I wish I had my own camera in my hands as he slips into photograph poses with the guests.

'Would you like me to take a group picture?' I ask, accepting a phone from one of the women who is literally swooning over the rock star. *Yeah, I get it.*

I'm also irrationally jealous for no good reason that Guy could choose any woman he wants. As I take his picture, I know he's watching me, rather than looking at the camera, and I try not to react but feel every cell in my brain exploding on the impact of his attention, remembering the feel of him, the touch of him.

'How about it, Lyra? Will you come?' Dave asks when we reform our group.

'Ah, no, I have, erm, things—'

'Please?' Guy asks, speaking only to me, surprising me with his lack of shits given in front of his friend.

I want to go. If nothing else, to indulge in that body wearing only swimmers on the hottest day of the year. I have to force myself not to see us frolicking in the sand when I next blink.

But he didn't call and I'm not spending the next two weeks pining after him.

Not that anything would happen between us, I just mean — *See! This!* This ends *now*.

'No.' I direct my rejection to Guy. Flipping him the proverbial bird. Thinking, *Enjoy it, the way I've enjoyed your brush off*.

Then to Dave, I say, 'Thanks for the offer, it sounds great but I've things I should be getting on with at home.'

I don't bother launching into the story of moving house and for some reason failing to unpack after three months. I don't tell them that I'll probably end up sitting in my small yard of empty plant pots, writing an article that no one will ever read about a man who loved his cows more than his bride. I already sound dull enough.

'Have a good day, everyone,' I tell them, scuttling away to my car before I change my mind.

Right before my car door closes, a large hand gets in the way, keeping it open.

Guy hangs over the top of the frame. 'Did I blow it?'

I want desperately to say no but I'm not the kind of girl who's going to fall for his charm. Or his voice. Or his frighteningly blue eyes and rugged dark features.

'That implies there was something to blow, Guy.' I peel his fingers from my door frame. 'So, no, you didn't blow it.'

His face twists into a grimace then his perfect teeth dig into his disastrously great-at-kissing-lips. 'Burn.'

'Now you know how it feels,' I tell him, pulling my door shut and accelerating away harder than necessary, watching him through my rear-view mirror as dust kicks up from the car park in my wake. Feeling bloody thankful that I pulled off that proverbial mic drop without stalling the car or running into a wedding guest.

Because I know the truth... There is something between us. Something I want more than I've wanted anything else in my life.

19

GUY

July 2025
The Afternoon of the (Aborted) Cow Wedding

I sent Lyra a message one hour and sixteen minutes ago, telling her where we are on Rocker beach, in case she changes her mind and wants to join us.

Dave was right – Kylie and her friends are outrageous, especially when they're drinking. But in a fun way.

Their conversation has covered kids, schooling, work, general gossip and Chris and Rosie Ramsey's comedy podcast, *Shagged, Married, Annoyed.* Which led to the beef they have with their husbands and the male species in general.

The number one complaint of all six women is a lack of domestication. I'm booed when I tell them I just don't think men are innately programmed to competently do household chores – choice words to elicit a response, which I do. One of the lasses throws a flip-flop at my head, which sails over me and lands in the lettuce that was supposed to dress-up the burgers Dave and I are cooking on his coal barbeque.

They flirt when I'm topping up their wine in plastic glasses from Dave's prized picnic set, but I'm not remotely interested and neither are they. If I wasn't in such a foul mood, my amusement would probably be heightened, and genuine.

When the conversation shifts to peri-menopause, I decide it's a good time to retreat to my own blanket. We're set up on the beach directly in front of my apartment building, which would have been handy, except I still had to lug all of Dave's man-equipment from his van parked nearby – including a set of barbeque utensils that are far too big for their purpose – and the barbeque itself, that might as well be made of bricks.

It was high tide at lunchtime, so the North Sea is slowly retreating, giving us more beach and more space. A good thing, since a few passers-by have done double-takes in my direction, something that wasn't happening regularly before that video of me and Nanna Winnie went viral, and now guests from other weddings have started posted me all over socials, too. Me singing Aerosmith today already has a ridiculous number of views, according to Dave, as if it's more important than the fact the bride got jilted.

I lie back, feeling the heat of the day on my naked torso, and reach for my phone.

Still no response from Lyra.

I really did blow it.

I meant to, obviously. I actively chose not to contact her over the last fortnight. For multiple reasons. I genuinely had a lot going on, with work and seeing Trev again, and having this constant and growing sense of guilt about ignoring my sister's invitation to go to her birthday bash, or even meet up with her.

Mostly, I've spent my time stewing, playing my Martin into

the early hours of the morning – receiving a few thuds on the walls from neighbours telling me impolitely to shut the fuck up – thinking a younger or different version of me would have called her. Would have told her to come to my place, enjoyed every inch of her body, *then* not called her back.

But with Lyra, it doesn't feel right. Maybe I've changed. One thing's for sure, though, she's better than a one-night stand. Better than me. That's why she didn't ask for my number after kissing me at that hen party. I tried to get her to admit it earlier when I asked why she never got my number then. And her mum's reaction to me even being in her house that Saturday night was case in point.

Lyra and I come from different walks of life. Even if we didn't, she's selflessness and hopefulness and *I'm*... the antithesis of those things.

I was holding steadfast. Strong. Resolute.

Until I fucking saw her today and I knew it would be hard to ignore the pull I've felt since the first day I met her in that broken lift. But when she turned up today, looking exactly like the girl from my dreams, the girl who has recurred in my dreams for seven years, all resolve was lost.

I think she's *become* the girl of my dreams. When I close my eyes, even now, behind my sunglasses, under the sun, I can't see the girl from That Night any more, I only see Lyra, as if she *had* been there, as if the girl That Night *was* her.

So I'm lying here, grumpy as sin, holding on to a fine thread where a lifeline should be, clutching at straws, hoping she might still come.

Because, damn it, even the way she sassed me and slammed her car door in my face earlier was... fucking hot. I like the fact that I seem to be the only person who elicits from her these less controlled emotions. At least I know I'm getting to her in some way. A trace of the way she is well and truly under my skin.

'Afternoon, lads and lasses.'

I'm dragged from self-wallowing by Trev, who's holding the hand of a heavily pregnant woman wearing a stripy dress that tugs across a well-brewed baby bump.

We've seen each other a few more times in the last couple of weeks, always at the gym, skirting around any mention of the band, Scott, Jay, old times.

Standing, I brush sand from my swim shorts. 'I didn't know you were coming.'

'Are you match-making again, Dave?' Trev asks.

Dave wags a spatula and a pair of tongs in our direction. 'I had to do something to drag Guy's face out of his backside.'

'My face isn't up my backside!'

'Oh, it is, hunny,' Kylie says, patting my shoulder as she heads over from her towel and pulls Trev into a hug. 'How are ya, love? And *you*!' She tugs Trev's fiancée into an embrace, bending over the bump. 'You look gorgeous, Tally.'

'Urgh, thanks. I feel like a house end. My feet are swollen up like water balloons in this heat.'

'Been there, hunny. I feel for you having a summer baby.' Kylie leads Tally over to her friends and calls back to me, 'Guy, bring Tally a deckchair, would ya?'

I carry over a chair and help Tally settle into it, then head to the barbeque where Dave and Trev are talking up the meat – they're cooking bog-standard sausages, burgers and marinated chicken but anyone listening to them would think it was Cut at 45 Park Lane.

'Beer, mate?' Dave asks Trev.

'Just one, I don't drink much these days. Not least 'cause Tally threatens me with going into labour every time I do.'

I get him a bottle of beer from a cooler and another can of pop for myself.

'You really are gonna be a dad,' I tell Trev. 'That's a bump and a half.'

Trev nods as he drinks from his bottle. 'Aye. It's happenin'.' And the way he beams at Tally makes me surprisingly envious.

The sun must be going to my head.

'What's this about you being in a foul mood, then?' Trev asks me.

'Dave talking bollocks, as usual.'

Dave shakes his head. 'The lass he's after isn't interested.'

'I'm not after anyone,' I lie, sounding petulant in the process.

Dave clears his throat and points his beer bottle along the beach from us. 'Not even her?'

As soon as I see Lyra, before I even clock her legs beneath tiny denim shorts, and her perfectly rounded breasts in her bikini top, barely covered by the open checked shirt she's wearing, I'm rooted to the spot. Stunned by a concoction of adrenaline, relief and excitement. As if I've been performing on stage for the first time, waiting to see how the crowd will react, and finally, they erupt.

'She came,' I say, either inwardly or outwardly, I'm not sure.

'Ya might wanna go over there, mate,' Trev says, pushing my back until my legs kick into gear.

Fuck. She came. And now I need to stay calm, be cool, pretend like I don't want to pick her up and take her back to my place, where I can have her all to myself.

'Is that her?' I hear Kylie ask behind my back.

'Hi,' I say to Lyra when I reach her. We're two feet apart and I'm trying my best not to gawp at how fucking incredible she looks, not least because I'm not wearing boxers under my shorts.

'Oh, hey,' she says. 'Fancy seeing you here.'

My lips break into a smile that's so wide it feels like a long-lost relative, and when she reciprocates with her own, I swear my insides explode. She made me wait more than two hours. Tortured me for one hundred and twenty-odd excruciating minutes.

That smile is worth every single one of them.

'Just out for a stroll, are you?' I ask.

'Exactly.'

'Well, Dave's brought a butcher's shop with him, so you might as well come and get some food. Since you're here anyway.'

She checks her watch. 'I suppose I could spare a few minutes.'

I chuckle, slipping her full beach bag from her shoulder and leading her over to the gang that suddenly feels much more tolerable. 'I'm glad you came,' I tell her, glancing her way in time to see her cheeks blush in that way they do.

She looks like a rock star but she embarrasses like a girl next door.

'Everyone, this is Lyra,' I announce when we're with the group. 'She's just passing by.' I smirk at her and she sticks out her tongue in response.

'At last, he smiles,' Kylie says, standing to give Lyra the kind of greeting that suggests she's already one of the crew.

Kylie has always been the mam of the band, and having

Lyra here feels like I'm bringing her home to meet my family. It's weird and new, and I'm astonishingly cool with it.

'Come and sit down with us, Lyra,' Kylie says. 'Put her towel out and bring her a glass of wine, Guy.'

I expect Lyra to look doe-eyed under the pressure and next to Kylie's mammoth-sized personality, but she seems entirely at ease as I set her up with a towel.

When I hand her a glass of wine, she hesitates to take it. 'Oh, no, I'm okay.'

'It's okay,' I whisper. 'I'm used to it by now.' Though grateful for the effort.

Her shoulders drop and her lips turn up. 'Thank you.'

Our fingers graze as the drink transfers between us and that smallest of touches puts my entire body on high alert. *We like her,* it's screaming. *We like her a lot.*

I practically have to drag myself away from her and back to the barbeque with the lads, both because Kylie tells me I have to – I expect some female interrogation is about to take place – and because I need to take a pause, get my head around the fact she's here. I'm not having some kind of respiratory failure; I'm just feeling things that I've never felt before.

And it's fucking petrifying. As petrifying as it is exhilarating.

Dave and Trev are talking across me and I hear bits of their conversation, making appropriate noises, all the while unable to take my eyes off Lyra and seriously grateful for my polarized lenses.

When the food is ready, I use the excuse to extract her from the others and bring her over to my blanket to eat. After dishing out plates of grub to everyone, I take a pew next to Lyra, not moving my leg when the bare skin of our thighs graze, feeling the connection in her touch that I felt two weeks ago.

I know I had reasons to try to ignore what happened between us, but I'll be damned if I can remember them now.

We slip into easy conversation about today's wedding, joking about the cows, Lyra telling me about other wedding disasters, me sharing gossip I've overheard from the hen parties I've been working at in the evenings. It feels good to laugh, as if my body is lighter somehow.

Once we've eaten, I lie on my side, propped on my elbow, and Lyra faces me, sitting cross-legged. It's as if there's only the two of us here, despite the busy beach. I'm lost in her easy company, until the increasingly rowdy voices of Kylie's friends start moaning about the 'shite' music playing through Kylie's beach speakers.

I reach for Lyra's phone next to her on our blanket. 'Can I?'

She nods and I take her phone to the speakers to pair it, then hand it back to her. 'Put Lyra's music on; she's got awesome taste.'

'Coming from a pro, that's quite a compliment,' she tells me quietly as I come back to lie next to her.

'I *was* a pro,' I remind her.

She shakes her head, reaching down to nip my chin between her finger and thumb. 'You forget I watch this face on stage and listen to that voice every other weekend.'

She's leaning over me, her shirt fallen open, exposing her body an extra inch to me. An inch that drives me wild with the urge to roll her over and continue what we started in her parents' house.

I open my mouth and take her finger between my teeth. Her own lips part and I can't resist tasting her, drawing my tongue over her knuckle, which sends something like a power surge to my groin. I want more and I'm stuck on this public beach, in a group of increasingly drunk friends, wishing I could carry this woman off to my apartment that is teasingly close by.

'Yer sister's still on me back to get ya to go to her birthday party, Guy,' Kylie says.

'You and me both,' Dave says from where he and Trev are both scoffing another burger beside the barbeque.

Talk about a mood kill. Lyra sits up straight and I shift my position to see Kylie.

'She shouldn't've brought you into it,' I tell her. I point to Dave. 'That plonker shouldn't've told her I'm back in the north east.'

'She's yer sister, mate, come on,' Dave says.

'Plus,' one of Kylie's friends pipes up, 'anyone on Facebook knows you're singing at Earl's Castle these days.'

This is precisely the problem with social media, the reason I don't have accounts and the reason I never used to give interviews when I was in the band. People think they have a right to comment on your shit when they know nothing about it.

'It's her quarter century,' Kylie adds.

I come to sit, rubbing a hand roughly across my two-day-old gruff. 'That's not even a milestone, and like I've told Dave, she's in the market for a present, not a big brother.'

'Hardly,' Kylie says. 'I don't think yer sister or yer mam can expect anything else from ya these days. Ya skint yourself to buy them both a house.'

I can feel my nostrils flare and stand to walk away from saying something I'll regret to a woman I ordinarily have a lot of respect for.

Dave has the sense to tell her, 'Alreet, Ky, ya can pester him later.'

I feel them having an unspoken exchange behind my back but I ignore it, grateful that the line of conversation has shifted.

Until I'm plating up chicken I don't really want and Trev's beers have clearly gone to his head too, because he asks, 'Do you ever see Matty?'

And by Matty, he means my nephew. Scott's son.

The instant his words hit me, I feel myself flip into fight-or-flight mode and it's Trev I'm looking at, so I want to go with flight but there's nowhere to fly when I'm trapped on the beach. I don't know why but I turn away from him to seek out Lyra and I hate what I see in her expression. Even behind the tinted glasses she's wearing, it's there – *pity*.

Imaginary walls begin to close in on me. My chest is tightening as if I'm locked in a tiny space with no ventilation. There's pressure building behind my eyes and I want to run. Or lash out. Or... I glance down to the cool box of booze. I won't, I know I won't, but—

Two cool hands take hold of my face, so soft they make me close my eyes and lean into them. I've held my blink and when I open my eyes, Lyra is standing in front of me, brighter than the light of the sun, beams bursting from around her, putting sunspots in my vision.

'Hey,' she says. Simply. Quietly. Spellbindingly. I watch her next breath and realise I'm inhaling with her, exhaling as her chest falls.

'Hey,' I croak, my gaze falling to lips I want to kiss so much it's making everything north of my waistline ache.

Then the track changes in the background and in a cruel twist, I hear the opening chords to one of The Hand Me Downs's songs.

Lyra's hold is suddenly gone. She goes to her phone and changes the music to a song by Sam Fender.

'Ah, they could have sung for us,' one of Kylie's friends says.

'Sorry,' Lyra says, chuckling. 'It would be really mortifying for him to find out I had a massive crush on him all through my late teens.' She looks my way and heat rises on her neck. 'My twenties, too.'

'Did ya?' Kylie asks, practically squealing with delight as my lips twist in disbelief because here she is again, Lyra, rescuing me. Making herself uncomfortable to spare me.

'Oh yeah,' she says, watching me watch her. 'Bad. Like, posters on the back of my bedroom door, playing the songs he sang on repeat until my university roommate threatened to cut the plug off my speakers.'

The ladies are laughing and remarkably, so am I. This *woman* is remarkable. And all I can think is, *I had a crush on you, too. I think I fell for you before I ever met you.*

So I set my plate aside and cross the sand, taking her cheeks in my hands the way she just did for me, and saving her from her self-humiliation.

I press my mouth to hers, showing her exactly how she just made me feel. Like no one has tried to protect me since… *ever*.

Either everyone has fallen into silence, *finally,* or I've just stopped hearing the noise. As I tear my lips from hers, Lyra gives me the sweetest half-smile I've seen in my life. Creases tugging on one side of her mouth.

'Thank you,' I tell her, for her ears only.

'Aww, look at my baby, all grown up,' Kylie says, making me look skyward as I shake my head. 'Lyra, has Guy told you that I used to babysit him? Long before the band. When he was just a spotty kid who'd lock himself in his bedroom with a guitar for hours on end.'

'Ah, no, he hasn't,' Lyra says, lips curved in a completely different way now that it's for Kylie's benefit.

With half an ear on the conversation, my mind only able to comprehend how much I want to take Lyra off this beach, I lounge next to her, listening to the banter of the group, occasionally throwing a putdown Dave's or Trev's way.

At some point, as the evening starts to drop cooler but the sun is still alive, Trev says, 'It's like old times this, all of us down at the beach, having a laugh, drinking beers. We're only missing a couple of guitars.'

I understand the sentiment but there's a lot different to those days. I don't think I show it but Lyra's fingers slide on top of mine, where our hands rest next to each other on the blanket. Times have changed. People have changed. I've changed.

'Maybe Jay could come next time?' Kylie asks, and I feel every morsel of my body lock.

'No.' My statement is emphatic and ends the conversation. Good. I hold my tongue enough. When it comes to Jay, the guy who introduced my brother to drugs, it's a hard no.

I take hold of Lyra's phone and scroll through her music, looking for a distraction, landing on a Stereophonics album.

'I love this song,' she says as 'Just Looking' begins to play.

She's sitting up, arms hugging her knees, and I'm sick of not touching her, wishing we were alone.

Trev starts to sing to the music and others follow suit. No one cares what I'm doing any more.

Sod it. I move to sit behind Lyra, my legs either side of hers, her back against my chest, and I wrap my arms around her, leaning my chin on her shoulder. I wonder briefly if I've crossed an unwritten line, but she rolls her head to one side and when her neck is exposed to me, I press my lips to her throat, the scent of her subtle perfume making me dizzy.

Then I sing into her ear, feeling and hearing her sigh against me.

'You're killing me,' she whispers, and I know that feeling. She's been killing me all afternoon.

Standing, I offer her my hand as I grab a towel and hook it over my shoulder. She lets me lead her down the beach to the water, as close to alone as we've been all day.

20

LYRA

July 2025
Roker by Sunset

'So you had a crush on me, huh?'

'Shut up,' I tell him as we stand near the receding tide. 'I only said that so you didn't have to get all embarrassed listening to yourself sing.'

'Yeah, right, Lyra.' He rocks his shoulder into mine.

'Go on, tell me. Did you back your school books with my face? Cut my head out of posters and sleep with it under your pillow? Kiss my face before you went to sleep at night?'

It wasn't quite that bad but I did fall asleep listening to his songs on repeat. 'I was lying, obviously.'

'Aha. Sure you were.'

Urgh. 'I'm so pleased the arrogant rock star finally showed up because that down-on-your-luck routine was getting really old.'

He throws his head back, guffawing. A sight and sound

that makes me freeze, mesmerised as I listen to him. Stunned by the brightness of him.

I could watch him like this as if time doesn't exist but I'm barely able to stand on wobbly legs. When he quietens, his eyes on my lips, the mush my mind is reduced to with him semi-naked and happy, standing inches from me, is only capable of registering that I want him to kiss me. Desperately. The last two weeks of waiting and uncertainty are a memory my hippocampus is unable to hold on to.

'You get a dunk for that,' he tells me, eyes narrowing on mine.

'In that sea?' I point across his shoulder to the ocean, knowing that despite the sun, it will feel like diving into the arctic.

'Yep.'

I drop my hands to my hips, life coming back into my legs and rooting me firmly to the spot. The warm, dry spot. '*You*, pink-Fiat-driving musician, think you're brave enough for that ice box?'

He ties his red swim shorts, hands me his sunglasses, and walks to the edge of the water with confidence, but as soon as his feet connect with the North Sea, he recoils.

'Fuck me, it's freezing!' he shouts, running back to our towel and jumping up and down on the spot.

It's my turn to guffaw. 'Big baby. You call yourself a northerner?'

'I lived in the south for a long time,' he protests.

Shaking my head, I slip off my own sunglasses and set down both pairs on the sand. I unbutton my shorts, one... button... at... a... time. Then slide the cut-off denim down my legs with the kind of brazenness I didn't know I had in me. I soak up the way his eyes hungrily roam my legs – bare but for my hot-pink bikini – ridiculously turned on. He's lost in me now, the way I am drowned by his proximity every time he's near me.

I let my shirt fall down my arms and I bask in the subtle parting of his lips as he takes in my boobs, teased together by the bikini I stopped to buy on my way to the beach.

Then I stride into the water as if it's the Indian Ocean, throwing a mental high-five to my inner Aphrodite.

'You're fucking crazy,' he tells me.

Over my shoulder, I call back, 'Where's my rock god now?'

And where the hell did that performance just come from, girlie?

The temperature of the water is a necessary cool off because I feel like I'm going to combust if I spend one more second around Guy Walker without him making a move on me.

Bravery or stupidity, I'm not sure which, causes me to dive under the water – it's not excruciating once you're in. I touch the sandy bottom, then push up, letting my head fall back, the water sweeping my hair from my face as I break the surface.

And he's here, standing taller than me, reaching his arms around my waist, wide pupils and crooked smile. 'Say that again,' he says. 'Tell me I'm yours.'

My lips curve up. 'My rock god?'

He moves his face closer to mine, holding my waist harder against him, our skin sliding together as the ocean drains between us. And finally... his lips meet mine. Finally, my hands are free to explore his naked body, my tongue invited to taste his. When he scoops me up, wrapping my thighs around him, there's no side tables or ornaments or Dad sleeping upstairs. There's just us. Him and me, kissing in the vastness of the sea, where nothing else can touch us.

I feel him grow beneath me and groan into his mouth, holding his face in my hands, craving more of him even as we're locked together. As if seven years of lust I've had boxed away have been unleashed. I'm back there, That Night, free and hopeful. Excited. And today, I'm fuelled by the kind of desperate desire no one before Guy has evoked in me.

I pull back from him because I need to know if he's here with me, and I'm greeted to the kind of smile he seems to rarely give.

'Are you going to ignore me for a fortnight now?' I ask, tongue-in-cheek.

'Where did that sweet girl in summer dresses go, eh?'

I nip the end of his nose between my teeth. 'What can I say, you bring out a bad side of me.'

He presses his forehead to mine and I indulge in the feel of his biceps, holding me up as if I weigh nothing. 'Good. I'm better equipped to handle a bad girl.'

'Kiss me like that again.'

He makes a move to do just that, but our mouths collide too eagerly and I knock him off balance. He staggers back, his feet losing grip in the sand and tumbling us both back into the water.

We're in hysterics when we splash back to standing, chest high in the water. 'That was smooth, Guy Walker. Cool as ice.'

'Well, it's probably a good thing because I need something to cool me off before I get out of this water.'

The reminder of his want is enough to heat me through, until we walk out of the water, replace our sunglasses, and I'm shivering.

Guy wraps a large beach towel around us and kisses me again, sweeter this time. 'It looks like the others are packing up,' he tells me.

He's right. Much further up the beach, Dave and Trev are dismantling the barbeque. The ladies seem to be tidying away.

'Do you want to go with them?' I ask, hoping I already know the answer.

He takes hold of my chin and tells me, 'I don't want to be anywhere other than here. Will you stay for a while?'

'Yes.'

He kisses me briefly again, then wraps the towel tightly around me and picks up my clothes.

'We're going to leave you kids to it,' Kylie says when we make it back to the group, humour dancing in her expression. 'That water looked hot.'

Guy flicks a towel at her and they share the joke. It was hot. Wholly hot. And I can't wait for everyone else to leave, but it takes an age to pack them up and help them back to their cars and taxis. All the while, my craving for Guy is increasing a million-fold.

The sun is dipping lower on the horizon, so low that the wisps of cloud now decorating the sky are starting to turn shades of orange, but the air is still warm.

'Don't do anything I wouldn't do,' is Kylie's parting line, to which Guy replies, 'We'll have a fucking brilliant night in that case.'

It does nothing to help the inferno raging inside me.

We head back to the beach and lie on Guy's dry towel, talking, kissing, groping, him rolling on top of me, staring into my eyes, stroking my face, pulling my hair. And once the sun sets, it feels as if the heat of the day has transferred from it to us.

Guy's on top of me, the weight of his bottom half pressed deliciously onto my thighs, his top half supported on his fore-arms. 'You can say no to this, but I live right there.'

'Right where?' I ask, following his pointed finger. 'That building?'

He nods. 'Right behind us.'

'All day, *that's* where you've lived?'

'And yesterday, and the day before that, and the day before that.'

'Why didn't you say that?'

'I didn't want to seem presumptuous.'

'Guy, your arse has been gyrating for the last hour, and you don't want to seem presumptuous?'

'When you put it like that... Grab your stuff. You've pulled.'

***

He unlocks the door to his fairly modest apartment. A reminder that he isn't the man who performed for tens of thousands of people just a few years ago. It's still baffling to me that he had it all one day and it was gone the next but, honestly, I don't care about who he was; I care about the man I'm sinking fast with today.

Inside, he takes my beach bag and can't wait to ditch his things either. He switches on a standing lamp in the corner of his lounge. Through the large glass windows, the beach is now in the light of dusk.

'Would you like a drink?' he asks whilst I'm enjoying the view.

I turn to watch him moving around his kitchen and notice on top of the cupboards, a line of twenty or thirty empty bottles of alcohol. The end of the line is the bottle of gold tequila I recognise from the night of the hen party when we first met. The bottle he'd started drinking when we were trapped together in the lift.

He must catch my gaze because he responds to my unspoken question. 'I don't drink any more but those are bottles I've wanted to drink. Every time I've wanted one, I've poured it away and put the empty up there, to remind me that I don't need it.'

One minute, this man is easy and simple. The next, he reminds me of a man haunted. But seeing the effort he's gone to, pulling himself back from a place I can't even imagine, is awe-inspiring. He's making changes and maybe there's a lesson there for me, too. Maybe I'm already taking his class.

'The tequila bottle,' I say.

'I'd filled it with water before I got to Charlotte's hen party. But I wanted it to be alcohol when I was afraid in the lift. When I stood in that penthouse and realised how far I'd fallen. Forced to take my clothes off to stay above the breadline.'

'Guy...'

He shrugs. 'It's okay. I don't want sympathy. It is what it is.' He sets down a glass of water he's drinking and takes slow and steady steps towards me, each one making my next breath shallower. 'I haven't wanted to drink a bottle since I met you in that lift, Lyra, and I think, I can't explain it yet, but that's part of the reason I didn't call or message you.'

His fingers reach for my hair and he fixates on the movement of it. Then his eyes flick to mine and darken.

'I'm glad I met you now,' I tell him, unsure what I'm trying to share.

But some kind of understanding passes between us and when his lips meet mine, it's slow and tender, not like the hen party, not like it was at my parents' house, or even on the beach. It's deeper.

His lips move from my mouth to my neck, along the sensitive skin of my collarbone, bringing pimples to my skin as if it's never been kissed before.

He slips my shirt down my arms and I take his t-shirt off over his head, moaning when his mouth finds my breasts and his hands tug open the string tie at the back of my bikini.

'Is this okay?' he asks.

'More than,' I tell him, unable to find more words because finally... I'm getting what I want. And what I want is *him*. The wedding singer. The naked butler. The complicated soul. The man behind the lyrics. All of him.

Hands on his face, I pull him up to kiss his mouth because my need to taste him is overwhelming. He's barely touched me and bright spots are already filling my vision.

Somehow, we work back towards his sofa and he lies me down, crawling on top of me. The intensity is like nothing I've known. Almost too much.

I place a hand on his chest, I think trying to compose myself. Trying to see straight and think straight. Not because I don't want this. I absolutely do. But because I want to remember it if tomorrow never comes.

He's looking at me, waiting, and for some bizarre reason, I say, 'Before we go any further, I should probably check, you don't have any weird cow or other barnyard animal fetishes, do you?'

That crooked smile teases his delectable lips and he whispers, 'The only thing I'm obsessed with is you, Lyra.'

That does it. I pull him to me, our mouths connecting, my hands reaching for his shorts and helping him take them down, exposing him where I've felt him all evening. And seeing it, him, in the flesh, steals my breath.

He unbuttons and frees me of my shorts, then unties my bikini bottoms at each side, discarding them onto the floor, where our clothes are scattered.

I take him in, all of him, and he does the same, until at last, he works his way back to me, slides his hand between my legs, then moves his whole body over me again.

21

GUY

July 2025
The Morning After...

I'm having the same dream again and there's no doubt in my mind that the woman I'm seeing is Lyra. Any trace of a face before hers is gone. I'm standing on stage, playing, singing back-up to Scott, when my chord becomes stuck. All other music has stopped and everyone in the venue is watching me play the same chord over and over again, painfully slowly.

I open my eyes into my dark bedroom in Sunderland, and the first thing I notice is that my room smells of sex. Better still, it smells of Lyra. The way she smelled when she turned up to the beach yesterday. How she smelled when her perfume had mixed with the salt of the sea. The scent of her after we'd washed each other in my shower, then she curled into my chest and I listened to her fall asleep.

The second thing I notice is the sound of that same chord from my dreams being strummed on repeat.

Folding back the blanket, I climb out of bed, pull on a pair of shorts and move in the direction of my guitars, not prepared for what I find when I reach the doorway into my lounge.

Lyra is sitting on the sofa where we made love last night. Where I got lost in a way I can't ever remember, as if all of the other shit that kicks about in my head every minute of every day was gone, wiped out by her.

She's wrapped in the white sheet from my bed, hair kind of mad from sleep but as beautiful as she was last night. There's a guitar resting on her lap, her fingers clumsily making a chord on the fret board, her right thumb gently playing the bottom four strings in succession, over and over.

It's testament to how distracting I find her that it takes me a moment to realise which guitar she's taken down from the wall. When I do, I brace myself against the door frame, leaning my shoulder into it for support. Because I'm waiting for it to strike me, for the chips to fall, for the world to disappear from beneath my feet.

Unexpectedly, it doesn't come. Nothing happens, until I take my next breath. I'm drawn to them both, pulled by the image of both Lyra and the guitar.

She glances up to me as I warily cross the lounge, but the sincerity of her gaze and the warmth of her smile keep me together.

'I hope you don't mind,' she says as I stare at the instrument in her control. 'I couldn't sleep and I didn't want to disturb you. I thought I was being quiet.'

Do I mind? I'm not sure yet. That guitar hasn't been taken down from the wall or even touched since I moved in. Before that, it had hung in my London apartment, untouched.

Because... I step onto the sofa and come to sit behind her, legs either side of hers. 'This is Scott's guitar.'

'Oh God, I'm sorry, I—'

'It's okay,' I tell her, allowing my chin to fall onto her shoulder, my lips to press to her throat, and my hands to rest over hers on the fret board, across the sound box. It's as close as I've come to holding Scott's Gibson in the way it should be played since the last time we were in a studio together, mid-recording a new album. The same day he died.

'You're trying to play a D,' I tell her, repositioning her fingers, adjusting her left wrist. My own fingers touch the guitar and it's not strange or painful, it's *fine.*

She nods and I manipulate her right hand into a better strumming position, slowly moving with her, up and down the strings.

'Better,' I tell her, feeling her cheek rise against mine with the tilt of her lips.

I move her fingers into a C chord, then a G, and we work through the sequence until she relaxes into it, each change of position becoming easier.

'Was he a good player?' she asks.

'Scott?' I chuckle, my chest moving against her back at the memory of how Trev, Jay and I used to mock my brother when we'd play in the studio, not a song necessarily, just messing around until sometimes we came up with a record unintentionally. 'Not at all. But he was a trier.'

'God loves a trier,' she says, reminding me of the times I said those exact words to Scott in jest.

'And hopefully tambourine players,' I tell her, surprising myself with how easy it is to talk to her about him.

She turns her head so we're nose to nose and she's smiling back at me, making me realise how rare it is that I sit in a memory of my brother and enjoy it. Enjoy him. Our kid.

And I think, *You'd like her, Scotty. You'd like her a lot, kid.*

She kisses me shortly and shifts out from between my legs, handing the Gibson to me. 'Would you sing to me?'

I stare at the guitar across my knee and I expect myself to say no, but my fingers shift on the strings and for the first time in three years, I start to play one of my own songs. Slowly, tentatively, uncomfortably at first, I sing through the verse of a record I wrote in my bedroom one night, long before I ever thought anyone would hear it. When I could hear my mam arguing with my stepdad.

Scott was lying in his single bed, parallel to mine in our small bedroom, barely any walking room between us. It was late, the shouting was loud, Scott should have been asleep, we both should have been. He had school the next day and I was holding down a job on a market stall then, making minimum wage selling fruit and veg for a local shop. His eyes were wide open as he lay and I sat, the street lamp outside our window the only light inside.

I sing the lyrics, as if I wrote them yesterday:

'I'm just a local boy,
Spending my days,
Dreaming of what will never come.
Selling fruit and veg,
To people who don't know my name.

'Thinking, thinking one day,
I'll stand on a stage,
And become someone.

'We'll shine beneath stage lights,
Sweating in the heat,
Throats croaking through each song,

Playing like no one believes we can.

'One day.
Some day.'

At some point, I get lost in the music, playing like I would to thousands of people—

Until someone bangs on the ceiling above us. I open my eyes to Lyra and laugh. *One day. Some day.* But there's nothing bigger in my world right now than the woman standing in front of me.

She watches me as she lets her sheet fall to the floor and with the light of the moon turning her perfect body into a silhouette, I go to her. We make love again, against the glass doors of the balcony, the ocean roaring behind us.

Sinking inside her is better than the best feeling I know – standing on stage in headlights. The arena quiet, expecting. The first depression of the drums. The strike of the symbol. The first note of the bass guitar. All playing a song I wrote. Mine.

A thousand barriers are crossed in this moment. I'm bared to her in every single way. Unravelled. Raw, exposed, and desperate for more.

* * *

The next time I wake up, my bedroom is hot, the sun shining in and heating the space. The smell of coffee sifts through the apartment and I grin at the ceiling as I remember... she's here.

I pad into the kitchen, dragging a hand through my bedhead as I watch her move around my place like it's her own. She's found an old t-shirt of mine and it rides dangerously close to the fine globes of her arse as she makes...

'Eggs?'

'You found the one thing in my fridge.'

'It's a bit sparse. Don't you plan on staying?' she jokes.

'I'm a day-by-day kind of shopper.' I move behind her, wrapping my arms around her waist and gently biting her neck until she flicks me off with a spatula.

'The chef is working here, sir.'

'Sir? I like that. Makes me feel powerful.'

'As the woman who's about to feed you, I'd say I have the power. There's coffee.'

'Are you trying to get into my knickers, Lyra?'

'Please, you're so easy.'

Chuckling, I take a coffee. 'What can I do?'

'Toast, please.'

I set to work under her instruction, all the while thinking, this is... *nice.* Besides staff on tour, I don't know that anyone has ever made me breakfast. I don't even remember my mam doing anything other than pointing me in the direction of the cereal cupboard. Domesticity is new to me.

We sit on the sofa to eat, facing each other from opposite ends, plates on our laps, me occasionally trying to glimpse her knickers beneath my T-shirt. When she objects, I explain, 'You broke the seal.'

'Once you pop...' she says, playfully relaying the words of the renowned crisps advert.

She's right. I don't know that I'll ever be able to stop.

When Lyra goes to get dressed, I check my mobile and see multiple messages from Dave: one telling me to have a good night; another two giving me updated analytics on the video of me singing Aerosmith yesterday that has, in his words, 'blown-up'.

She returns wearing yesterday's clothes and I turn the phone over without sending a reply. I'm much more interested in what's right in front of me. The woman I've finally conceded I want more than I can manage to resist.

'Dave,' I explain. 'Last night, telling us to have a good night.'

She bites her lip and blushes, the confident woman who has absolutely rocked my world in the last twenty-four hours sweetly shy again.

'I have to go,' she tells me. 'I have work to do, and I usually help my mum make a roast on Sundays. Plus, I have things I promised I'd help my sister with for her wedding.'

'Lyra, you don't need to explain.' Though I can feel myself coming down from the high of her.

'I know. I just—' She sighs. 'I'm not very good at this, Guy. I hardly ever... ah, date? And really never... you know. Not like *that*.'

I can't help it, I'm smirking at her discomfort because she's so unbelievably cute.

'Are you mocking me?' she asks.

'Yes.'

'Huh.'

I cross the kitchen to her and tuck the hair from her temple behind her ear. 'I like you being here.'

'Now you're just trying to get into *my* knickers.'

I kiss the tip of her button nose. 'Too right I am.'

22

LYRA

July 2025
Sunday Lunch at Mum and Dad's

Mum and Dad have friends visiting for lunch. Brian and Jean are both consultant doctors, predictably, and godparents to Livy and me. They've driven up from York for the day, which they do every couple of months. Livy and Joshua-not-Josh are here, too.

They're all in the lounge, enjoying wine and conversation that's ranged from Livy's big day in September to Brain and Jean's life since they both retired last year. I've been adding very little to the group, preoccupied about the one thing I don't want to talk about with my family. So I'm tucked away in the kitchen. Mum always makes the meat for a Sunday roast – a north-east staple, despite the stifling air temperature today – but I make an epic Yorkshire pudding and the best stuffing balls in the family. Accolades I have to hold on to because, you know, I'm not a doctor and it's one of few things I do that doesn't make Mum look at me like I eat kittens for breakfast.

I open the oven to place my stuffing inside and the wave of hot air that engulfs me thrusts me back to last night, standing in the steam of Guy's shower, with him.

I've never had sex out of a bed, let alone been made to see stars on a sofa, been held up against glass balcony doors because my legs are giving out, or feeling a man as perfectly sculpted as Guy through the slick moisture of soapy water.

Falling asleep in his arms, against his chest, sated, was easy. Staying asleep was much harder. I felt... *alive.* With anticipation, excitement, fear of what morning would bring. I thought about leaving in the middle of the night to spare me the uncertainty but there was a big part of me that thought Guy would have to be the best liar in the world to have faked the looks, the touches, the words he whispered against my ear and the sounds he made that drove me crazy with lust.

I've never felt more womanly, more desired. More confident and... *sexy.*

When he came to me in the middle of the night as I played guitar, Scott's guitar, he was afraid; I felt it. He was exposed and vulnerable, too.

I stare at the stuffing and roast lamb cooking in the oven, my hands roaming my neck, my collarbones, where his stubble grazed and his mouth caressed.

'I still can't be*lieve* you cut your hair,' Livy practically snarls, leaning into me to make sure I can hear, an unopened bottle of white wine from the fridge in her hand.

Ah, yes, one of the perks of being late to arrive. Brian and Jean were already here and spared me – for a while, at least – the fallout of me cutting off my hair yesterday, which Livy has taken as massive shade.

It was. It is. But it's also for me. It's only a haircut but it has reminded me in a small way of someone I was the last time I think I was truly happy.

I haven't been *un*happy since I dropped out of university but with hindsight and whatever has come over me recently, I haven't been living my best life.

Maybe I can't completely have a do-over but maybe I don't need to be acting as if I have a million obligations and a thousand people to please, all more important than my own wants and desires.

'You don't like it, then?' I ask my sister.

'I told you not to cut it before the wedding.' She slaps her free hand to her thigh in exasperation. 'You've already had your hair trial.'

'I'll pay for a new one.'

'Lyra, it's not about money. And, for the record, I do like it. I think it looks great on you. But my wedding is in six weeks. Couldn't you have waited *six weeks*?' She raises her arms out in question. 'I don't know what's got into you recently. It's like—' She cuts herself short with a gasp. 'Are you seeing someone?'

Because, of course, my sister drives me crazy, as mad as I make her, but she can also read me better than anyone else. We've spent twenty-eight years in each other's company.

'Ah, erm, *no*.'

'You *are*!'

'I'm not. I— It's new and I don't know where I'm at or where he's at yet.'

Livy pulls two empty wine glasses from a cupboard and sets them down on the kitchen table. She opens the wine bottle and pours some into each glass. She sits into a chair and pats another.

'I'm not doing this,' I tell her, knowing my pinkened cheeks and curved-up lips are betraying me.

'*We* absolutely *are* doing this. It's about time you let me live single life vicariously through you.'

The sound that escapes me would be best placed on a teenage girl at a sleepover. It's a giggle that says, *I have a crush on a boy and he kissed me.* That's how it sounds in my head and it obviously sounds that way to Livy too because her eyes practically burst from her head.

'You've slept with him!' She's leaning into me, shout whispering like we would in our bedrooms when we didn't want Mum and Dad to hear our secrets.

Good thing, too, because when Mum finds out I slept with the wedding singing naked butler, she's going to flip at best, and disown me at worst.

'I'm still furious with you about your hair but I want *all* the details.'

I'm almost certain I'm not going to spill any details until words are tripping out of my mouth. 'It was…' I cover my face with my hands, shaking my head. 'Fuck, Livy, it was…'

'Oh my God. *That* good?'

I nod, sipping my wine. 'Yeah.'

'Who is he, this Adonis?'

I full-blown laugh now. 'You don't know him.' Which is true, though she for sure knows *of* him.

Her eyes narrow on me. 'Oh, Lyra, no. Not Guy Walker?'

Her words kill my laughter because I know what she's thinking; I've thought it, too.

'Sweetie, he's…'

'Go on, Livy.' I drain the wine in my glass out of temper more than want. 'What is he? Or, what is he not?'

She sits back in her chair, no longer in gossip mode but older, brighter, got-her-shit-together big-sister mode. 'He's not boyfriend material. I mean, come on, Lyra. I know you used to love The Hand Me Downs but he's not in a band any more and if his current profession is anything to go by, he's a deadbeat too, these days.'

I push out my chair, the rub of its legs loudly scraping the floor tiles as I stand. 'Would *everyone* stop with that? I agree, he might not be boyfriend material. I have no idea yet and, honestly, who's to say I want to be his girlfriend anyway? But I didn't sleep with him because he used to be in a band. I slept with him because I've fallen for who he is now.'

'Lyra—'

'No, Livy.' My voice is raised far beyond where I intend it to be. We're no longer two sisters having a secret talk in our unicorn bedrooms. 'What everyone seems to forget is that *I* am in the wedding industry too, and every time someone says he's worthless, do you know how that makes me feel? It makes me feel like I'm nothing, too.'

I can't believe it but tears are forming in my eyes, because this day that started out so incredibly well has turned to crap and it's only lunchtime. Because every word I'm saying is true – my family think I'm *nothing,* and perhaps I've thought it too, before now; perhaps I've allowed them to make me feel like that since I gave up on medicine. But yesterday, someone made me feel like I was *something.* So today, my family's view of me feels like it's breaking my heart.

I turn my back on my sister and her protests, her outstretched arms that I'd usually give in to when we fight so that we can end it all sooner, no matter which of us is in the wrong. Because today, I just don't feel like hugging it out with her.

Before I leave the room, I tell her, 'I *did* cut my hair to spite you.'

* * *

After I'd pulled myself together, sitting on the bed in my room, I faked cheeriness for my godparents, finished making lunch and poured the others wine. Now, I'm listening to Jean trying to sell my mum on retirement, again, wishing I was anywhere else than at this immaculately set dining table.

As Livy and Joshua dish out their contribution to lunch – an overpriced, pre-bought fruit flan – my phone pings. No one seems to notice as I slip it out of my dress pocket under the table, but I think everyone notices my Cheshire cat grin.

I knew I wasn't going to be first to call or message and I guess I can admit now, I was afraid I misread last night. That Guy and I would do what we seem to have been good at – kiss and don't call. So when I read his words, I can't hide my relief.

Can I see you tonight?

I want to reply with *Yes, duh.* But I play it slightly cooler, I think.

Depends. What do you have in mind?

Honestly, barring swamp swimming or bog sampling, he could say anything and I'd go.

It's a surprise. Can you be at my place by 7pm?

I leave it a minute to reply. Ignoring the eyes on me around the table, pretending like I'm not messaging against Mum's no-phones-at-the-table rule, when blatantly I am.

Okay.

He fires a message straight back.

Don't sound too excited, will you?

I chuckle, my eyes shooting straight to Mum and her disapproving face. Then, for some reason, to Dad, who is also staring at me, only he's smiling. His quirky smile, which I see more in the brightness of his eyes than on his lips.

What should I wear?

Typing...
Typing...
Typing...

Is this a trick question? Start the night in those tiny little shorts you wore yesterday. Maybe not a bikini on top, though. I'll let you decide what to wear at the end.

* * *

He meets me in the car park of his building at six fifty-six, wearing washed-out jeans and a t-shirt and, though I've seen him naked and I've seen him in a perfectly tailored suit, it's this look that makes me want to tear him out of his clothes.

God, last night has sent my hormones into overdrive.

I need to play it cool, I remind myself as he opens my car door and I climb out. *Play. It. Cool—*

Guy decides not to. As soon as I'm standing, his fingers slip into my hair, tugging at the base of my neck, and his other hand runs a tantalizing line up my thigh to the hem of my probably too-short shorts. Similar but different to last night's. It's still reasonably warm but I've worn my old leather biker jacket over my plain t-shirt.

I'm thrilled I didn't have to make the first move. Even happier I didn't have to wait a second longer to taste him again.

'I want to tear you out of these clothes but we've got somewhere to be,' he says when we part.

I run a thumb along my still plump lips, from last night, this morning, just now. 'You know, a polite man might have led with hello.'

He narrows his eyes. 'What gave you the impression I'm polite?'

'Good point. You're actually extremely grumpy.'

He's still scowling at me as he sniffs the air. 'What's that smell?'

Oh. I reach back into my car, knowing Guy is watching my arse as I lean over the driver's side to the passenger seat, unabashedly teasing him in a way that is completely unlike me.

Then I hand over a foil-covered plate and a gravy boat. 'Leftover Sunday roast. Lamb, Yorkshire puds, stuffing, the works.'

There's humour in his expression as he takes the food and thanks me.

'Is it weird that I brought you leftover food?'

'Ah, no?'

He's still staring at it, contrary to his words.

'I assure you, I make the best Yorkshire puddings and stuffing balls for miles.'

'Then I'm looking forward to it.' He nods in the direction

of the entrance to the apartments. 'Come on, we need to get going.'

'Where *are* we going?' I ask, honestly, kind of disappointed to not just be staying here with Guy, taking him out of those jeans and that top that is clinging to all the right places on him.

23

GUY

July 2025
The Arctic Monkeys

We pull up to The Stadium of Light's executive entrance in a cab. Not because I'm trying to be flashy – the tickets were free. Definitely not because I want to draw even a tiny amount of attention to myself – these social media numbers Dave keeps telling me about are something I'm trying not to worry about. But because I couldn't keep my hands off Lyra in that outfit.

I've officially lost my mind – that jacket looks exactly like the one I've dreamed about for years. I know it's Lyra's and my brain is making a fool of me, but damn it, I had to have her before we came out and since she was keen too, there was no holding me back.

We took a cab instead of walking half an hour to the home of Sunderland football club because we're running late.

I've never planned a date. Come to think of it, I'm not sure I've ever been on a date, really. Wining and dining someone was ruled out for a number of reasons. First, it's not my thing – posh restaurants and extortionately priced food that leaves me hungry. Second, at the age most people start dating, on my market-stall wages, I'd have done well to afford a Happy Meal from Maccy D's. Third, once I could have afforded something better, the girls who were throwing themselves at me were never the kind of girls a young man has to feed first.

This is different.

Lyra is different.

I've called in a few IOUs to get us tickets in a suite to see The Arctic Monkeys.

We get out of the cab and I pay the driver, then autograph his cap.

There's security on the entrance, which is conventional, yet the memories it evokes for me catch me off guard. Getting off a tour bus, turning up to arena venues with screaming fans lining the carpets that were rolled out for us.

Before I realise I'm doing it, I've slipped my hand into Lyra's, I think as comfort, honestly, but when we step inside the shiny marble foyer of the stadium, it occurs to me she might not want to hold my hand, she might not want the flashes from cameras going off around us to capture her, *us.*

I glance down at our interlaced fingers, then at her, and I'm rewarded with her smile, sparkling in her eyes brighter than any stage lights ever could, and a firm squeeze of my hand tells me, *This is okay.*

We're led through corridors, some people stopping to say hello to me, until we make it to the suite.

Inside, I point Lyra to the balcony, where other guests are gathering – some I recognise from days when the music scene was all I lived and breathed. The countdown to the main act has started.

'I'll get us some drinks. What would you like?' I ask. 'Beer? Wine? Fizz? They'll have everything.'

'Something soft, please. I am literally buzzing right now. I definitely don't need to add alcohol into the mix.'

'Are you sure?' I ask, though I'm really asking, *This isn't just because I don't drink?*

'Absolutely. Something like lemonade or Coke would be amazing.'

Though she's as giddy as a kid in a sweet shop right now, there's a sincerity about her that makes me kiss her, impulsively. 'Head on outside, I'll be there in a sec.'

I watch her go, leaning on the bar as the barman pours two glasses of lemonade. He eyes me as he does – he knows who I am. In this setting, I guess it's easier to imagine I was a someone once. I also know that he's been told to be on his best behaviour and he isn't allowed to ask for autographs and pictures from the guests who come into these suites.

'I can't believe we're here!' Lyra shouts as the lads open with 'I Bet You Look Good on the Dancefloor', an absolute classic, a crowd pleaser. 'This concert sold out in hours when the tickets went on sale. How did you pull this off?'

'I still know a few people.'

She stares at me for a moment and I see it in her look; she's thinking about Guy Walker from The Hand Me Downs. I wonder if this was the worst idea in the world. I'm trying to show her that I'm not him any more, then I do the exact opposite, pulling strings that *that* Guy had available to him.

But she shakes her head and twists her cute-as-hell button nose. 'Weird.'

I guess it is.

Then she sets down our drinks, raises her arms above her head, and starts shouting out The Arctic Monkeys' lyrics.

Nah, this was the right decision. If my brother could see me now, he'd laugh in disbelief, because standing on this balcony with a girl I can't get enough of, I let go of all my usual inhibitions and yell the song words right along with her.

I remember what it feels like to have fun.

24
LYRA

July 2025
Gravy Fondue

That saying about over-egging the pudding… well, I don't want to over-egg the pudding but tonight has been incredible. It still is. Despite the concert being over and Guy and I almost being back at his apartment.

I should be exhausted because for the entire time The Arctic Monkeys were playing, I didn't stop dancing like something out of *Trolls*. When they started 'When the Sun Goes Down', I video-called Cami and let her watch the entire song. Tonight, I danced the way I bounced around to that song with Cami so many nights at uni.

I felt like someone I used to know, like I was with a version of Guy who didn't seem to give a damn about anything except the music. I've realised in recent weeks that there's a side to Guy that isn't the gloomy, brooding man I met at the beginning of the wedding season. But tonight, he was like a man unleashed.

So many people in that suite knew who he was, watched his every move. I was aware of it and he must have been too. Yet he jumped around with me, screamed for an encore with me, as if we were the only people in the packed-out stadium.

We shout-sang and laughed and joked and rocked out shapes that should never be seen outside a person's own bedroom as they sing into a hairbrush for their own ears.

So yeah, I should be tired but I'm absolutely on the ceiling. High on life, music, *Guy*. I feel like a dream version of myself; invincible.

He lets us into his apartment and I don't want to outstay my welcome or be presumptuous. I'm not really sure what the protocol is here. He invited me on a date. We've already slept together multiple times. I haven't been drinking, which means I can drive home, though neither one of us seems to be inclined to end the night yet.

'Are you hungry?' he asks, making his way into his kitchen.

'Starving, actually.' There was food on offer in the suite but neither of us left the balcony to eat.

He opens his cupboards, which are bare but for a box of breakfast cereal, a loaf of bread and a few tins of baked beans.

'I can order in.'

I take off my leather jacket and hang it over one of the kitchen stools. 'Have you ever had gravy fondue?'

'Gravy fondue?' He raises an eyebrow in a way I'm kind of envious of – I've always wanted to master that expression – *Are you for real?*

Rolling my eyes, I tell him, 'Step aside, amateur.'

I heat through the gravy I brought earlier that was tucked away in his fridge. Then I slice everything that's not already sliced on the Sunday roast plate and pop it into the microwave. Five minutes later, I place on the coffee table a bowl of thick gravy and slices of meat, veg, stuffing and Yorkshire puddings for dipping. I cast two sofa cushions onto the floor and sit down, cross-legged, waiting for Guy.

He pairs his phone to speakers and The Script's 'At Your Feet' plays quietly into the room. Then he comes to sit opposite me, his arm lazily draped over one knee.

'Is this a posh girl's doner kebab?'

'I'm not posh.'

'You have a tennis court in your back garden.'

I take a piece of Yorkshire pud, dunk it in the gravy, and let the excess drip back into the bowl. 'Actually, I have four currently empty plant pots in my very small back yard.'

I offer the pudding to him, which he takes, making the kind of noise that tells me simultaneously that he hasn't had a homecooked meal in a while and that I may never be able to get my fill of this man.

'My parents have a tennis court. I'm not my parents, much to my mum's dismay.'

He nods, watching me like he's reading song lyrics from my expression. 'Me neither, which is definitely not a bad thing.' He looks away, dunking half a stuffing ball in gravy. 'Is this Lyra's famous stuffing that I need to try?'

'Yep. I defy you not to like it.'

'Bold statement,' he says, putting the food into his mouth. I watch, waiting. 'Aye, all right, that's probably the best stuffing I've ever tasted.'

My mouth falls open in fake shock. '*Probably?*'

He laughs and I won't say it but I think, he really ought to make that sound more often. Delighting in the fact I can make it happen. Thinking I'd happily expend a lot of time and energy into forcing the tune.

'Okay, the best.'

'Better.'

At one point he tells me, 'It mightn't surprise you to know that I didn't grow up eating fine cuts of meat and homemade Yorkshire puddings. You're really slumming it with me.'

And I tell him, 'I have more respect for you because you didn't. You achieved everything you worked hard for regardless.'

'Having a door or two opened for you isn't a bad thing, Lyra.'

All I can do is nod as I wonder whether I've slammed those doors in the faces of the people who were kind enough to have opened them for me.

We eat our way down the plate of fondue, listening to music, taking about the artists, about how Guy got into guitar at school, about the years he, Jay and Trev waited for Scott to mature enough to become their frontman.

'Can I ask you something?' I venture, unsure, even as the words leave my mouth, whether I should.

He nods, warily, I think.

'Your songs must be played all the time. Don't you get royalties?'

'I do. So I guess your next question is why am I skint?'

'I— That was invasive. I'm sorry, I shouldn't have asked. I guess I've just been curious. It's unlikely that someone like you would end up being a wedding entertainer. And I say that as someone who loves weddings and photographs weddings most weeks of the year, so it isn't intended to be a derogatory comment. Equally, *I've* never made anything of myself. I've never done anything special.'

His eyes narrow on me and again, there's hesitation before he speaks. 'The easiest narrative is that I spent all the money.'

'On the houses you bought for people?' I remember Kylie's comments at the beach yesterday.

'No. I bought my sister and my mam houses but I bought those back when the band was doing really well. Before...' He takes one final slice of lamb from the plate between us, offers it to me and, when I shake my head, dunks it in the gravy bowl. 'Scott has a son. My nephew, Matty. He's four years old. He was still a baby when Scott died. The kid won't ever know his dad and I should've—' He stares at the tabletop, as if his next words are written on it. 'The royalties go into a trust for Matty, so that he can at least get from life what Scott would've wanted for him.'

So that's how – he sacrificed himself for Scott's son. For his sister and mam, too.

I realise I should respond to what he's just told me but I can't seem to articulate my thoughts. There are many facets of Guy and I think I could fall hard for them all.

'Guy, that's—'

'The least I can do?' He looks at me and his eyes that have shone with brightness, even in the black of the arena tonight, are dark, raw with pain. 'It won't ever be enough. What I should've done was stop Scott from getting messed up in the first place.'

What I want to ask is, *How?* What I want to tell him is, *Scott was a grown man who made his own mistakes.* But something holds me back. Maybe the knowledge, even though I'm barely scratching the surface of getting to know Guy, that he doesn't want to hear it. Or I'm not the right person to say it.

Instead, I ask, 'Do you see Matty much?'

He rests an elbow on the coffee table and props up his temple with his fist, the anguish in his eyes receding, the midnight blue creeping back. 'Never. He lives in London with his mam and I'm sure I'm the last person she wants to see.'

I choose my next words carefully. 'Possibly. Or perhaps she and Matty would be really happy to have Uncle Guy around.'

I wish I could read his thoughts because I certainly can't read his expression, and I don't want to have meddled where my opinion isn't welcome. I don't want to have ruined tonight.

So I change tack and ask him, 'Kylie used to babysit you, huh?'

It takes a beat but amusement finally breaks the intensity of his look. 'She did. Worst babysitter ever. I watched *Pulp Fiction* when I was seven or eight. I also saw her get her first love bite on my mam's doorstep, wearing shorter hot pants than even Sabrina Carpenter would wear.'

My laughter feels good; it cuts through the last few minutes of tension. 'I bet you've never let her forget it?'

'Not a chance.' He scoffs. 'Does it all sound a bit incestuous?'

I shake my head. 'It sounds like you had a community around you. I never had that.'

'I guess I did, when it came to friends.' He stands and takes the gravy plate through to his kitchen.

'When did Dave come onto the scene?' I ask, following him and locating my leather jacket in the process.

'Those guys met in school. I've probably known Dave since I was fifteen or sixteen, through Kylie. Then when we formed a band and started gigging locally, Dave offered to manage us.' He leans back against the kitchen units, hands braced either side of him, muscles taut. Despite the ungodly hour, and being stuffed from my second roast of the day, my mind is transferred straight to the gutter, without passing go.

'What happened with Dave? How come he stopped managing the band?'

'The band was offered a pretty lucrative record deal, on the proviso we went with the label's management. We were going to refuse, I think. I'm fairly sure we wouldn't've agreed to drop Dave. But we didn't have a choice. He stepped aside. We were all gutted but at the time, it felt like it was the right thing for the band. If we'd been ready for what came, that is. But we weren't. It all got so big so quickly and we were just lads. Dave was like a protector. Our shield. Until he wasn't.'

He drags a hand back through his hair and I watch the motion, remembering the feel of my hands in his hair, before the concert. He shrugs. 'Then piece by piece, the wheels fell off, for all of us. You know how the story ends.' He holds out his hands, as if to say, *Here I am, the ending.*

'It's hard to remedy the man standing in this kitchen with me, in a perfectly lovely but humble apartment on Roker beach, who works alongside little old me, with the guitarist and vocalist from The Hand Me Downs,' I tell him honestly.

And that inability to comprehend that the two people are the same is part of the reason I'm afraid. He *is* the rock star, the musician, the untouchable. He's also a man I'm falling hard for. A man I want to know everything about, the good and the bad.

There's a spidey sense ringing alarm bells in my brain, telling me... *You're going to get hurt, Lyra.* I know I'm way out of my depth here.

I pick up my leather jacket and slip my arms into it. 'You know I'm not the kind of girl who gets VIP access to anything, let alone a sell-out concert from one of the nation's favourite bands, don't you?'

His face is deadpan as he folds his arms across his chest. 'I think that's why I like you so much.'

Oh boy. Oh boy, oh boy, oh boy.

'I'm going to go,' I tell him, already making a move for the exit. 'It's...' I check my watch. 'Jesus, almost 3 a.m., and I have work in a matter of hours.'

I'm so busy scarpering to the front door that I'm not even sure he's showing me out until his hand is braced on the door frame above my head, making me want to turn into him.

'Are you running, Lyra?'

'Yes. No. Ask me a less complex question.' Like, *Why?* I know the answer to that one – I'm leaving to protect us both. To protect myself.

My teeth find my lip as I mistakenly look into his blue eyes, again, which threaten to unravel my resolve. 'I don't know if this is the right time to ask or if the answer should be obvious, but are you seeing anyone else, or are we...?'

He brings his other arm to the door above my head so that I'm encased by his body. And if he asks me to stay, I know I'll cave.

'No, Lyra.' Just the sound of my name from his lips is teasing the lower part of my body. 'Not for a while. There's no one else I want to be seeing either. You?'

Laughter bursts from me.

'What's so funny?' he asks.

'Oh, Guy, I'm so not the kind of girl who has a different man on offer every night.'

He drops his face to within inches of mine. 'Good, me neither.' Then he winks, that insanely devilish lopsided smile displayed, and my knickers are pretty much begging me to take them down.

'Goodnight, Guy Walker.'

He exhales heavily and I wonder if he's going to let me go or if he's going to ravish me. One option is sensible. The other is highly appealing.

'Thank you for a great night.' He kisses me softly, briefly, then steps back, reaching to open the door for me.

'Shouldn't I be thanking you? You arranged everything.'

'But the highlight was the gravy fondue.' He gives me the kind of smile that would be fitting of a frontman.

Only when I close the door of my car, shielding myself from desire I can barely control, do I let out what feels like my first breath for too long.

I'm in big trouble.

25

LYRA

August 2025
The Malpass Wedding

The next twelve days pass in a blur of beach walks and sea frolicking, snogging on a blanket with crashing waves making a soundtrack to our romance, rolling around in the sand like no one else is watching.

I feel a constant push and pull. The want to let go versus the fear of uncharted territory, not knowing when but certain that this whole dream will come crashing down at some point. But every time I decide to take a step back, have us stay apart for an evening and try to keep a semblance of real life, Guy is the first of us to message or call.

He teaches me how to play guitar when we're in his apartment, and when he comes to my parents' house one night whilst Mum is at the hospital and Dad is sleeping, I teach him how to play the piano, until his hands stop roaming the keys and start caressing me. And my secret hideaway becomes another place that Guy and I are bared to each other, exposed in the very best way.

At his place, we cook together, mostly chopping salads as the heatwave from the continent continues to affect the usually cold north of England. He also gets me to show him my grandmother's recipe for Yorkshire puddings and tells me that anything doused in my gravy has become his new favourite meal.

And I think to myself that my new favourite meal is anything I eat with Guy, laughing, touching, exploring each other, teaching each other new things, learning about each other's favourite songs and quirks as we eat.

He asks me about the articles I write as a hobby and I tell him about the dark room at my bungalow. We go out for fish and chips, eating them from their wrapper as we walk along the beach. At the weekend, we take a trip to Finchale Abbey, sitting amongst old priory ruins, with a picnic, dipping in the River Wear to cool off.

Guy's recent videos from weddings continue to gain viral popularity on TikTok. Old concert videos of The Hand Me Downs are making a splash, too.

It turns out that the royalties from the very first record he wrote, which he doesn't give directly to Matty's trust, are increasing enough that he can quit being a naked Butler. I'm not sure how true the financial piece is. But I choose to accept when he tells me that I'm the only woman whose hands he's interested in having on him.

When we go out, Guy wears his cap and sunglasses. I pretend not to see people conspicuously taking his picture or making a video with their phones when we're doing something as innocuous as throwing chips in the direction of seagulls to fend them off at the beach.

The fact is, I don't care. I feel like I'm in a bubble that I don't want to pop.

One night, I arrive at Guy's apartment after work to find him sitting on a stool in his kitchen with a stack of a trashy weekly magazines in front of him. Our image is splashed across the front page: kissing on the beach, me wearing the bikini I bought the day we barbecued with Kylie, Dave and their friends.

'Are you okay?' he asks me.

There's a heaviness about him that I don't like, especially when it comes from him worrying about me. So, hoping my family don't happen to stumble across a copy of the gossip rag, I pick up the stack of glossy paper from the benchtop in front of him and toss every last copy into the bin.

'I don't read that one anyway,' I tell him, my palms on his cheeks, forcing him to see the meaning in my words. All that matters is what we think.

I don't know when this shift started to happen but it's true. If we aren't hurting anyone, then why can't we be happy? If people are perturbed by us, maybe we need to question their right to dictate or opine on what we do.

I remember a part of me that's been buried for too long, a part of me who truly believed that I had a right to be happy, and I think I'd like that piece of my puzzle back.

Today, we're both working at Earl's Castle for the Malpass wedding.

We've spent the morning apart, him going to Trev's house for brunch with Dave on account of Trev being told by his girlfriend that he can't be more than ten metres away from her, since she's now overdue to give birth to their baby.

I laughed when Guy told me because I couldn't help imagining the panicked calamity that would ensue if Tally were to go into labour with Trev, Guy and Dave as her doctors.

Guy called me 'cheeky' and spanked me on my backside as he kissed my temple, making me feel a heady mix of closeness and undeniable arousal.

Meanwhile, I spent the morning working on developing an old camera film that I found in one of my moving boxes. I'm unsure when it's from, though since it's amongst my Newcastle University sweaters and notebooks, I suspect it's from then.

I stopped taking and developing pictures for a while after That Night. I think I wanted to forget what I'd done, what I'd caused by switching my courses, and what I'd decided to give up when I dropped out of university altogether.

But there was one film that made me pause because I think, I *know*, there's more to the reason I didn't develop that one. I know it has pictures from That Night.

The night that changed everything. But maybe now, there's more to the memories than just everything going pear-shaped. Perhaps now, I could face that film.

It's at the Malpass wedding that the film in my personal Pentax finally runs out, containing all the pictures I've taken through the wedding season so far.

The wedding is an elegant black-tie affair, with Dave's string quartet playing through the ceremony outside. In the day-to-evening interlude, though my camera lens is directed at the family and friend feuds taking place over Jenga and pétanque, I'm focused on the fire that ignites in my lower abdomen when Guy arrives to set up for the evening entertainment.

Mandy is officially on duty tonight, but since there's nowhere else I need to be and no one else I'd rather be listening to, I stick around for Guy's set.

He opens with 'Show Me How' by the Stereophonics, making me wonder if he's chosen the song himself because it works so well with his voice, or if the bride and groom happen to have exceptionally great taste in music.

He sings the words looking my way and I'm cast back seven years, standing at his gig, as if there's no one else in the room besides us. It occurs to me that I've fallen for him in a way I've never fallen for anyone. Deeper than my imagination could have possibly conceived, faster than any sane, rational woman would think reasonable, harder than a rock falling from a mountain top, with no end in sight, only an abyss.

It's a beautiful, scary, freefalling sensation, and I'm fairly sure I'm starting to experience that little thing called love.

After the happy couple have cut the cake, Guy welcomes the new Mr and Mrs Malpass onto the dance floor. He's standing on stage, wearing grey trousers, a crisp white shirt I'd like to tear off him later, and the braces I've pinged against his nipples now more than once. Backing music to Michael Bublé's 'Haven't Met You Yet' starts to play and I smirk in his direction because I know just how much he loves to sing Michael Bublé songs – not. The problem for him is that he sings it remarkably well. So well, there are more cameras in the room videoing Guy than there are videoing the newlyweds as they make choreographed shapes across the dance floor.

And tonight, Guy seems to sing this song better than every other time I've heard it from him in the wedding season so far.

I come to stand by Dave, who is similarly leaning back against his sound box, and tell him, 'I genuinely think he might be enjoying himself.'

'He looks like the frontman he swears he'll never be,' Dave replies, watching his friend, the fallen rock star. 'I don't think it's just the music that's turning him into a showman again, flower.'

I try not to react to his statement. He could mean anything. Guy's job, reconnecting with his friends, spending time at the beach in the fresh air. But there's a definite part of me that's delighted by the thought that maybe, *just maybe*, I'm making Guy a little bit happier, too.

Then, something entirely unexpected happens. Something more unexpected even than the last few weeks. Something bizarre and implausible.

Guy is... *dancing?*... on the stage as he builds to the crescendo of Michael Bublé's lyrics. The tempo at peak, the pitch at its highest, the joy in the room at fever pitch.

And Guy... *twirls?*... on the spot, then takes hold of his microphone and dips it, bending to catch it, looking up at me as he does with as wide a beam on his face as I've ever seen.

Laughter bellows out from the depths of me as he winks at me in that way he does, simultaneously kicking the bottom of the mic stand with his shiny shoe and standing upright for his grand finale.

'Did he just dip his mic, Bublé style?' Dave asks.

I can't respond to him because of the ache in in my cheeks from smiling, the pain in my ribs from delirium, and because my current happiness seemingly knows no bounds.

26

GUY

August 2025
The Dornan Wedding

'It feels too easy,' I tell Dave and Trev as Dave finishes his last reps on the pectoral fly machine in the gym, Trev and I waiting to switch in. 'When I'm with her, I can switch off everything else. Forget all the noise. She—'

I want to say *consumes me, takes me out of my head*, but I'm not the kind of man who talks about fluffy stuff. That's what music is for.

Trev climbs onto the machine as Dave comes to stand next to me.

'When I'm not with her, I'm waiting for the punchline. I'm waiting for whatever it is that's gonna come along and ruin it.'

It could be any number of things – her family, my family, my demons, my past, my addictions. I'm scared of stifling her because even with the knowledge that something bad will come of this eventually, I can't stop the craving.

'I'm way out of my depth. I've never had a...'

'Girlfriend?' Dave asks when I don't say it myself. But I am thinking it. I feel it.

Trev finishes his set and rests his arms on his lap. 'Not everything has to be hard, man,' he tells me. 'I know that's news to ya but sometimes, something good comes along and ya should grab it with both hands.'

I'm too dumbfounded to respond, not because the concept is too difficult to comprehend, though it is quite for me. Because Trev and I, none of us in the band, ever mastered heart-to-hearts.

It hits me that we might just be older than the kids who started The Hand Me Downs. Maybe a tiny bit wiser than the boys who found fame and fortune too young.

I still don't care for the fame, though. When Dave and Trev start rabbiting on about the media surrounding me and, irritatingly, Lyra and me, I shut it down, deciding to take a spin on a bike with my headphones plugged in.

When I hear my brother's voice singing into my ears, I don't turn it off. Not today.

As my brother belts out the lyrics to 'Addicted,' I shake my head at him in my mind, knowing he's sitting on a cloud messing with my song selection on my phone because I could have written every word of that song now about Lyra. And the spirit in the sky knows it.

I'm clock-watching whilst Dave and Trev order a second coffee after our Saturday-morning post-gym brunch – another thing turning into habit. When I leave the lads, I have hours until I have to be at the Dornan wedding. But instead of wallowing about having time on my hands, alone with my own thoughts, like I would have done a couple of months ago, I'm excited to get home.

As soon as I'm showered, I settle onto my sofa, guitar in

hand, notepad and pen on the coffee table. The novel I'm reading for inspiration, a thesaurus and a dictionary are scattered around me. I didn't think I'd ever write music again. I had no desire to. But in the last few weeks, something's changed, a door's been unlocked, and I've realised that the world won't fall down around me again just because I pen a new record.

* * *

Fitting my Martin and its hard-shell case into my Barbie car is no easy feat. If it had been anything other than my best guitar, I'd have kicked it into the back seat and slammed the door shut on the thing. But not my Martin. We've only just reconnected.

As I pull into the staff car park at Earl's Castle, I notice I have a voice message from my sister. Reluctantly, I listen.

'Guy, ya can't ignore me forever. It's my birthday on Saturday and I really want ya to come. I really want to see ya. Dave and Kylie'll be there and if ya want to, ya can bring yer new lass. Mam and Dad would be chuffed to see ya. Please come. Love ya.'

Tossing my phone onto the passenger seat, I drag my hand roughly across my chin. So Dave and Kylie have been talking to my sister about Lyra. *Great*. I feel as if nothing could kill the conflicting mix of guilt and anxiety I feel just weighing up being in a room with my sister, my mam and my stepdad, versus not going at all.

The one exception comes into my view just when I need her to. I watch Lyra taking pictures of wedding guests who are mingling on the lawn, waiting for the marquee to be turned around for the evening. Minutes pass and all I'm doing is watching her. The way she works, her easy manner with others, the way her body moves in her white linen trousers and beneath her fitted tank top. When she spots me, her smile grows wider and I feel ten feet tall.

I step out of the car, willing her to walk faster in my direction, eager to take her in my arms and kiss her.

'Hi, you,' she says.

Two words. Two simple words and every synapse in my body feels like it's jump-started. I encourage her towards me, hooking a finger into the leather camera strap around her neck, and when our hips connect, my body is ready to drive zero to sixty in record time.

Her lips meet mine and I forget, or don't care, that people in the distance are watching us, pretending as if their camera phones aren't taking pictures that will surface on social media within the hour. Because the only thing I care about right now is her.

'I saw you watching me from over here,' she says mischievously as her fingertips run a teasing trail up my neck and into the base of my hairline.

'Have I crossed into stalker territory?' I ask her, thinking I could come dangerously close to being that obsessed with her.

'You have seen the car you drive, right?'

I tug her to me, chuckling into her neck, unbelievably, given the voice message I just listened to. 'You're full of cheek.'

'Is that your Martin in the back seat?'

We both move away from the car and stare at the guitar case that's wedged in the tiny vehicle.

She doesn't ask me if I intend to play it or what I intend to play on it if I do, but there's something like excitement dancing in her eyes and it's the final nudge over the line that I need. The woman who's reminded me that I love to play has also sold me on playing in public for the first time in three years.

'How's your day going?' I ask.

'There've been a few wedding glitches. Minutes after the ceremony and before even half the official photographs had been taken, the groom spilled an entire pint of Guinness down the bride's dress. The bride's parents both chose to introduce each other to their respective new partners, which has resulted in them having to be separated for the foreseeable future. Oh, and the page boy threw up down the flower girl. Oh, *oh*... and during set up this morning, the top tier of the cake was dropped in the kitchen and irreparably wounded.'

'Sounds like the Dornans aren't meant to be?'

Lyra shakes her head. 'Look at them,' she says, nodding in the direction of the bride and groom, who have their arms around each other, laughing and joking, despite the bride's brown-stained dress. 'I think it just shows that they can weather a few storms. They're rolling with it.'

She's an optimist. My polar opposite. But God knows I could use an optimist in my life and if it's going to be anyone, let it be the woman I am falling absolutely head over heels for. Maybe. Definitely, maybe, this thing could have legs.

* * *

An hour or so later, I've sung through the bride and groom's first dance – 'Can't Help Falling in Love' by Elvis Presley – and through Take That's 'Greatest Day', amongst others. The lights in the marquee are dim and Dave has got me standing under a spotlight.

The dance floor is packed, as much about the lively playlist as the nature of the Irish, I think. I give Dave the nod to tell him, *I'm going to do it.*

Then into my microphone, I tell the wedding party, 'When I was looking at the playlist for tonight, it was obvious that the bride and groom have great taste in music. In particular, they're big fans of Oasis.'

Dave carries my guitar onto the stage and hangs it around my neck to the background noise of shocked guests and squeals from the sweaty bodies closest to me on the floor.

'Now, I'm told there's been a few wedding hiccups today.' I glance to Lyra, who's made her way to the side of the stage and has hold of her personal camera, trained on me. 'I'm also reliably informed by the same woman, who's reminded me how good it feels to pick up a guitar again, that sometimes shit happens, and you've just got to...' I strum my opening chord, Dave kicks in the backing track, and I tell the crowd, 'Roll With It'.

The marquee erupts as I begin to sing the Oasis song.

Ten covered tracks later, I congratulate the newlyweds one more time and leave the stage to the small but loud crowd shouting for more.

I hand my guitar to Dave and he tosses me a towel in exchange. As I mop sweat from my brow, he asks me, 'Did that feel good?'

I glance back across my shoulder at everyone still singing and dancing, now singing out lyrics to The Hand Me Downs track that Dave has played first and I admit, 'No, mate. It felt fucking incredible.'

Uncharacteristically, he yanks me into an embrace, thumping my back, not letting me go until I push him away and tell him, 'Enough, man. Be cool. Did you get what I asked for?'

He hands it to me – the precisely cut metal small but heavy – and I slip it into my pocket. Then I find the woman I've watched dancing and taking my picture for the last forty minutes. And I see it in the way she looks at me – crooked smile, eyes shining – she's seen a small glimpse of a man she's resurrected. A man she saw rock a stage in Madrid.

She tugs the ends of the towel around my neck and tells me, 'Welcome back,' right before her mouth meets mine.

* * *

Half an hour later, right on schedule, Dave tells the guests to head outside to the lawn and I take hold of Lyra's hand, leading her in the opposite direction.

She giggles as we wind through the castle's corridors, past *no entry* signs for guests, and up a spiral staircase.

'Where are we going?'

At the top of the staircase, we're confronted by a hefty wood door and when she tells me that going up into the castle turret can't be done, I pull the key Dave gave me from my pocket.

'How did you get that?'

I hold up crossed fingers. 'Pearl and I are like this since I saved her business.'

'Oh, *you* saved it?' She raises her eyebrows. 'Your modesty is humbling.'

I chortle, leading her outside onto the castle turret, where we have the best view of the Earl's estate, and a phenomenal spot to watch the Dornans' fireworks.

'Oh my gosh, they're beautiful. It's stunning up here,' Lyra tells me as she leans on the old stone wall and I come to stand behind her, chest to her back, hips to her waist, arms wrapped over hers, our fingers entwined.

How could I stand here and not agree with her? It's isolated. It's breathtaking. And *she* is truly exquisite. My heart is racing, my body is more alive than when I'm standing in a football stadium playing to tens of thousands of fans, but only in the best way, because Lyra keeps every other part of me calm.

I can't resist pressing my lips to her neck. She's all I want. All I need. And if I have her by my side, I think I could cope with anything else.

So, in the understatement of my life, when the fireworks fall to just the sound of a fizzle going up into the black void of time and space, I whisper, 'I really fucking like you, Lyra.'

She leans back into me and tells me, 'I really fucking like you, too,' right as literal and proverbial fireworks go off around me.

27

GUY

September 2025
My Sister's 25th Birthday Bash

We're in Lyra's car, pulling into the car park of the pub where my sister is having her quarter-century birthday bash in Newcastle. I look across to her from the passenger seat. She looks incredible in a tight-fitting pair of jeans and a pair of heels I'd really like her to keep on later. In truth, my superficial brain being partially distracted might be the reason we've managed to get as far as the venue.

Lyra's driving because she told me she's intimidated by the eyelashes on my Barbie car. But what I'm coming to realise about the woman to my right is that she has a sixth sense when it comes to looking out for people. In this case, she made the right call, because I'm sitting on my hands to stop myself fidgeting.

'Are you sure you want to do this?' I ask her, again, staring at the few smokers standing outside the back of the pub.

She pulls into a parking spot and kills the engine. It's early

September and though it's only 8 p.m., I can sense that summer is fading.

She unbuckles and twists to face me, one knee bent up on her seat, letting me know that we aren't getting out of the car, not yet.

'You don't need to see where I came from, Lyra.'

It's a partial truth because she doesn't need to see just how working class my roots go – *working* class is being generous. I know Lyra won't care. I know that later tonight, when I make excuses and apologise for my family, she'll tell me something like, *It doesn't matter where we come from, it's about the people we are that matters.* The rest of the truth is, *I* don't want to be reminded about where I came from.

'Would it freak you out if I said I do?' she asks, leaning her temple against the headrest. 'I want to know everything about you that nobody else gets to see.'

I mirror her position, relaxing into my seat, thinking, so long as she comes, I can just about stomach an hour here. Honestly, if she hadn't offered to come when I told her my sister had invited her, I still wouldn't be here.

And if she hadn't whispered to me, as I lay on her lap on my sofa, that my family love me, no matter what has happened in the past, because that's what being family means, I wouldn't have even found the will to reply to Bex's voice note.

Because Lyra is smarter, funnier and kinder than any other person I know. I trust her. I believe her. Despite knowing that on some level, that's because I want to believe her words.

I let my family down when I failed Scott. But they've begged me to come tonight. Bex has pleaded with me to be here. So maybe Lyra is right. It's possible that they love me in spite of everything.

I watch her breathe, listening to her inhalations and exhalations in the quiet of her car, not pressuring me at all. Eventually, I ask her, 'Would it freak you out if I told you I think I dreamed you into existence?'

Her response is a lazy tilt of her lips that gives me the strength I need.

Outside the car, I take her hand in mine and squeeze it as if *I'm* reassuring *her*, and I wonder if she can see straight through my façade.

We walk through a plume of cigarette smoke that actually doesn't make me want in on it at all. In fact, it irritates me that Lyra has to walk through it. The carpet in the pub is an old nineties-style pattern. It's worn and sticky. The smell of beer – yeast barrels – hits me at the same time Blondie's 'Brown Eyed Girl' assaults my ears.

I'm sixteen again, sneaking into the local boozer on Christmas Eve. All the oldies rocking out like they've been unleashed for one night of the year. The underage teens hiding out of view with their acne and alcopops so that the bouncers will turn a blind eye until the place is at capacity, or a fight breaks out and threatens to bring in the coppers.

I give Lyra a tight smile, still holding her hand, fingers entwined, as she follows behind me.

In my free hand, I'm holding a gift bag of beauty products and a spa voucher. Lyra insisted she contribute to the gift, so I let her pick everything out and got Dave to give me an advance on next week's paycheque to buy them.

I stare at the bottles of hard liquor on the shelf behind the long oak bar, disappointed to think, for the first time in months, that I wouldn't mind sinking a few shots of Dutch courage. Lyra's hand comes up to my bicep as I hold my next blink and I know she's reading my mind.

'Alreet, lad?' Dave and Kylie are two of the first people we bump into as we reach the back room that's been hired for Bex.

I doubt it's coincidence that they're hanging near the doorway and I'm grateful to them both for it.

We chat to them for a few minutes before going in search of my sister, who's tucked into an alcove at the far side of the large room, next to a table full of presents and two large foil balloons – 2 and 5. En route, we pass the buffet that has everything I'd expect – sausage rolls, dips and bread sticks, fried chicken, fried fish goujons, fried chips, fried scotch eggs, pork pies, salted nuts and crinkle-cut crisps in bowls.

I try not to make eye contact with my sister's guests, who make no effort to pretend they aren't talking about me, shouting 'Guy Walker' to one another above the music. I do check that Lyra's okay but *still* she seems to be taking it all in her stride. Remarkable, really, because all this party is demonstrating is that she and I are worlds apart. She should be walking into places like Earl's Castle, on the arm of a doctor or a lawyer, not a deadbeat who has to check in with his addictions every time he gets anxious.

'Guy! You came!'

Bex charges at me, near bowling me over and making me lose Lyra's hand in the process. I spot Lyra across my sister's shoulder, laughing, and her reaction makes me settle into my kid sister's hug.

'Happy birthday,' I tell her, pulling strands of her long blonde hair from my mouth and holding out the gift bag. 'This is for you.'

'Aww, *Guy*, ya didn't have to get me anything,' she says, already untying the bag on top of her gift table and rifling through the contents.

'Well, Lyra picked everything out,' I tell her, which is a neat segue into an introduction.

'Hiya, babe,' Bex says, thrusting her arms around Lyra. 'It's lush to finally meet ya.'

If Lyra's uncomfortable by my sister's over-familiarity, she doesn't show it, and I'm grateful that they drop into conversation about beauty stuff whilst I come round. My heart rate eventually starts to calm, as my anxiety slowly begins to recede. This isn't so bad. Bex is happy to see me. Maybe, now that I've crossed the line, we could start seeing each other again. Get a coffee. Be half sister and brother, like we were once.

Lyra could be right. Families love each other, no matter what shit has passed between them.

* * *

The party isn't my scene and though Lyra is trying, I can tell it isn't hers either. We mostly chat to Dave and Kylie and it transpires that Bex invited Trev and Tally too, but Tally is having twinges that she thinks might be early labour.

I bet she is

I message Trev, who sends a laughing emoji back. He would want to be here as much as I do.

Checking my phone tells me we've been here for a whooping twenty-seven minutes and I haven't yet seen my...

'Mam.'

She's walking towards our group of four. Unsteady. Eyes already glossed. As if she started drinking long before the party started. Her arms are outstretched, though, and as much as they're unexpected, they're welcome, too.

Her hold is only as familiar as it used to be – we weren't a physical family, at least not in a caring sort of way – but it's better than what I've been expecting, which was something much darker. Hate. Spite. I don't know for sure but dark enough that I've avoided it since Scott's funeral.

'Is this Lyra? Our Bex was just telling me about ya.'

'Hi, yes, I am. It's lovely to meet you, Tracy.'

'That's me, love. This one's mam, for me sins.' She cracks up but Lyra, usually so affable, doesn't match it. Instead, she watches me across my mam's shoulder, asking me in a look if I'm okay.

I'm annoyed by the insinuation. *Why wouldn't I be okay?*

I'm also annoyed that there's some kind of unspoken stand-off happening between my mam and my girlfriend, which is completely unlike Lyra.

'Guy, love, get yer mam a wine, would ya?' Mam asks. 'A pink one, love.'

Lyra gives me a stiff smile as I head to the bar. I order my mam's drink, two more of the same for Dave and Kylie, and a soft drink each for Lyra and me, then lean back on the bar to keep an eye on what's happening between my mam and Lyra.

They're just talking. I can't hear what's being said but it seems okay. Mam is overly touchy and staggering as she speaks but Lyra seems *fine.*

'It's Guy, isn't it?' a lad asks me, sloshing lager from his pint glass as he moves closer to me.

'Ah, yeah, Bex's brother,' I tell him, already knowing that's not why he's asking.

'Bet it's a comedown walking in here after playing at Wembley, eh?'

Then his mate joins us and I check how my order has advanced – sadly, it's not ready, because I'd really like to walk away now.

'Ha way then, give us a tune, mate,' the drunk friend says.

'Another time, lads,' I reply, turning my back on them and facing the server.

'Ahhh, ha way. You're billy big time, aren't ya? Too good for this lot?'

He chortles into his beer in a way that's more sinister than friendly, and I can feel every sinew in my body tightening, getting ready for what I know will come.

'Lads, he said no.' *Dave.* 'He's just here to have a good time with his sister, alreet?'

'Who're yey like, his security?'

Dave grins threateningly. Equally as sinister as I'm anticipating the lads' next move to be. 'Fuck off or you'll find out,' he tells them, baring teeth.

Now I turn, braced. I wasn't in the market for it but if shit's going down, I'm not leaving Dave to fight my battles for me.

Wisely, thankfully, the lads move on, but that was my warning. One more drink and I'm taking Lyra home. Getting myself out of this shithole.

I'm on edge again. I don't want to be here and I don't want Lyra to be here or seeing this or thinking that I'm like this. Maybe I was. I know I was. But I'm not the kind of man who's going to pick a fight over nothing because I've had too much beer. Not any more.

Back in our group by the door, Mam is slurring her way through recounting childhood memories of me, though I don't remember most of what she's talking about – trips to parks, swings, beach ice creams. It sounds nice, loving, but I have no recollection of it.

Every time she mentions Scott, I want to curl in on myself. When her glazed eyes fill with unshed tears, she kills me, because we both know I should have been better. And she lets me hug her – an apology that's long overdue.

It feels like a moment, something special, an invisible barrier that we've needed to cross. It leaves me hopeful that we could salvage a relationship. Have lunch together. Go somewhere or do something nice.

I'm buying into it. More than believing it, I'm wanting it. Wanting her time.

* * *

The nostalgia lasted for minutes. Until Mam pulls me aside and says, 'Bex wouldn't want me to ask, love, but she's having her kitchen done and she's had a right time with the builders. They've kept adding costs on and...'

I zone out, knowing the punchline in any event, understanding why I'm really here. And the fucking thing is, the joke's on me, because when they hugged me, I thought they really hugged me. And when Lyra said families love each other no matter what, I wanted to have faith in her.

'How much does she need?' I ask, not knowing how I can help but knowing I'll try.

28

GUY

September 2025
The Fallout

Lyra and I leave without saying goodbye to my family and when we exit, we aren't holding hands the way we were when we arrived.

'Are you going to give me the silent treatment all the way back to Roker?' Lyra asks after ten minutes of silence that's only served to elevate my temper.

'Maybe, Lyra, because I was always told that if you don't have anything nice to say, don't say anything at all.'

I hate how shitty I sound but the fact is, I'm pissed off. Mostly with my family but with her, too. I'm pissed off that she convinced me to go there tonight, to take her with me, to let her have that insight into who I am. And I'm really fucked off that my palms are sweating and my pulse is through the roof and even when I'm not speaking, I feel as if my lungs are being squeezed and it's getting harder and harder to breathe.

'I don't know what happened, Guy. Talk to me.' God, she's not even irate, she's annoyed but typically calm, rational.

'I don't want to talk, Lyra. I don't want to fucking—' I inhale deeply, dragging in an unsteady breath that doesn't feel like it's enough.

We're coming off a dual carriageway and getting closer to home and I think, if I can just hold it together for a little bit longer, she won't have to see me fall.

'Are you okay?' she asks, glancing my way then back to the road.

I wind down my window, the fresh air welcome but still not shifting the tightening in my chest.

'Fine,' I manage, physically holding my ribcage as my heart tries to explode right out of it.

'Guy.' Her voice is softer now. 'If this is going to work, you have to let me in.'

That does it. Her bringing our relationship into this. Exactly like I knew would happen. There were two certainties tonight and I stupidly chose to ignore them. One, I would be reminded of how I let my kid brother down catastrophically, the only person who's ever really loved me. Two, Lyra would see where I came from and we'd be ruined, too good to be true.

I respond how I've learned to over the years – offensively. 'I don't need saving, Dr Lyra. I'm not someone you can fix. I never asked for your help. I don't need it and I don't want it. So take your do-gooding somewhere else. Maybe your next boyfriend will be a fuck-up, too.'

God, Jesus, the pain in my chest.

She thinks she isn't like her family, not worthy of them, but she is like them. She's caring and good.

'Guy?' She sounds panicked. I can hear it in her voice but I can't see it on her face because my eyes are squeezed shut, one hand on my chest because I can't breathe, the other braced on the dashboard because I feel like I'm going to black out.

'Pull over, Lyra. Pull over,' I gasp.

She does. Into the car park of a McDonald's drive-thru, but I don't notice that until I've crawled out of the car and I'm propped up against the wheel, legs splayed out in front of me.

'You're having an anxiety attack, Guy. Breathe, baby. Just breathe.' I look at her now, hunkered down in front of me, full of compassion, and it's the straw that breaks my back and obliterates the dam that's holding back a reservoir of tears.

'I'm sorry,' I say as hot tears roll down my cheeks and I try but fail to steady my breathing.

'Shh, shh, shh. You have nothing to be sorry about. Nothing at all.' She drops to her knees and holds my face in her palms, wiping my cheeks with her thumbs. 'Big breath in for me. We'll count to four.'

And she does count, though I can't hold it for four. But she repeats it again and again and again, still stroking my face, making me feel like I'm not alone, until finally, my lungs are expanding and retracting with some semblance of rhythm.

What I'm left feeling is drained, remorseful, guilty, heart-broken and grateful for the woman sitting next to me on the dirty ground of a Maccy D's car park, holding my hand, catching me as I fall, in a way no one has caught me before.

* * *

She doesn't leave my apartment once she's driven me home, though I tell her to go, guilt free.

Instead, she asks me, 'Why would I leave the man I love when he needs me?'

And I stop short of crying again but she'll never know how much her words mean to me, how much I desperately want them to be true. How ready I am to be loved by someone.

When we're lying in my bed, her exactly where I like her to be – curled onto my chest, her leg entwined with mine – I tell her what happened with my mam.

'They always saw us as an ATM. Before the band, when I was told to get out and get a job instead of going to school. Especially when the band started doing well. And you can imagine how frequent and sizeable the demands for money got when we were successful.'

'But you bought them houses,' Lyra says. I know she's trying to keep her tone neutral and mostly listen but every now and then, she responds to me and I can hear it in her voice – *shock*.

'I tried to give them everything they wanted to keep them away from Scott.' Her hair feels like silk beneath my fingers and the simple act of stroking it makes it easier to talk somehow. 'I would tell him, don't be daft, kid, they're your family, they love you. Blood means everything.'

'Like I told you about going to the party tonight?'

'I guess, yeah. The stupid thing is, part of me believed it. Even though I knew they liked the money, despite every memory reminding me that the love wasn't there, I believed it.'

'Because you wanted to.' She props herself up on my chest, looking into my eyes in the dark room.

'I think that's why I was mad at you tonight. I'm sorry, Lyra, none of it was your fault and I was a dick to you in the car.' I hate that I was. I tuck her hair from her temple behind her ear. The very last person in the world I want to be shitty with is the woman I'm holding right now. 'I think I wanted to believe what you were telling me, so I let myself go back there. I let myself fall for it, again. Like I have so many times before. Stupid.'

She turns into my palm and kisses it. 'We all want to be loved, Guy, for who we are, not what we're worth in gold coins. That doesn't make you stupid.'

I take the kind of breath that makes her rise and fall against my body, tracing the outline of her beautiful face with my fingertips, and tell I her what I've known for weeks. 'I love you, Lyra.'

And now, I get to wait for it all to fall to wreck and ruin. For the ticking time bomb to go off.

29

LYRA

September 2025

Two and a Half Weeks Until My Sister's Wedding

Guy Walker Breaks Out of his Bublé

The catchy headline of yet another post in my social media feed.

I fight against the urge to read the thousands of comments on the online news post, but curiosity wins out. I skim over the posts that mention the mystery woman in the pink bikini and guesses about who she is, and try to ignore some of the hideous and unnecessarily nasty comments.

The overriding message is this: his fans want him back. They're calling for The Hand Me Downs to make a comeback.

As much as I agree that would be amazing, I can't imagine it will happen whilst Guy can't stand the thought of seeing Jay again. And until he realises he can be a lead vocalist, entertain a crowd, I just don't see him coming back without a band.

'Would you like a glass of wine, darling?' my mum asks, already heading to the kitchen to get herself and Livy a drink.

I'm sitting on the floor of my parents' lounge, Dad in his usual chair chatting to us, Livy sitting next to me as we make small boxes and fill them with fancy foil-wrapped chocolates for her wedding favours.

'Thank you for helping today,' Livy says out of the blue. 'I know you have work coming out of your ears at this time of year. I also know there are people you'd rather see.' She rocks her shoulder against mine in a way that makes me look in Dad's direction but he's pretending not to eavesdrop, which I can tell from the ghost of a smirk on his unique mouth.

'I want to be here,' I tell her honestly. 'I should also say sorry. About cutting my hair. About being sharp with you recently. I've just been...' I shake my head, trying to articulate how I've been feeling since meeting Guy's family and seeing how despicably he's been treated all his life. 'I've been figuring a few things out lately. Thinking maybe it's time I decide what I really want to do with my life. But that's about me and I might have been taking it out on you. I mean, you have been a bridezilla in places...'

She laughs.

'But I love you.'

Mum comes back into the room and hands us each a glass of wine.

'And Mum and Dad. We have a pretty decent family, don't we?'

Mum rears, as if I've slapped her in the face, then glances to Dad, who shrugs. Whilst Livy and I lean our heads together for a moment, Mum takes her glass of wine to his chair and plonks herself on the arm, taking hold of his hand.

They're not perfect but nor am I. As a family, we're far

from it. But they've always loved me. Guy is right, they may have been oppressive but it's always been driven by them wanting what they think is best for me.

It's been a weird few days since I last saw Guy. When we woke up together the morning after his sister's birthday party, there was a strange vibe. Everything he did and said would have read like normal. He kissed me the way he does, we drank coffee on his balcony, we hugged goodbye when I left his place late morning. But there was something between us that hadn't been there since we got together. Something not dissimilar to how it felt being trapped in an elevator with him back in April. As if he was holding back, his actions clouded.

He's messaged me and I've been busy with wedding stuff and editing photographs for work. I've even managed to get into my dark room and start developing my completed camera rolls – my most recent one and the one I found from university. I've been writing before bed, my silly article snippets, some of them about Guy, as I've watched photographs of him develop one by one from this summer and from That Night, seven years ago. Pictures I'd forgotten – or intentionally buried – and never developed because I haven't felt ready for reminders of That Night before now.

Oddly, it's made me feel more distant from him. The photographs of who he was, the person and the band that fans are crying out to make a comeback. I'd hate him not to. But I don't feel like that version of Guy belongs to me at all. Except in one photograph, in that moment he sang 'You and Me' That Night and it felt as if he was singing the lyrics to me, only me.

Crazy.

As I'm lost in thought, mindlessly crafting, a message comes through to my phone.

Come over tonight? I'll cook? X

I don't realise I'm grinning at my phone until my dad says, 'That will be Guy.'

I roll my eyes at him but he chuckles in response. A sound we hear too rarely these days.

* * *

When Guy opens his door, he's freshly showered, his hair still wet, his skin smelling of grapefruit and black pepper shower gel. There are a smattering of water droplets seeping through his white t-shirt and his jeans are not yet buttoned up.

The effect is... damaging for someone who has a complete hormone imbalance around this man.

He kisses me and I hand over a homemade trifle that's going to take two people some real eating. He takes the dessert from me to the kitchen as I look around his lounge in something of a daze. There are a multitude of dirty coffee cups, tossed food wrappers, crumb-decorated plates. Pieces of balled-up paper, scrawled paper, a dictionary and a thesaurus are scattered like a crop circle around his guitar that's lying in the middle of his sofa.

'Wh— Ah— Should I ask?'

'Sorry, I meant to clear-up before you arrived but I lost track of time,' he tells me, taking a puff-pastry-topped pie out of his oven, burning himself on the rim of the dish in the process.

'You've been writing?'

He turns away from the food, sucking on his burnt finger, to assess the state of the place the way I'm seeing it. 'Yeah, I guess I have.'

'For how long?' I laugh. 'A decade?'

I cocks his head to one side. 'Feels like it.'

Funnily enough, whilst I'm no songwriter, I think I understand the sentiment. 'I use photography in the same way,' I tell him.

To explore how I'm feeling. To get lost in someone else's world. To process.

When he nods and that half-moon tugs on his cheek at one side of his mouth, I know I've hit the nail on the head.

'That pie smells incredible.' I'm suddenly starving after not feeling hungry for the last few days.

'Steak and ale,' he tells me with a grin. 'It's actually a reheat from Kylie, on Dave's instruction because he's got in his head about— Anyway, I promise it's good home cooking and better than the beans on toast you'd have got if I'd cooked myself.'

Dave wants him to write. Of course he does. Him and half the world. Me included.

So why, as I take up a stool in Guy's kitchen, do I have a horrible sinking feeling in the pit of my stomach like I'm about to fall from Cloud Nine?

We've barely made a dent in what is, unequivocally, the best pie I've ever tasted, when there's a rap on Guy's door, followed by the sound of a key in the lock.

We look at each other, then he says, 'Dave has a key.'

'Not indecent are ya, lad?' he calls through the door before opening it fully. As Guy gets up and heads his way, Dave says, 'Sorry, Lyra. I didn't know ya were here, flower.'

'Clearly,' I say, chuckling whilst trying to kick meat from between my teeth with my tongue. 'Hi, Dave.'

It's all jovial, until it's not. Until Guy stills like he's been cast in bronze, boring holes in someone on the other side of the open door. It's an expression I haven't seen on him before. It isn't sad or angry, not shocked or afraid. It's something else entirely. Crazed. Wild.

Before his fists clench at his sides, before I see red mist descend on him as if it's a physical presence in the room, I think I know who he sees.

'It's about time you lads have it out,' Dave says, his tone fatherly. Like a father who's about to strap boxing gloves on his kids and throw them into their garden to fight to the death.

I want no part in whatever is about to happen but that doesn't stop my legs from carrying me to Guy's side, in time to see Trev, then another man, whose eyes widen, right before Guy all but snarls at him. 'Outside.'

'Guy,' I say gently, putting a pointless hand on his arm in an attempt to placate him. I'm mute to him. Invisible. Because every single part of him is focused on the old drummer from The Hand Me Downs. Jay.

Guy lunges for him. Jay is thrust back against the wall, head banging against the surface so hard it makes me wince. And they fight like animals, tearing at each other's clothes, until Dave and Trev somehow usher them into the open lift.

I hear them scrapping and run back inside to the balcony, from where I see them tackling each other onto the beach, drawing the eyes of passersby.

30

GUY

September 2025

Down and Out

I can taste the metallic of blood in my mouth. I can see it running from Jay's nose. We lie panting, side-by-side, backs on the sand, halfway down the beach in front of my apartment.

'I think you've knocked my tooth loose,' Jay groans.

'That's the least you deserve,' I gripe, coming up to sit, wiping blood from my cheek without knowing where it's coming from.

Jay brings himself upright, sitting next to me. I've no clue where the others are; I was blinded by rage when I saw Jay standing at my front door. This has been a long time coming.

'I miss Scotty every fucking day, Guy,' he tells me, making me want to hit him again.

'You don't get to say that.' I can feel pressure at the back of my eyes that I don't think is a result of our scrap. 'You introduced him to the hard stuff, Jay. I told you and I told him. Weed, beer, fine. The rest—'

'I kick myself every day, Guy. So ya can go on hating me if ya want to, but ya won't cause me any more damage than I've felt already.' He wipes the back of his hand under his nose and it comes away looking like it's been coated in red paint.

'I wasn't in the right frame of mind myself to think better of it, man. None of us were. You included. But I've accepted, and you need to, that if Scott was hell-bent on finding drugs, he would've got them from somewhere. That accident could've happened whether he was high or not. I didn't make him get in a car that night, just like I didn't force him to take drugs.'

I can't move my blurred focus from the grains of sand around me, but I sense Jay shrug and hear his sigh. 'Fuck it. If ya need to make me the scapegoat, I'll be it. But I've done a lot of work on myself in the last few years, man, and I'm not the same kid I was then.'

I hate myself for looking at him and seeing genuineness in his expression. For hearing sincerity in his voice.

'I've got a wife now and a kid of my own,' he says.

'I didn't know that.'

He shrugs. 'It's not like we've spoken a word to each other since Scotty's funeral.'

I wipe the stream of red from my face again. This might need medical attention.

Jay stands and offers a hand up. 'You need to forgive yourself, too. He was yer brother, not yer kid to babysit. He made his own choices and his own mistakes and he'd be fucking irate if he knew ya were broke and singing along to karaoke for a living in his honour.'

I don't know that I agree with his words, or him, not yet. But I heard one word – scapegoat – and maybe he has been that for me. Someone to take a small amount of responsibility from my own shoulders.

He's still holding out his hand and after long seconds, I bring mine to meet his, letting him drag me off the sand.

'Got that out of yer system now, lads?' Dave asks from somewhere behind us.

He and Trev are standing like bouncers: stances wide, shoulders broad, arms folded across their chests.

I consider the scene, like something out of an underground fight club, and the onlookers we've drawn. Rubbing my hands over my filthy, sandy, bloody and beat-up face, I scoff. 'This is gonna look great splashed over the web tomorrow.'

'Show us a rock star who doesn't have a temper,' Jay says. 'Can we get patched up now?'

His words have a double meaning, I'm sure, but before I can respond, I remember...

'Where's Lyra?' I ask Dave and Trev.

'She left, matey.'

Ah fuck.

'We'll have to deal with this mess another time, lads. I've gotta go after her.'

* * *

I knock on the door of the address she texted me, hoping she didn't lie. Despite being near inseparable for weeks, we're always at my apartment or out somewhere, or sometimes at her parents' house if her mum is working.

Lyra lives in a tiny bungalow that looks as if its owner should be about eighty. Outside the door are two empty plant pots and, honestly, the place looks uninhabited.

I'm relieved when she answers. Then, I immediately realise how badly beaten up I look as she gasps in response.

She holds on to the door frame, not offering to let me inside to her hallway that's untidy with what appear to be stacked moving boxes, giving me a clue as to why we haven't spent time here.

'I'm sorry you had to see that, but it was— It was something I needed to do for Scott. I'm not like that any more. It's not who I want to be. But the old me had a score to settle.'

A crease forms between her eyes as she exhales.

'I'm a broken record, I know, but I swear it's done.'

'I didn't leave because I was mad at you or disappointed in you, Guy. I left because I didn't want to be just another bystander looking on to something you didn't invite me to see.'

Despite her words, her reticence is clear from the way she's standing, the way her jaw is gently moving from side to side. Yet she tells me, 'Come in, let's get you fixed up.'

I sit on the side of the tub in her small bathroom that notably gives no insight into who she is. It's as sterile as a doctors' surgery, which is fitting, because she cleans me up with stinging alcohol wipes and puts tape strips along a cut she tells me could use a stitch at the corner of my eye. Meanwhile, I hold a tea towel packed with ice against my fat lip.

She works in silence, and I don't dare speak and undo her patchwork, until she starts packing things back into her first aid kit. 'You should stop seeing yourself as two different people. There's the you from your past and the you now and it's okay that they're the same person. We can learn and grow and become different, better versions of ourselves.' She zips the bag shut and meets my eyes. 'The man sitting in front of me now wouldn't have changed anything, if it wasn't for the things he'd seen and done even yesterday.'

She gently takes control of the ice on my lip and peels it away, dropping the cubes into the sink and looping the tea towel over a heated rail to dry. 'When you're ready to let me in, I'll be here for all of it. The good, the bad and the downright chavvy.'

I give a short laugh, wincing as I feel a tug on my broken skin.

'But if you can't learn to love yourself, what chance do I have of you letting me love you?'

She presses a quick kiss to my temple on the side of my face that Jay hasn't messed up. I feel drained, exhausted, and I rest my head against her stomach as she holds me. I want to beg her to keep me here, in her arms, in the sanctity of her place, because I'm barely holding it together. I'm falling apart all over again.

She takes her first aid bag and leaves the room, leaving me sitting on the edge of the tub in my boxer shorts. Alone.

I'll be damned if I'm going to make her part of it. Damned if I'm going to let her see it. But she's going to have to be the one to walk away because I'm in so deep, there's no way out for me when it comes to her, the woman I've conjured up from my subconscious.

When I pull myself together enough to find her, she's made me a cup of tea and left out one of my own t-shirts that she's previously borrowed. My blood-stained jeans are already cycling in her washing machine. I feel guilty to be such a burden. A thug and a burden. So I decide not to tell her the outcome of the fight with Jay, that maybe, at some point down the line, I could see us being civil.

Maybe he's right. Scott might have found hard drugs from somewhere else, if not from Jay. He might still have become an addict; we were all guilty of that to some degree. But it doesn't excuse my failings in it all. I should have stopped it and I didn't.

Lyra and I drink tea, lounging on her sofa. She tells me she just hasn't got around to emptying her moving boxes yet, but I reckon there's something more to that story.

She shows me around her place, which is small but something she's proud of because it's hers and she pays for it with her own earnings. I get that.

The one room she doesn't let me inside is her dark room, even though I'd like to take a look and see her hobby. She has photographs developing and doesn't want to let in light that could contaminate the film and paper she uses. Since I have zero clue about this stuff, I don't push it.

Instead, we watch a movie and, though it's late when we go to bed, there's something I like too much about being in her room, in sheets that smell of her, in her house, to go to sleep.

We make love, slowly, gently, cautiously, and I hate that I can't kiss her with my beat-up lips. There's something about it that's different to every other time we've slept together. It feels heavy, loaded, as if our actions mask unwanted and unspoken conversations.

She falls asleep exactly where I like her to be, but I don't manage to. There are too many thoughts flying around in my head.

I think if I can just write it all down, I might be able to rest. So I slip out of bed and go in search of a pen and paper.

It's dark in her home but I've been awake for so long that my eyes have adjusted. I don't find paper and a pen but I do have a glass of water in her kitchen, where I find myself looking at more empty plant pots in her small yard through the window.

Then I remember the dark room. There's no light to upset anything right now, so I let myself inside the room, which is dimly lit by a red light, so faint my eyes would need to adjust if I hadn't already been up lying in the dark for hours.

And nothing could have prepared me for what I find in here...

Clipped along multiple rows of string, interspersed with handwritten notes, are pictures of me.

They aren't just pictures of me. Some recent, at Earl's Castle. Others that go way back.

I'm on stage with the band, with Scott, Trev and Jay. I recognise the stadium we played at in Madrid.

Then I see a picture that takes my breath away.

My dreams from a different perspective.

She was *there.*

That Night.

Seven years ago, she danced like a bird opposite me, she hung her head back and sang every lyric, and when I sang 'You and Me' directly to her, she took my picture.

This picture.

It was her, all along.

It was always her.

And the sight of it, the thought of it makes me stagger back, stumbling against the wall.

She knew.

All this time, she's known, and she hasn't mentioned it. Not once.

We were supposed to meet.

We were about to meet.

Then she ran, and set in train the beginning of the end.

If I hadn't followed her That Night. If I hadn't had my head so far up my arse after she left that I didn't want to stay out and party with the lads...

Scott would never have taken Class A drugs for the first time.

We would have met. Lyra and me.

The world would have been different. *Everything* could have been different.

She knew.

And she's hidden it from me for five months.

My vision is blurring, somewhere between subconscious and reality, semi-lucid, and when it comes into focus, I scan the pictures of me from this summer. They start back at the hen party in April and walk through the wedding season at Earl's Castle like a storyboard.

I move in closer to read the notes clipped next to each picture, and I read the handwritten text. Quotes. Snippets of... *an article? The fallen rock star*, she's written. And words like *rock bottom* and *unloved* leap out at me from the pegged pages.

This is what she's wanted all along. She wants to be a documentary photographer and I'm her source and subject.

All the crap she's told me about wanting me to open up, so that she can love me. It's all been about this.

Just another person who wants to use me for financial gain.

'I can explain,' she says in the dark space with me, her voice quiet across my shoulder. Her presence makes this all more real.

She doesn't love me.

She used me.

'It doesn't matter, Lyra,' I tell her with as little energy as I feel. 'None of this matters.'

I leave the room without looking at her, head to the bathroom and pull on my jeans that are now clean and dry on the towel rail, and make to walk back out of her life.

'I found an old film in one of my university boxes that I'd never developed and it happened to have pictures from a night The Hand Me Downs played in Newcastle seven years ago.'

I turn sharply to face her. 'And the recent ones?'

Her forehead creases, as if she's surprised by my asking. 'You know I take pictures of you, Guy. Of you, of everything I see and do. I take pictures of us.'

'And the article notes? Do you write those about yourself, too? Are you going to try to document your life story? The fallen rock star, Lyra. That's what you wrote about me.'

'Those scribbles mean nothing, Guy. You know that's what I do. I can show you hundreds of notes and articles I've written about people I find interesting.'

I scoff as I pull on my boots. 'No, Lyra, those notes are different. What's your end game? Sell the unprecedented first-hand account of my life story? Tell me, did you start writing about me before or after those fucking videos went viral and everything started blowing up again?'

'Do you hear yourself?' She's shouting. Something I haven't heard on her yet. Raised voice, a bite in her tone, both to match mine. 'I didn't kiss you at Charlotte's hen party for the right reasons but the attraction between us was real, before I even knew who you were. I didn't sleep with you because you used to be a rock star. I slept with you because of the man you are now, today. But I don't see two versions of you, I see one incredible man, who's been influenced by music all his life. Who *loves* music, and has it running through his veins, and who hides away because he feels a guilt he shouldn't own.'

I'm not listening to this bullshit. I turn my back on her and twist the key in her front door, needing to get out of here, away from her.

'You didn't kill your brother, Guy; drugs did.'

Her words still me, the door partially open and the cool night's air blowing inside, making me shiver.

'Despite what you want everyone else to think, you didn't force Scott to take drugs, either. *He* did that. Not you.'

'*You* weren't there, Lyra,' I grind out through my teeth. '*You* don't get to tell me what is or isn't true or right.' I open the door wider. I'm going. But first, I do a one-eighty to look at her, wishing I hadn't when I see hunched shoulders, glazed eyes by the light of the moon in the near-black hallway. 'Scott would never've been in a band if it weren't for me. He would never've been the frontman of The Hand Me Downs. And if I'd been there for him properly, he never would've taken drugs.'

I walk into the night, down the pathway towards my car, her next words falling on my back. 'Yes, Guy, he would. With you, without you, he was talented. With or without you, he would have turned to drugs. The setting might have been different, the circumstances changed, but things in life don't just happen.'

I want to say, by the same token, *I saw you and never met you that night for a reason, and I found you again in a lift going to a hen party that neither one of us wanted to be at, yet you decided not to tell me that it had been you all along. That didn't just happen.* But it sounds trivial when we're arguing about Scott's death. So I don't. Instead, I shake the thought from my head, dragging a hand through my hair, fingers gripping so tightly onto the roots, it's a welcome pain.

'If there can ever be anything between us, you have to show me all of you, Guy, the broken bits and the best bits. You have to love yourself before you can love me.'

'And what about *you*, Lyra? Do you love yourself? Do you love your life? Have you ever fought for something you want?

Because as far as I can tell, you're trapped as the person your parents and sister and the idiots who used to be your friends see you as. Maybe you need to accept that you are like them, but you don't have to be a doctor and that's fucking okay because you have a life of your own to live. Right now, you're wasting it hiding away in a place you don't want to live, writing articles you'll never even try to publish, denying yourself anything that might make you happy because you want to punish yourself for something that was never your fault. You're living in a bubble. Too terrified or naïve to pop it.'

'Are you calling me out or yourself? Because from where I'm standing, if that's true, I'm looking at my own reflection.'

'I'm not doing this, Lyra.' I open my car door. 'I knew this was a bad idea from the off. It should've never started. I'm on my own because I'm better that way. Without all this extra shit.'

She's walked down the path, halfway between her house and me. 'Shit like feelings? Is that what you're hiding from? Is that why you're driving me away?'

'Lyra, believe me, I've done nothing but fucking feel for years and I'm exhausted. I've got nothing left for myself or anyone. Definitely not this.'

'So you're walking away over an article, over some pictures? Hurting me just so you can give yourself another reason to leave?'

'No.' I make the mistake of looking at her right as she swipes a knuckle under her eyes, and if there was any piece of my heart that hadn't been broken before, it just broke now. 'I'm not walking. I'm running.' Because this is all too much for me to take.

'Fuck you, Guy,' she spits. A version of her I haven't witnessed. A version of her I've brought out by hurting her.

'Race away from me and keep going until you make me just another bottle of something you wanted to drink once. Another cigarette you'll never smoke.'

She goes back to her house and that's exactly what I do. I leave thinking I could really use a drink, knowing I won't let myself have one but really fucking wanting one.

It's only when I'm halfway home that it dawns on me that her dad's stroke was That Night. And That Night, she was at my gig. I'd invited her backstage.

The reason she ran, the reason we never met, was because her dad had a stroke.

And I just threw it in her face like the absolute twat I am.

If there's one good thing I can do by her, it's to keep driving.

31

LYRA

September 2025

One and a Half Weeks Until My Sister's Wedding

I used my sister's hen party – an all-day spa in Northumberland – as an excuse not to cover the Stroud wedding last weekend. As it turns out, Mandy told me Guy didn't show anyway, and one of Dave's other singers replaced him.

I'm sure the Strouds were disappointed but hey, every wedding has a glitch, and they still ended up as husband and husband by the end of the day, so all's well that ends well... for some people.

Meanwhile, my sister asked me today if I intend to bring Guy as my plus one during the day at her wedding because she needs to submit the final table plan to Earl's Castle. So I told her honestly, 'I don't know. Though, given I haven't heard anything from him since our blow-up a week ago, my best guess is no.'

And when she turned my hurt into panic about *her*, that

Guy needs to turn up because he's supposed to be performing on her wedding night, I told her, 'He's a professional. He'll be there.'

Honestly, I hope he doesn't drop her in it but I just don't know.

Tonight, Mum has been held up at the hospital, so I came over to my parents' house to make Dad's dinner but, in truth, I'm happy to be here with company.

Dad has insisted that he load the dishwasher tonight, since I roasted a chicken and made us both Caesar salad. I'm sitting in the hideaway on my piano stool, occasionally striking a note, mostly staring into space, trying not to help Dad every time I hear a dish fall too heavily into the machine.

I've started playing Coldplay's 'Sky Full of Stars', falling into the tune after playing the same few chords on repeat.

Dad near shocks the life out of me when he appears in the doorway. None of my family come in here these days.

'Keep playing,' he tells me, coming to sit into the wing-back chair closest to me. 'I always liked listening to you play.' He speaks slowly, steadily, thinking about each word and forming it as best he can, which is pretty good these days, especially considering he was close to non-verbal at one point.

When I'm finished the song, I stop, hands on my thighs, staring at the sheet music in front of me.

'Play me something from the man who's put the biggest smile on your face that I've seen in as long as I can remember.'

I breathe in, not sure if I want to, knowing I'll do it because Dad has asked. Also knowing that I don't need sheet music for a few of Guy's songs, not least because I've been teaching him to play them himself recently.

So I play, and in my tone-deaf voice, I sing intermittently

too, mostly in the choruses. When I stop, Dad asks, 'Why are you sad?'

Sighing, I close the lid on the piano and shuffle on the seat to face him. 'We had a fight. Probably *the* fight. I haven't heard from him since.'

'I'm sorry to hear that,' he tells me. 'But in my experience, couples only fight over things they care about.'

'I'm not so sure, Dad.'

He pats the arm of the chair and I go to sit by him.

'Tell me about him.'

'He swears too much. He dropped out of school when he was sixteen. He grew up in a council house in Jarrow. And he's a wedding entertainer with no clear view of what his next step is in life.

'His band was... Well, you know how much I loved The Hand Me Downs. But he's broke now because he gave all his money to other people. He carries the weight of the world on his shoulders so that others don't have to.'

I glance down to find Dad smiling at me.

'And he's the most talented, incredible man,' I admit. 'He makes me feel like I could be anyone and go anywhere, do anything.' *Pierce my bubble*, I think. 'He makes me dizzy with how much I want to be near him even when I can't get any closer to him. He's perfectly imperfect.'

Then I tell him about the fight, spilling it all until there's nothing left to say.

Dad nods. Just *nods*. Choosing now to revert back to being a man of few words, when I've basically just poured my heart out about the man I'm in love with. Who I've screwed everything up with.

Dad squeezes my hand where it rests on my leg. 'Lyra, I pretended to myself when you lived here that you weren't babysitting me but now that you've moved out, I know that's what you're doing. I love you, but do you know how undignified it feels to be watched over by your daughter? I'm a grown man. My issues are my own and I don't need to be hand-held through life.'

'Dad, I—'

'Don't deny it. It is possible that Guy wants to stand on his own two feet before he lets you carry his load.'

'What are you saying, Yoda?'

'Don't give up on him yet.'

I lean my head against his and sigh.

'Also, I've asked your mum to retire, at last,' he says. 'Life's too short to work this hard for this long and I'd like to spend some time with her, doing things we've always wanted to do.' He shifts to kiss my scalp. 'I suggest you do the same.'

'That'd be great, Dad, if I actually knew what that was.'

'I think you do know, you have just stopped yourself from wanting it. You knew when you dropped out of medicine, then life got in the way of your dreams. It's time for us both to move on now.' *Sweetheart.*

Half an hour later, Dad insists I stay downstairs whilst he settles himself to bed upstairs, and I pick up a notepad and paper.

After breakfast the next day, I choose one of my favourite photographs from my dark room at home. At work, in the studio, I frame it and wrap the whole thing in brown paper. Then I type and print my article about Guy and stick it to the front in an envelope marked *Guy* on one side, and on the other, *If you want to know what my article would have said, this is it. If not, don't open it, but the picture is a gift. I want you to keep it.*

I deposit it against the wall beneath Guy's mailbox and walk away from his apartment building.

32

GUY

September 2025
The Greatest Gift

'Then she left me the best gift anyone has ever given me. It's a photograph of Scott and me, laughing on stage together, really laughing. She took it That Night. Before the shit hit the fan. I've never seen it before. She left it by my mailbox with her article taped to it... The things she says about me in it are...'

I'm standing in the window of my therapist's office in London. I've driven down because being spotted has become as frequent as it used to be and, frankly, the petrol was cheaper than a train ticket. Jon has given me an emergency appointment on a Saturday because I basically begged him for one.

He's sitting in his usual leather armchair, one leg casually resting on his other, as if I'm not having a complete meltdown two metres away from him.

'You don't believe them?' Jon asks.

'No one would believe them.' There's a tree beyond the

window and it's blowing in the wind. A green leaf breaks loose and seems to glide from side to side like a feather before landing on the lawn of the kept garden in Fitzrovia.

'What are you so afraid of, Guy?'

I respond whilst watching a young boy play with a man, most likely his dad, in the garden, kicking a ball between them, and I think of Matty. Of the footballs he'll never kick with Scott.

'At this point, I'm scared of getting addicted to my own fucking shadow,' I tell him.

'Lots of people have addictive personalities. Motivated people, driven people. Normal people. The trick is to channel your addictions in a healthy way.'

I reposition myself, back against the old Georgian sash windows, water glass in hand, focusing on Jon and the calmness of his voice.

'You go to the gym every day; you just need to make sure you're going to stay healthy and to focus energy in the right way. By the same token, you can let yourself fall in love. You can love her harder than you love anything else in your life. But you need to remember who you are without her, who you want to be with her, and that you don't want to stifle or lose either of yourselves.'

'I don't want to need her. I don't want to mess with her.'

'That's all in your gift, Guy. I've seen what you've come through, as a young man and as a grown man. I reckon you can do anything you put your mind to. Including loving and respecting Lyra in the right way.'

I hate the way my body reacts to his words, the way it excites at the thought of us somehow making things work, that I can love her. And, hell, that she could love me.

'Try to relax and go with it. Talk to her. Communicate.'

I scoff. 'That might be a problem, since I haven't spoken to her or even messaged her since I yelled in her face and walked out on her for doing... absolutely nothing wrong, other than preying on my own demons, inadvertently.'

I like that Jon doesn't sugarcoat anything. He doesn't push back when I admonish myself. It reminds me of Lyra, actually. The way she sits back and listens, doesn't push a view on me that I haven't formed myself.

'If she's the right girl for you, she wants to make this work. She'll be afraid, too. Of feelings, of getting hurt. We all are, Guy. Shadows can be scary. But we want the sun to shine, so we work with the shaded patches.'

I smirk around my glass as I take a sip of cool water. 'Can I steal that for my next record?'

'Will you give me royalties?'

'Mate, I can barely afford to pay you for today.'

We share the joke.

'I've seen the interesting choice of car you've driven here in. What's the deal with that?'

I chuckle again. 'Dave's daughter's. I'm borrowing it whilst she's doing what young lasses should be doing at twenty years old – travelling and living her best life.'

Lyra wasn't, it occurs to me. Lyra was too busy doing exactly what I do – wearing guilt, doing what other people needed her to be doing.

But not That Night, before she slipped from my grasp.

'Where did you go then?' Jon asks, zoning me back into the room.

'To That Night,' I tell him truthfully. 'The thing that's scared me the most, I think, in all of this mess. It's hard to compute that I could've met Lyra on the night when everything started to go wrong. Is that a bad omen? Should I look back and think it was a good thing? It's blurred lines and confused me. You know uncertainty and me don't mix.'

'You always see that night as negative. The night it all started to go wrong,' Jon says. 'Can I put something to you? What if that night was a great one – on the cusp of all your dreams coming true, the band happy, your brother happy, and you're about to meet a girl full of possibility? Life changed because all those things started being pulled from under you one by one against your will.'

'The thing is, I don't know if I want them back. Not without Scott.' I bring myself to sit in the chair opposite Jon's. 'This isn't rock bottom. I found that at the bottom of a bottle. Anything better is a bonus. But I don't know if I need all that noise. I don't know if I want it all. How do I even know for sure that I can cope with it? Especially without Scott.'

'What do you want, Guy?'

I don't miss a beat as I tell him, 'Lyra.'

'Then go get her. Sacrifice yourself on the altar of dignity and get her back. But remember, she's only human. As much as you want to put her on a pedestal you can't reach, she's going to mess up sometimes, too. That's what humans do. You need to give her the freedom to get things wrong and not run into the wind every time she does, or you do. You're sitting here asking me how to love her and my advice is, ask her. Ask her how she wants to be loved.'

We talk for another ten minutes or so, me mindful that as much as I like Jon, I'm paying for his time, or rather, Dave is today.

He walks me outside to my Barbiemobile and fondles her lashes.

'Steady, lad, she's shy,' I tell him.

'You know, we'd need a whole other session on this but

you could consider stopping giving all your money away. You've punished yourself enough for things that were never your fault.'

* * *

I don't realise I'm driving to Matty's house in North Finchley until I'm sitting in my car outside his mum's terrace, watching Matty and Lou move around inside.

I've stunned myself enough by being here, so why not get out of the car and really set my head into a spin?

When Lou answers the door, she says, 'I was wondering if you were going to come in.' She starts walking inside and surprise at her lack of animosity makes me falter before following. 'Nice wheels, by the way. Swish.'

People need to leave my car alone. Poor girl.

I follow Lou to the kitchen and freeze when I see Matty sitting at their kitchen island, eating a yoghurt, which has dropped all down his front.

I freeze because, 'He looks just like Scott.'

Lou smiles softly, gently, as if there's nothing but love still there for my brother. 'Yeah, he does.'

'Daddy?' Matty asks.

'Yes, baby,' Lou responds. 'And do you know who this is, Matty? Do you remember?'

Matty shakes his head and though it's obvious he wouldn't remember me, given I haven't seen him since before he could even crawl, I'm gutted.

'This is Daddy's brother. Uncle Guy.'

'Uncle?' Matty asks, and Lou nods.

I end up spending a couple of hours with them, mostly

playing football (sort of) with Matty in their small garden, and it's fucking awesome.

'He's such a great kid,' I tell Lou.

'He is. He reminds me so much of Scott, too.'

I come to sit with her at the outdoor patio table. 'Would it be okay if I saw you both sometimes? I'd really like to.'

'We'd love that.'

Then I tell her about Matty's trust and the seven-figure sum amassed for him from my royalties. 'I'm gonna give you control, so you can get him whatever he needs whenever he needs it,' I tell Lou, who hasn't uttered a word since I told her about the money.

'Guy, I don't know what to say, I— Are you sure?'

'It's the least I can do.' But as I say those words, I try to remember Jon's, too. I've got to stop punishing myself. And that's why, after today, I'll take my royalties back and maybe stock my food cupboards with something other than baked beans.

I say goodbye to Matty with a ball of emotion in my throat and tears in my eyes that threaten to fall when he hugs me – not because he presses strawberry yoghurt into my white T-shirt, but because I absolutely adore him. My nephew. My brother's son. Scott's doppelganger.

They walk me out to my car and Lou hugs me in a way that tells me honestly, she doesn't resent me or blame me, and it's *that* hug that finally makes me pull on my sunglasses to cover my tears.

Unable to hide the weakness in my voice, I tell her, 'When Matty's ready, I've been keeping his Dad's Gibson for him.'

* * *

Three days after getting my head closer to straight and my finances more like a functioning human being's, I finally agree to Dave's request to get me, Trev and Jay in the same room again.

When I walk into the living room at his and Kylie's place, the lads are already there, sitting around the sofas and chairs. Kylie's latest sofas and chairs – she loves upgrading the house décor.

I'm not sure what I'm expecting from Jay's reaction to me or my own to him, honestly, but when I see him, there's not the level of hostility there was before we had it out on the beach.

I don't know that we've said our last words to each other on the subject but I think I'd like to draw a line under it all and finally try, or start trying, to move on.

The lads and I give our usual short hello and before I take a pew next to Trev on the leather two-seater, Kylie comes through from the kitchen, holding a baby with a shock of dark hair, like Trev's, and a brand new, chubby and sort of squishy face – cute in a fugly way, like a pug.

'Here's yer Uncle Guy, babba,' Kylie says, cradling the baby in her arms.

'Meet Katie,' Trev says, chest puffed out and full of pride, as he should be.

'You're a cutie, aren't you, girlie?' I say as Kylie hands the baby over to me, indifferent to whether I'm terrified of holding a miniature human or not.

But you know, she's okay snuggled against my chest, curled like a seahorse. She smells like baby, whatever babies smell like, and she's a warm bundle of undeniable cuteness.

'Congratulations, mate, she's a little belta,' I tell Trev.

I hug Tally when she appears from the kitchen. The whole scene brings Lyra back to the forefront of my mind.

After handing Katie to her mam, I sit down next to Trev, where Dave adopts a kind of Chair of the Band role.

I know why we're all here, of course. We're talking about a reunion, or just a coming back together – the band minus one. Minus our frontman. A thought that wrecks me.

At the same time, I can't deny how good it's felt to pick up the guitar again and, even though I was playing other people's songs, to play for a crowd again. To be writing, letting everything I feel and am too inarticulate to say in conversation spill out of me onto pages, as easy as knocking over a drink.

The only part I'm not enjoying is the same piece I never did like – the encroachment on my privacy. That's for me to work out, to deal with differently this time. But we all have demons, and that's why I tell the lads...

'If we do this, we do it right this time. We do it for as long as we're happy and if we're told *no*, fuck 'em, we walk away. We've never been in it for fame and fortune, lads, and we need to remember that.'

Trev and Jay respond by chanting, 'Wallace', which is a random *Braveheart* movie reference from our touring days but also quite funny. I guess I am giving something of a pre-war speech.

Once I've tossed sofa cushions at them and Dave has scurried to pick them up, telling us, 'Not the new ones, lads. She'll kill us,' we settle back into our conversation.

'Wives, kids, they come along for the ride this time,' I tell them. 'All of us in it together.'

'For my two penneth,' Dave starts, 'I think having something else, something more, is a good thing. You lads didn't have anything to root you last time. It's easy to forget what really matters when nothing else does.'

He's right. And I think, finally, I'm ready for some roots, but not the kind that tie you down and drain everything you have to give. The kind you want to come home to after a long, sweaty night on stage or two weeks on the road.

'We'll be the only sober rock band topping the charts,' Jay says, only half in jest.

I let out a short laugh too, then rub the jaw I really need to shave and tell him seriously, 'We do it for the love of it or we don't do it at all, because I've seen rock bottom and I don't wanna go there again.'

'Same,' Jay says.

'D'you know what's different this time, though?' I ask rhetorically. 'I also know that if I get there, I can come back.' I look to Dave. 'With a few helping hands.'

He nods, leaning across to thump me on my back.

'We're stronger. Older. Wiser. Greying and wrinkling,' Trev says. 'But we still know how to put a record together.'

I wonder whether Scott is listening in on this and telling us he's still a spring chick, suspended in time, free of character lines and grey flecks. 'We still need a frontman, though,' I say, stating the obvious.

'We've been turning you into a frontman for an entire wedding season, matey,' Dave says.

Trev shrugs. 'You always were the leader in my eyes.'

'Second that,' Jay adds.

'None of that,' I tell them, wondering whether I have what it takes to talk to a crowd, to entertain in a way that came naturally to my kid brother. 'We're all equal.'

'I'm in,' Jay says.

'Me too,' Trev adds.

'And I'll manage ya lads, if ya want,' Dave tells us.

''Course we do, you dafty,' I tell him, tossing another sofa cushion his way. 'I do have an idea, though. Dave, do you have the number for the violinist and the cello player from your string quartet?'

'Aye. Why?'

'Before we do anything else, I'm gonna need a favour, lads.'

33

LYRA

September 2025
Livy's Wedding

The morning has passed in the same frenzied way most weddings do. Usually, I'm photographing the chaos but today, I'm in the thick of it, as Mandy takes the official pictures of my sister's big day.

Livy, her four bridesmaids – including me – Mum, Mandy, two hair stylists and a make-up artist are all packed into the bridal suite at Earl's Castle. It's funny, seeing it from the perspective of a guest, and I'm surprised how easy it's been to switch off from my day job and enjoy the build-up of it.

I've been enjoying it, or parts of it at least. Livy let me do my own make-up and there was very little the stylist could do with my hair except stick a pretty bridal clip in the back. If it wasn't for the fancy blue silk dress that I'd never wear, that's lower cut than I remember at both the back and the front, I'd feel reasonably like myself.

Livy looks incredible. I know it's cliché but she does look

the best she's looked in her life – hair in flawless, glossy waves, her face perfectly contoured, a dress that makes her look like a glamorously chic princess. Above all of that is the sparkling beam she's worn all morning, only faltering now as she's photographed holding her bouquet. It's clear the enormity of the day she marries the man she loves is dawning on her and it's... nice. I love her, I love them. And, yes, the old story about how Joshua preferred her over me is still one that's been over-told but honestly, I'm pleased he did. Livy and Joshua will be perfect together.

The only moments of today that I'm not enjoying are when my mind drifts to Guy and the fact we still haven't spoken since the night he found my pictures and the notes I'd written about him.

Maybe I got it wrong. Maybe I shouldn't have written the article and left it by his mailbox. Perhaps giving him a picture of him and his brother was a step too far. It was the image I loved, of them sharing a joke together, brothers before band-mates. But I can see how it could have been invasive. How writing the article, no matter the content and what my intentions had been, my attempt to show him how in awe of him I am, might have been perceived as doing exactly what he hates – exposing him, even if it was for his eyes only.

The thing is, I'd like to put it all out of my mind, at least for today, and be present, be here, focused on helping Livy have the very best day. But I can't because Guy is supposed to be the evening's entertainment and I have no idea if he's going to turn up. I doubt it.

So once Mandy is finished and tells Livy that she'll next see her downstairs for the ceremony, I slip outside the bridal suite and ask my friend, 'Has he arrived to set up?'

'No. I'm sorry, Lyra.'

'Sorry, Lyra, like you know he isn't coming? Or sorry, Lyra, like you just haven't seen him or Dave drop off any equipment yet but maybe they're doing the set-up later when the room is switched around?'

She twists her mouth. 'Sorry like Dave's dropped off equipment. Lots of it. It looks like one of his bands'll be stepping in for Guy.'

I drag in a breath and try to hold my back straight when really I feel like a deflated balloon, the last bit of helium turning my voice unnaturally bright. 'That's good. Dave's come through. I can stop worrying.' I force a grin but the expression Mandy wears tells me I'm not fooling her.

* * *

The ceremony goes off without a hitch – no one passes out, or pukes down Livy's dress, and at the end of it, my sister has married her best friend.

My dad hands me a tissue afterwards and I try not to smudge my mascara before the group pictures Mandy takes outside. I'd love to pretend my waterworks are entirely to do with rainbows, unicorns and happily ever afters, but I think that's a cover for the fact I'm going to take a seat on Table One alone. Alone because I don't have a plus one.

I'm fixing Livy's dress for a shot of her tossing her bouquet in the same place I have snapped countless brides, at the top of the palatial stone steps between the lawn and the towering castle, when Mum tells her, 'She's here.'

'Oh my goodness! She made it!' Livy says, undoing all my hard work as she grabs my hand and hotfoots it down the steps – remarkably steady in the high heels she'll swap for flats later – dragging me after her.

'Who made what?' I'm asking as I'm tugged along.

'It's time for your bridesmaid gift,' she says.

'Isn't it me who's supposed to give you a gift at this stage in the day?'

She's still dragging me through slightly uncertain onlookers, towards the gravel driveway, where a black cab is parked.

The door opens and I'm waiting for the punchline, flanked by Mum and Livy. 'Happy My Wedding Day, little sis,' Livy says, hugging me. 'Thank you for all your help making today extra special.'

'A little something of thanks from Dad and me, too,' Mum says, handing me an envelope.

Dad has stick-hobbled over too and I'm not sure if I'm supposed to be watching the cab or opening the envelope, until Mum tells me, 'Go on then, open it.'

Watching them suspiciously, I tear open the envelope and find two tickets. 'Flights?' Then I read the details on them. 'To Brazil?' I see my name on the top ticket, then move it to expose a second. 'With Cami?'

Now I see who steps out of the black cab and Dad hangs an arm around my shoulder, whispering, 'It's time to do things you want to do.'

Step out of my bubble. I kiss his cheek, then run to Cami, almost bowling her over as we both squeal, 'We're going to Brazil?' and, simultaneously, 'You're coming to Brazil with me!'

And if I had only looked at the table plan, I would have seen, in the seat right next to mine, is Cami Withers.

My family might get on my nerves sometimes but God, I'd bury a body for them and I know they'd do the same for me. I need to find my voice with them; I'm working on it. But I'm bloody lucky, too.

* * *

Cami and I eat and drink and catch up about our summers, getting excited about Cami showing me around Brazil. When she asks about my night at The Arctic Monkeys, I let the wine take over and absolutely spill my guts about Guy. How I messed up. How he messed up. How, basically, we're screwed.

Then I cry listening to Dad make a short but stunningly beautiful speech, and I have tears of laughter streaming down my face listening to Joshua's best men. Their jokes are close to the bone in places and feel a bit like karma for that time Josh ditched me for my sister.

And it's okay. I'm fine. Better than fine. It's just that, 'I miss him,' I tell Cami when we're taking a break from wine, pacing ourselves, hanging out in the toilets for some reason. I'm sitting on a chaise longue, giving my feet a rest from being in heels all day, and Cami is sitting on the side of the marble sinks, as if we're on a night out at uni, only in much fancier clothes.

'I'm not going to get sad on my sister's wedding day but... I...' Sighing, I accept a tissue from Cami – *garghhhhh*, what is it about weddings making everyone emotional? 'I've never felt like I do when I'm with him. Like I could be anyone, do anything, go anywhere. He's the antithesis of me in so many ways and my mirror image in others. And it's so stupid and cliché but part of me thought that if I loved him the right way, it would be enough to make him... *urgh*, I don't know.'

'Change?' she offers.

'No. Yes. Not *change*. I love who he is. Just... open up and take a chance. I thought it was happening, I'm sure it was. Then I blew it. I should have told him about that night when we saw The Hand Me Downs in Newcastle. I guess I thought he'd see me as some kind of super fan or groupie and that's not who I am. Then time passed and it became impossible to tell him. Plus, *he* didn't remember me, so I couldn't have expected it to be a big deal to him. Could I?'

'You kind of were a super fan, though,' Cami adds, making me chuckle, against the odds.

'Yeah, I was. I *am*. But my point is, I didn't want him to think I fell in love with a rock star, rather than everything else he is. Then I showed him the exact opposite anyway.'

'He also sounds like he massively overreacted, Ly. He ran scared and unless he comes back, cap in hand, with a gesture like something out of the movies, I'd say *he's* the one who messed up.'

I blow my nose less than gracefully and toss the tissue into the bronze bin. 'We both did.'

Cami hops down from the sink. 'Right. Enough wallowing and self-pity; I'm supposed to be bringing the party.' She checks her phone from inside her clutch bag. 'And the party should be getting started by now, so let's end this wine hiatus and get to the free bar, shall we?'

I smile. Some things never change. 'Let me just take a wee and I'll meet you out there.'

'Ly, we've been in here for thirty minutes; why haven't you had a wee yet?'

'I only just realised I need one.'

I do the deed and Lyra heads to the bar. Once I'm done, I tidy my face with a make-up retouch and get ready to dance.

In the mirror, I see Mandy and Cami push through the bathroom door together.

'Lyra, you need to get out here,' Cami says.

'You're gonna wanna see this,' Mandy adds.

Frowning, but also weirdly vibing their shared excitement,

I follow them to the wedding reception, stilling at the back of the room as soon as I see the man standing in the middle of the stage, a full set of lights on him. A drummer and guitarist I recognise are backing him up, and on stage with them, a violinist and a cello player.

Despite being a full room length away, I know Guy Walker of The Hand Me Downs is looking my way when he tells the room, 'This one's called "Addicted".'

My heart thuds as Trev strikes the first note on his electric guitar. My stomach tightens as Jay pounds the foot pedal against his base drum. And my lungs fill sharply when Guy strums the first chord on his Martin. My hand comes to my mouth as I comprehend the enormity of what I'm seeing on stage.

'Oh my God!' Livy crashes into me, rocking me backwards so hard it takes both Mandy and Cami to keep us upright. 'You've played it cool all day, all *week*, and all along, you knew he was coming. You brought The Hand Me Downs to my wedding!'

'Nice one, sis,' Joshua says, patting my arm, which even in my discombobulated state, I know feels weird. 'We owe you big time for this.'

'Ah, you're welcome?' I manage.

As my sister drags my teen ex and new man-aged brother-in-law – totally bizarre – off to the dance floor, I'm left staring at the band on stage as a violinist that never used to be part of the arrangement kicks in to 'Addicted'.

It's The Hand Me Downs, the same music and lyrics I've known and loved for years, only different. Not better or worse, just new, modified.

'You had absolutely no idea this was happening, did you?'

Cami asks, flanking me at one side as Mandy, camera raised, stands at my other.

'None,' I admit.

But he showed up. He showed up in a bigger way than I could have imagined and the piece of me that thinks there's a chance he did this for me, at least in part, is whooshed back to Cloud Nine like the slide of Trev's foot against his wah-wah pedal.

'Is it okay if I'm massively crushing on your boyfriend?' Cami asks, making Mandy and me laugh.

'You'd better get used to people pining after your man, babes,' Mandy tells me.

As reluctant as I am to let myself hope, as much as I ought to protect myself, I fall even harder, even deeper for the man singing into the microphone with the voice I fell for more than a decade ago.

'Let's dance!' Cami yells, dragging me, running, into the crowd of people dancing and videoing what's happening on stage – the reunion of The Hand Me Downs. The rebirth of three rock stars – and two of a string quartet.

Guy watches me as I come into his field of vision and though he's singing words to another track, one that has nothing to do with him or us or even relationships, I know he's apologising.

Who knows what happens when he comes off stage but right now, my parents are making their way to the dance floor. My sister is married. I'm jumping around with Cami with an aeroplane ticket to start exploring the world in my clutch bag.

For the first time since That Night, I let my head fall back, hold my arms out wide, and move free and easy, liberated, like a bird. Happy.

My bridesmaid dress is sticking to me and there's as much

sweat in my hair as there is running down Guy's face and wetting his T-shirt.

The music stops while he takes a drink and Dave tosses him a towel.

Refreshed, he steps up to the microphone and says, 'Bear with me folks, I'm still working on this standing at the front and talking thing.'

I give him a gentle smile as the rest of the room catches his joke because I know it's not only a wisecrack for the crowd but genuine. He's trying. This is new to him. He adjusts his fingers on his fret board and starts gently thumbing the strings on his guitar, a move that seems to help his confidence.

Then he looks up to me, staring so deeply into my eyes, I feel like he's engraving lyrics on my soul.

'We're gonna bring it down a notch with a slow one.' He pauses and I can hear expectation in the room, despite the pounding of my own heart in my ears, because I know what comes next on his set list. It's 'You and Me'. My song. Our song. From That Night.

But he says, 'This is a new one. You're getting the first rodeo.' He clears his throat, his fingers still working his strings. 'I wrote this one for the woman who's responsible for making me fall back in love with music, life and her.' He nods, eyes on me, and I think he's telling me, *Yes. You.*

I'm rooted to the spot despite everyone else seeming to partner up and move slowly around me. I wouldn't miss them if they weren't here because when Guy starts to sing, it's only to me. There's only him and me.

'Move aside dark mood,
You've been around long enough.
And I've found your antidote,

The girl to fix me.

'She says she's not a doctor,
But she's the only one,
To save me from drowning,
And keep my head above water.

'Come into my world,
Let me into yours.
Teach me how to love you,
Like it's the last night of our lives.

'I saw you seven years ago,
And let you slip through my grasp.
Then I kissed you,
On the summer solstice.
And you know I won't,
Make the same mistake again.

'Come into my world,
Let me into yours,
Teach me how to love you,
Like it's the last night of our lives.

'Now I'm gone,
No going back.
Take my hand,
Let's fly together.

'Come into my world,
Let me into yours,
Teach me how to love you,

Like it's the last night of our lives.'

At the end of the song, it's not sweat running down my face but tears, *again*.

He whispers into his microphone, 'I love you,' then leaves the other musicians on the stage to play an instrumental as he hops down to the dance floor, to me.

His palms meet my cheeks and he runs his thumbs under my eyes. 'I'm sorry. I got scared and I blew it. Again. But I swear, if you'll have me, I'm gonna do my best not to fuck up at every bump in the road, Lyra.'

My fingers find his wet hair, which is just about the only response I can muster in this moment.

'There're gonna be times I need you to tell me where I'm going wrong. I might need you to show me how to love you properly, fully, without limitation. Can you promise me that, Lyra? Because I will mess up and I don't want to ruin this. I want to love you every day as much as I love you today. And I want to be someone you can love back.'

With every single part of me feeling as if I'm melting into him, I inch closer, our wet foreheads touching with zero shits given. 'I'm going to get this wrong, too, Guy. I already have, and for my part, I'm sorry. But I want this. I want us. And I'm ready to fight for it.'

His lips break into a smile and mine respond reflexively, doing the same, when he says, 'I really fucking love you, Lyra.'

'I really fucking love you too, Guy.'

34

LYRA

September 2027

The Last UK Gig of the World Tour

I check the time on my phone again from the back of the luxury car Guy sent to pick me up in London and drive me back up to Sunderland.

Ironically, he said the national rail system is too unreliable and he wanted me to see the final concert in the UK leg of The Hand Me Downs's World Tour. It's another sell-out show at the Stadium of Light and if I'm not there in thirty-seven minutes, I'll miss the start, because we've hit more road works and bumper-to-bumper traffic on the motorways than Guy's eaten my Yorkshire puddings.

'How long is the satnav saying?' I ask the driver again, foot bouncing against the floormat.

His name's Ed and he's driven me around enough times now that I don't have to spend the entire journey making polite conversation. Which is great because I've worked myself up into a giant ball of stress.

It's the Stadium of Light. Sunderland. Their home crowd – for all except the new guitarist who's from Manchester. I haven't been to every gig on the tour because I've been travelling for my own work, but I know tonight is important to the band, to Guy especially.

I want to support him in the way he does me. I wouldn't have even been in London today if it hadn't been for Guy sharing the crazy article I wrote about him two years ago with a contact at *Rock On the Edge,* the fastest growing music magazine in the *world.*

I'd never intended that article to be for anyone's eyes except Guy's. All I'd wanted was to show him how much I loved him, how inspired by his music and in awe of his strength I was, still am, every single day.

It was days after my sister's wedding when my now editor – one of them because I'm freelance – called me and said he'd read my article. He asked if he could publish it as the first exclusive interview Guy Walker had given since his brother died.

Despite the enormity of the opportunity, I'd refused to sell the story. It won't ever be for anyone else to read, only Guy.

But I had said I'd write him another one. An interview with original photographs. The first official comeback story for The Hand Me Downs.

So far as my career goes, the rest is history. I spend my days photographing people and places, in new countries, across continents, creating the kind of stories I've always wanted to write.

I spend as many nights as possible with Guy, listening to the voice I'll never tire of, singing lyrics I'll never stop feeling in the depths of me.

And I wake up all the mornings I can in the arms of the

man I am still, nine years on from the first time he asked me to meet him, utterly besotted with.

'Five more minutes,' Ed tells me.

'Are you coming in tonight?'

'I'll drop you first, then park and come inside.'

Every show, the band has a huge suite and one thing I love is that, in with their family and friends, amongst celebrity friends, there's always space for the team who tour with them and generally run around after them.

If there's a perk of coming right down to the wire, the stadium's searchlights already dancing against the dark September sky, it's that there's no traffic around the venue.

Ed pulls up to the main entrance and I hot-foot it inside, the security team waving me on. I pull up, sliding to a stop along the marble floor when I see Dave, not stage side where he should be but, 'Waiting for me?'

'Aye, flower. Guy's asked for ya to come and watch from the sound pit tonight, not the suite.'

'At the front of the stage?'

He holds out his arms and says, 'It's the best spot in the house.'

'Best spot for the best night of the tour?' I ask, stepping into the lift.

There's a roar in the stadium and the concrete walls of the corridors are literally shaking as we stop by the dressing room to drop my bag and leather jacket. I know from experience that I'm going to be hot amongst the lights and electronics, though not hotter than seeing Guy do his thing on stage makes me feel. The room smells of Guy's aftershave and makes me desperate to get out there.

'Ready?' Dave asks, and he looks at me weirdly.

Everyone is on edge for tonight.

'Absolutely.'

The sound from the stadium gets louder and louder as we approach the backstage doors. The rattle of the walls, the pounding of feet, and when Dave opens the door for me, I'm assaulted by the wild screams of fans. The place is electric. The voltage higher than any normal human could withstand.

It's all for them, the four extremely talented men on stage. Trev building the frenzy with his electric guitar, George on bass, Jay steadily increasing the pounding of his bass drum like a heart rate that's rising. And Guy, strumming his Martin, approaching the standing microphone. The stadium is exploding, literally with pyrotechnics, and with the wild voices yelling Guy's lyrics back at him as he plays the opening song.

'All the voices scream,
As we come home.
Out of the steam,
We're in the zone.

'Rock to the sound,
Let us hear you pound.
We're moving you,
Falling for you too.

'This is where we're from,
Back on the north-east scene.
We never went to prom,
Started rocking as a teen.

'Rock to the sound,
Let us hear you pound.

We're moving you,
Falling for you too.'

In the instrumental, he calls out to the crowd, 'Let us hear you sing, Sunderland!'

As the place hits the roof again, he looks to the sound pit and nods to me, that heartbreakingly sexy half-smile tugging on the mouth I get to kiss, and the women in the stadium ignite as he winks on the big screen, but I know it's mine. All mine. Even when he's not on stage, without a guitar in his hand, when he's putting up shelves in our home or we're falling out as we construct flatpack furniture, he's still *my* guy.

Someone puts a bottle of cold water in my hand halfway through the set and I glug it down without my hips stopping their unrelenting twist and swing.

'Thank you,' Guy tells the fans at the end of a song.

Then he looks my way again and despite my smile, he gives me an expression I can't read. One I'm not used to. He stops speaking and the arena is relatively quiet. He's just staring at me, until eventually he seems to remember what his job is up there.

'I've got something a bit different for you tonight, Sunderland. Something I've been working on.'

He unhooks his guitar from around his neck and sets it against the speakers behind him, then moves to the piano that George usually plays for a few of the slower tracks. The session violinists set their instruments under their chins – whatever this song is, it isn't a surprise to them.

Guy sits down to the piano and the sight has me biting my lip. I've been teaching him to play pretty much since the day we got together, but he rarely plays on stage.

'I wrote this song a couple of years ago. The woman I

wrote it about not only showed *me* the light, but she's the reason we're onstage tonight. She also taught me to play it on the piano. So this one's for her, always.' He adjusts the microphone overhanging the Yamaha. 'And she's standing right over there.'

I hide behind my hands when the cameras put my face on the big screens. Peeking through my fingers, I see Guy laughing, then move my hands to give him a teasing death stare.

Then he starts to play. The camera moves in close on his fingers, expertly working the keys like he's been doing it since birth.

And he sings the lyrics I love. My song.

He plays piano through two verses and two rounds of the chorus, then he picks up his acoustic and strums. The violins kick in, the guitars ramp up, and Guy walks across the stage, his gaze fixed on me.

He doesn't sing the next verse, he leaves it to Trev and the others, and he comes to sit on the edge of the stage, right in front of me. We're on the big screen and my heart is pounding harder than the drums because I don't *know* what's coming but... *God, is he going to...?*

I swallow so hard, my throat might burst.

'Marry me,' he says.

I blink. *Is he...? Is this...?* 'What?'

'Marry me. Because I'm so in love with you, Lyra, none of this matters without you.'

The Stadium of Light is as loud as I've heard it for any of their concerts.

Guy unhooks and sets aside his guitar, then jumps down from the stage to take hold of my face in his hands.

'Marry me.'

Oh. My. God.

'Yes,' I whisper, watching my toes to stop myself from crying on a big screen in front of sixty thousand people I don't know.

Guy gently nudges my chin until I'm looking at him.

And I nod. 'Yes.'

He crashes his mouth against mine as if no one else is watching, then wraps his arms around me and lifts me off the floor, twirling me around the sound box, ecstatic happiness bellowing out of me as laughter.

When he sets me down, he tells me, 'I really fucking love you, Lyra.'

And he watches me the whole way back across the stage, making it to centre stage, the frontman in all his beautiful glory, singing the final chorus of my song along with every single fan at the concert.

He only takes his eyes off me to look to the heavens.

I don't believe there'll ever come a time that Guy doesn't imagine Scott is still the frontman, that his brother isn't up there on that stage with him with every note he sings.

But from where I'm standing, Guy does a pretty good job of being the star of The Hand Me Downs. The brightest of all the stars in my life.

I think that's how it was always supposed to be.

* * *

MORE FROM LAURA CARTER

Another book from Laura Carter, *Stuck in Paradise with You*, is available to order now here:

https://mybook.to/StuckInParadiseBackAd

ACKNOWLEDGEMENTS

All I knew when I pitched this book was that the meet cute would take place in an elevator, in which the FMC and MMC would have a box of tacos and a bottle of tequila. Truly, this is how I pitched the book. Which was wholly unhelpful when the me of many months later couldn't remember what she'd been thinking! And I would never have predicted that my mind would take me back to where I grew up, in the north east of England.

Once I started delving deeper into my characters, I knew that the honesty, charm, humour and, for me, nostalgia of the north east were the same characteristics that Guy has. There was no better setting for this book.

Goodness, it was fun to revisit places, faces and accents from my childhood. There are so many hidden names and traits of my friends and family in this book. I hope you enjoy finding them and take them all as an acknowledgement of my gratitude for you. With this caveat... if you weren't mentioned, I just couldn't fit you in but I'm still grateful for you... and there'll be more books! Also, just because you're named, doesn't mean you behave like the characters in the book or that I perceive you in that way (mostly).

Thank you to the entire Boldwood team, from editorial, through marketing and sales, production and administration. But extra special fist pump to my wonderful champion and editor, Emily Yau, for giving me the freedom to venture wherever the wind blows me (within reason). Your dedication, support and hard work are so very much appreciated. You are all superstars, and I love being a Boldie!

Massive thanks to my incredible agent, Tanera Simons. I remember sitting in Covent Garden and telling you over coffee that I just had no idea where to go with this book. We talked it out and not long after that conversation, the ideas started to flow. I'm not sure you know how much you help me. I couldn't ask for a better team than you and Laura.

Finally, but most importantly, thanks to *you,* Reader. I would write words even if they weren't read because it's my passion, but you make all the hours spent and the times sacrificed completely worth it. To know you connect with these characters and stories is one of the best feelings in the world. Please stick with me. I adore you!

ABOUT THE AUTHOR

Laura Carter is the bestselling author of several rom-coms including the series *Brits in Manhattan* which she is relaunching and expanding with Boldwood. She lives in Jersey.

Sign up to Laura Carter's mailing list for news, competitions and updates on future books.

Visit Laura's website: www.lauracarterauthor.com

Follow Laura on social media:

instagram.com/lauracarterauthor

x.com/LCarterAuthor

facebook.com/LauraCarterAuthor

ALSO BY LAURA CARTER

The Law of Attraction

Two to Tango

Friends With Benefits

Always the Bridesmaid

Fake It 'til You Make It

Stuck in Paradise With You

Table for Three

Catch a Falling Star

www.ingramcontent.com/pod-product-compliance
Ingram Content Group UK Ltd.
Pitfield, Milton Keynes, MK11 3LW, UK
UKHW040235120725
6865UKWH00008B/66

9 781785 135903